Ophelia studied the ___
tried to keep her ex ___

"Perhaps we're both a little desperate, hmm? Why not see if it can work to both our advantages?" she asked.

She had always known Dane Montgomery would be the toughest recruitment of her career. But she had the feeling that if she could just spend enough time with him, get to know him, find some sort of compromise to their situations…

"Fine."

"Fine? I mean…you'll do it?" She knew that her face revealed her surprise.

"For $10,000, I'll be your personal tour guide…for this week only." He rose to his feet. "But let me warn you, Ms. Reid, that others with more experience than you have tried many times over the past three years to lure me back."

"I'm well aware of that."

He paused, seeming to consider her. "What makes you think you'll have a better chance than they did?"

She met his gaze with determination. "I don't know that I do," she confessed, "but I have to try."

He straightened at this, and did she imagine it? Or was there just the slightest hint of respect in his eyes to avoid repetition?

"Then let the games begin."

Dear Reader,

I've had the pleasure of visiting Hawaii a total of three times in my life. The first, I was barely three years old and recall little other than crystal clear waters, deliciously cool breezes and soft, pristine sand. The second trip was a family vacation in my early teens that created a wealth of treasured (and humorous!) memories. And the last was only a couple of years ago, not too long after I had the idea for *Gentle Persuasion.*

The impression of Hawaii that has always stayed with me is the unique culture and welcoming *aloha* spirit of its people, the complicated beauty of its native language, and the purity and diversity of its landscape.

Hawaii is a place where it's easy to fall in love. So it was no stretch of the imagination to consider characters who might be tempted to leave behind their mainland lives for the paradise of the islands.

Dane's dreams of running a coffee plantation on the islands afforded me the opportunity to learn more about the families who live and work the hundreds of farms along the coast of Hawaii's Kona region. Their daily struggles and triumphs helped give voice to the challenges of making such dreams a reality.

If you haven't already, perhaps one day you can experience the beauty of the islands for yourself, but for now, I hope *Gentle Persuasion* gives you a small taste of paradise.

If you'd like to share your own Hawaii experiences, contact me through my website at www.cerellasechrist.com.

HARLEQUIN HEARTWARMING

Cerella Sechrist

Gentle Persuasion

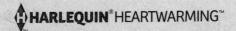

Recycling programs
for this product may
not exist in your area.

ISBN-13: 978-0-373-36651-4

GENTLE PERSUASION

Printed in U.S.A.

H HARLEQUIN®
www.Harlequin.com

CERELLA SECHRIST

lives in York, Pennsylvania, with two precocious pugs, Darcy and Charlotte, named after Jane Austen literary characters. She has won various competitions and a scholarship for her writing, which includes devotionals, full-length plays and novels. Her debut novel, *Love Finds You in Hershey, Pennsylvania,* recently was rereleased with Harlequin Love Inspired. Cerella divides her time between working in the office of her family's construction business and as a barista to support her reading habit and coffee addiction. Her novels exhibit her love for both the written word and food in fiction. You can find her online at her website, www.cerellasechrist.com, where she pens "Literary Fare: Fiction & Food," a blog for readers.

Dedicated to my mom, Cherie Sechrist, who gave me my first glimpse of Hawaii at three, my first taste of coffee at five and a love of stories from the moment I could understand words.

Special thanks to my editor, Laura Barth, and senior editor Victoria Curran, for their input, advice and support. You have been invaluable. I raise my mug of Kona coffee to you both!

CHAPTER ONE

IT WAS BALMY.

She hadn't expected it to be so…balmy.

Ophelia Reid squared her shoulders as she stood at the doorway of the Okina Inn, the bed-and-breakfast where she'd booked lodging until she completed her mission in Hawaii.

She'd endured merciless teasing from her co-workers in the time before her flight: how privileged she was, as the CEO's daughter, to snag this assignment. Yet, even in such lighthearted banter, there had been the glint of sympathy in their eyes. This was no simple placement such as those Reid Recruiting Agency normally performed. This was the assignment that would make or break her career and fulfill the dreams she had nurtured since childhood.

Clearing her throat, Ophelia raised her hand and rapped upon the door with solid determination. Only as her fist withdrew did she notice her hand was trembling slightly.

Frowning, she rested her arms at her sides and willed her fingers to still their shaking. She tapped out the seconds in her designer sling backs, resisting the desire to smooth her black slacks.

Minutes passed, and she again marveled at the temperate climate. Not too hot, not too cold—just as her assistant, Holly, had told her it would be. The trade winds offered a consistently sweet breeze, and the air held only the faintest hint of ocean moisture. Paradise.

For a moment, her shoulders sagged, and she let her head fall back, feeling the delicious pull of her tense muscles as they stretched along her spine.

The door opened, and she snapped her head forward, wincing at the abrupt movement.

A squat, round-faced woman with Polynesian features narrowed her eyes to slits at the sight of Ophelia standing on the doorstep.

"I'm Ophelia Reid." She paused, hoping this introduction would be sufficient.

Apparently not. The woman stared.

"I'm a guest of the inn. I've booked the Lilly…koloni suite." She stumbled over the Hawaiian name, and the stubby woman scowled.

"Liliuokalani," she offered in a slightly accented voice, her tone disparaging.

Ophelia's smile felt strained after her long flight. "That would be the one."

The woman huffed and folded her short arms

across her more-than-ample bosom. "Where's your husband?" she demanded.

Ophelia's mouth dropped at this question. "I don't *have* a husband." She winced at this statement, thinking of her longtime boyfriend, Cole. The two of them had broken things off shortly before she'd boarded the plane to Hawaii. The possibility of her moving to Paris had ignited an argument between them that could reach no satisfactory conclusion, and she had ended things after four long years of dating.

Her statement only served to heighten the woman's suspicions. "What sort of haole woman books the Liliuokalani suite only for herself?"

"Haole?" Ophelia repeated, suspecting she had just been insulted.

"Foreigner. White," came the clipped reply.

Ophelia flared her nostrils. "I will have you know that just because I am a single woman does not mean I cannot enjoy a luxury suite! This is the twenty-first century, and women are entitled to...to—" she flagged as she mentally cataloged her list of feminine rights "—to stay in luxury suites by themselves!" she lamely finished. "If they want to," she added.

The other woman looked Ophelia up and down. "Maybe you're single because you're too skinny. A man wants a woman who can feed him. That's the problem with you mainland girls. You starve yourselves and think that's what a real man wants." She reached out and pinched Ophelia's bare arm to demonstrate her point.

Ophelia gasped in indignation, jerking her arm beyond her criticizer's reach. "I can cook!" She automatically defended herself and then considered the relative dishonesty of this statement. "When I have to," she tacked on to the end.

This elicited another *harrumph* from the Polynesian lady. "Microwave dinners don't count. Neither do reservations at fancy restaurants."

Frustration and fatigue churned madly in Ophelia's stomach. "Are you going to show me to my room or not?" she demanded.

The irritating woman unfolded her arms to rest them on her wide hips. "The rooms are not ready. You're too early to check in."

"What do you mean the rooms aren't ready? My assistant made the reservation on Friday. She was assured I could check in as soon as I arrived"

"I *said*—" the little woman amplified her voice by several notches, as if this might impart understanding *"—the rooms are not ready!"*

Ophelia felt pinpricks of tension shooting

along her nerves. She had never been treated so abominably when trying to check in to a room. Except that one time in Paris when Holly had booked her at the wrong hotel. But even the most snooty of French concierges didn't compare to the feisty lady before her. "Well...what am I supposed to do in the meantime?"

The woman shrugged, as if this was a matter beyond her concern. Despite her upbringing, where appearances were everything, Ophelia suddenly wanted nothing more than to sink to the porch of the inn and cry with aggravation. It had been a long flight to the islands with a combined travel time of over twelve hours on two planes, and she had not expected to encounter such a greeting upon her arrival in this tropical paradise.

"Pele? Is there a problem here?"

The woman turned toward the voice at her back. Ophelia's weariness suddenly evaporated at the appearance of the man behind her tormenter. Six feet, two inches tall with a scruffy jawline, russet-colored hair and the most startling blue eyes she had ever seen, Ophelia immediately recognized the singular presence of Dane Montgomery. Her stomach jerked with what she could only assume was relief at the presence of the very man she had been sent to find.

"Mr. Montgomery." She smoothly extended a hand. "I'm Ophelia Reid."

This poised introduction caused Dane to hesitate for a fraction of a second before slipping his hand into hers. His grip was firm, cool and brief, his expression guarded.

"I'm sorry. Did we…have an appointment?"

Pele answered for her. "This haole woman booked the Liliuokalani suite…*for herself.*"

The sight of Pele's eyebrows, arched with meaning, stung.

Ophelia fought the blush threatening to stain her complexion. "There seems to be a bit of a misunderstanding," she explained.

Dane looked from Ophelia to Pele and back to Ophelia again. "My apologies. You're one of our guests?"

Ophelia nodded, trying to keep the pleasant this-isn't-bothering-me-at-all smile stuck to her lips. "The Liliuokalani suite," she confirmed, taking pains to pronounce the name correctly.

"I apologize," Dane repeated and attempted to nudge Pele's considerable girth from the doorway's entrance. "Won't you come in?"

"She has no husband!" Pele reminded him. "And the rooms are not ready!"

Dane carefully cleared his throat and steered Pele aside. "Well, then, why don't you see about making the rooms ready, Pele?" he suggested, and Ophelia noted he spoke the words through clenched teeth.

The stout woman glowered. "She wants the suite all to herself," Pele persisted.

"Which is absolutely not a problem." Dane directed these words to Ophelia with a contrite look. He continued to prod Pele toward the stairs, no easy feat considering she appeared to be digging her heels into the rug as Dane pushed her along.

"This is what comes of girls starving themselves," Pele muttered direly as her foot landed on the first step. "They lose all their senses!"

Her mumbling continued the entire length of the stairway until she disappeared onto the landing above. Dane turned with an expression of relief.

"I'm sorry we weren't able to greet you properly. My receptionist has the day off, and Pele is our housekeeping staff. The Liliuokalani suite is usually reserved by honeymooners. Pele must have misunderstood. She can be quite…set in her ideas of propriety."

Ophelia waved a hand to brush off the mix-up. "It's not a problem." Now that she had finally been allowed entry into the inn's foyer, she took some time to survey her surroundings. The furnishings were exquisite: beach-scape paintings in rich hues of cerulean blues, aquatic greens and ivory sand, a teak reception desk with track lighting, tropical plants dotting the end tables and a woven area rug covering the hardwood floor. Paradise kept looking better and better.

While Ophelia had been studying the main reception area, Dane had slipped behind the desk to consult the records.

"Here we are, Ophelia Reid. Liliuokalani suite. Paid for one week in advance." He glanced up at her. He seemed to consider querying her further on this before remembering his manners as the inn's owner and host.

"As you're well aware, the suite is not quite ready for you yet. Perhaps you'd like to take some refreshment on the lanai?"

Ophelia nodded with relief. "That would be lovely. Thank you."

He led her toward a set of glass-and-wood doors opening up onto a patio overlooking the gardens. She breathed deeply, once again enjoying the perfect weather.

"Would you like me to bring in your bags?" he questioned.

She shook her head. "They'll be fine in my rental car for now."

While Dane stepped behind the bar, Ophelia used the opportunity to regain some of her scattered composure. She tried to recall the speeches she had formulated on the flight from New York to LAX and then on to Kona International airport. She was good at this— a crack negotiator and a talented recruiter in her trade. But this was different. Everything— her career, the family business, her relationship with her mother/boss—hinged on this one man, this one job.

She was so deeply absorbed in thought that she jerked physically to awareness when Dane approached and set a tray of chilled juice and glasses on the table before her.

If he noticed her start, he didn't draw attention to it. Instead, he poured them each a beverage and handed one toward her before taking a seat.

"If you don't mind my asking, Ms. Reid—"

"Ophelia."

"Ophelia," he corrected, "how is it that you know who I am?"

She smiled easily at him. "It's only been, what, three years since you retired to these islands, Mr. Montgomery? Surely, you didn't think your celebrity status in the corporate world would be forgotten so readily."

She noticed her mention of his former life caused Dane to reflexively tense.

"Your face has graced the covers of nearly every notable trade magazine in business." And

Dane Montgomery's face was not a forgettable one, though she didn't flatter him by saying so.

His jaw, dusted with a fine smattering of stubble, hardened. "I don't grant interviews anymore."

"Oh, I'm not a journalist," Ophelia assured him.

He studied her intently, his mind obviously scanning its memory banks.

"Ophelia Reid…" he murmured thoughtfully.

She took a sip of her juice, its cool sweetness sliding easily down her throat. "This is delicious, thank you. What sort of juice is it?"

"Guava," he answered with some distraction before looking at her carefully. "We've never met," he noted with certainty.

"No," she agreed. "We never have."

He leaned back, his own beverage standing forgotten. "But I would presume to say you're not here for a vacation, reporter or no."

Ophelia took the seat across from him, settling into the cushioned wicker chair. "Not exactly," she admitted. She couldn't help admiring the lean, muscled lines of his arms as he crossed them over his chest. No wonder the media had so often portrayed him as something of a demigod in the business world. His famed good looks were even more evident in person than they had been in the articles she'd been reading about him. It filled her with intimidation, and she reminded herself that his looks had nothing to do with her mission.

He narrowed his eyes and watched her. She held his gaze and stared right back.

"I'm here to make you an offer," she finally said.

Dane dropped his arms and stood, his response short and sharp. "Not interested."

She sighed. Of course it wouldn't be that easy.

"You haven't even heard the terms."

He shook his head and placed several steps of distance between them, as though she were contaminated.

"Not. Interested."

She leaned back, looking out over the garden. "Fine. This job's not on commission for me, so…" She shrugged.

This statement apparently piqued his curiosity, as she'd known it would. Recruiters usually made their living solely on the commissions they reaped from placing high-salary executives in top-end jobs. Working an assignment gratis had to have a compelling reason behind it.

Sufficiently mistrustful, however, Dane did not nibble on this declaration, at least not immediately.

"Ophelia Reid." He repeated her name once more. "You're a headhunter."

Now it was her turn to tense. "I've never been fond of that term. I prefer the more noble title of 'executive recruiter' in my profession."

He scoffed. "You can paint it any color you like—it's all the same to me."

She took another sip of juice to prevent herself from rising to the bait. Dane Montgomery's dislike of recruiters was well known, and she chose not to take his disdain personally.

When she remained silent, Dane began to pace, scratching his jawline thoughtfully before finally snapping his fingers.

"Reid Recruiting Agency." He slid her a sideways glance. "You're Lillian Reid's daughter, aren't you?"

She suppressed a wince, as she always did, when she was labeled in this manner. Her mother's reputation forever preceded her, singling her out as the only child of the ferociously famous corporate negotiator.

"The one and only," she coolly owned, lifting her glass in salute.

He frowned, seeming to notice the subtle frost in her tone. "Lillian Reid as your mother. *That* must have earned you your fair share of therapy."

She tried not to glower at him for this observation. Her attempts caused him to grin, and she felt a strange stirring in her stomach at the sight. "So you work for your mother, then?" he confirmed, getting back to the subject at hand.

She nodded.

"How long?"

"Straight out of college. You can't expect me to confess how many years ago that's been."

Dane closed one eye and pretended to size her up. "Less than ten, I'd say."

She laughed, her tension easing slightly. "They told me you could be charming."

"Could be?"

"When you want to be."

"Ah." He paused. "So?" he prompted.

"So, what?"

"Am I right? Ten years or less?"

She rolled her eyes. "Twelve, if you must know. I'm thirty-three."

He clicked his tongue. "So young."

"As compared to your thirty-six years?"

"You *have* done your homework."

She swirled the ice in her glass. "I should warn you not to underestimate me."

He scoffed. "As Lillian Reid's daughter, you're probably right." He frowned. "If you're not taking a commission, there must be some other incentive. You didn't come here just for the weather, after all." His lips twisted into a smirk of disdain.

"No," she admitted. "I didn't."

He returned to his seat and picked up his glass. "Not to sound arrogant, but…the salaries I've been offered would have provided a, let's just say, *substantial* commission for you, should I accept the proposal. Any particular reason why you're foregoing your percentage?"

She placed her glass back on the table and leaned forward. "Some things in life are worth more than money."

He grunted in acknowledgment. "Well said." He waited a few seconds more before querying, "You're not going to tell me your reasons, are you?"

She leaned back in her seat but remained silent. Instead of responding, she swiveled the topic in another direction. Gesturing to the gardens before them, she observed, "It's easy to see why you gave up what you did. The islands are beautiful."

Relaxing farther into his seat, he followed her gaze. "This is your first trip to Hawaii?"

She nodded. "Travel comes with the job, of course, but I've never had the pleasure before this. You gave me a good excuse." Her eyes returned to his, and when they met, she found herself inexplicably unsettled. Diverting her attention away once more, she tried to keep herself on solid conversational ground. Her research had prepared her for Dane Montgomery's handsome features, square jawline and toned physique, but the reality of those liquid blue eyes and deep voice was something else entirely.

"How many employees do you keep on staff here at the inn?" she asked, anchoring herself to neutral territory.

"Three, in addition to myself. There's a set of rooms on the other side of the inn for them. They live here with me."

"And they're all locals?"

He cocked his head. "Why do you want to know?"

She sighed. She had known he'd be difficult, but she hadn't expected such open mistrust. She shrugged. "It's an interesting endeavor—giving up the corporate life like you did, buying a coffee plantation and inn, and setting out on a new venture. I'm curious."

"If you've done your homework, I'm sure you've read all about it already."

"Still…reading about a legend isn't quite the same as meeting one."

He arched an eyebrow. "Laying it on a bit thick, aren't you? If you'd bothered to compose a personality profile on me, you'd realize that flattery won't get you very far."

He had a point. She had made that very note in the margins of her paperwork during the flight over, and already, she had made the mistake of trying to play to his vanity. She had a flash of doubt as to her ability to accomplish this task. After all, she wasn't the first recruiter to attempt luring Dane Montgomery out of retirement.

"I apologize," she offered, "but before you turn me down flat, you should at least read the proposal."

He sighed and looked away, off toward the mountains in the distance. She sensed a weariness emanating from him, and rather than take advantage of this vulnerability, she attempted to alleviate it.

"I have the entire week at my disposal," she reminded him. "And I'm certain you feel a little ambushed by my arrival. Why don't you take the afternoon to let the idea sink in, and I can present you with the proposal later?"

He turned his eyes on her, the warm blue going a shade darker with what she could only hope wasn't loathing. "How considerate of you," he noted.

She bit her lip.

Clearing his throat, he rose to his feet. "I'll

check on Pele, see how she's coming along on your suite."

A deep exhaustion had settled into her bones. She wanted nothing more than a hot shower and a nap before facing the initial round of negotiations. "Thank you," she responded.

Dane turned to go, but then he lingered on the threshold of the lanai, frowning at her. She smiled cheerfully, though it felt tight and awkward on her lips. He did not return the gesture. As he stole away, Ophelia relaxed her face and rested a hand over her stomach, attempting to convince herself it was only the stress of the situation that had caused the restlessness inside her.

WHILE OPHELIA REID waited for her rooms to be readied, Dane found himself struggling to explain his dilemma to Keahi.

"She is not the first haole to try and lure you away from the islands," Keahi, his plantation manager, pointed out as he flipped through a sheaf of paperwork in their shared office.

"No," he conceded, "but she may be the prettiest."

Keahi looked up from his task with sudden interest, and Dane wished he could withdraw his offhand remark. He'd meant to make a joke of it, as much to convince himself that Ophelia Reid's unexpected beauty was of no consequence as to prepare Keahi for it.

"Pretty, eh, boss?" A wide grin split the older man's face. "You don't pay no attention to the pretty ones."

Dane grimaced. "I pay attention, Keahi. I just don't pursue them." After all, there had been no end to the beautiful women in his life—both those on the mainland, before his retirement, as well as the ones who came and went on the islands. But Dane had learned that most of them were still too interested in the successes of his past to appreciate the commitment to his new life in Kona.

Keahi rolled his eyes and reached for another stack of papers. "Leilani says you spend too much time alone."

"Leilani is young and full of romantic notions about love," Dane reminded and swiveled to face his own desk. "She thinks if I fall in love it will solve all my problems."

"Ah, she just cares about you," Keahi said. "She appreciates all you've done for her and Pele. She wants you to be happy." Dane heard the squeak of his friend's chair as he turned in it. "She knows you deserve it."

Dane pretended to study a list of items he needed to order for the inn to avoid having to respond.

"Boss?"

Dane suppressed a sigh and raised his head, turning in his chair to face his friend.

"You know the numbers aren't good, *brah*."

"We'll figure it out." He turned back around and bent his head over the paper before him. The list of expenses wasn't long, but it felt exorbitant in the face of the other bills piling up.

"The numbers don't lie," Keahi pressed. "Maybe you should cut your losses. Take the pretty lady's offer. Go back home."

"This *is* my home," Dane snapped. "I'm not going to abandon it. Besides, what would happen to you? And Pele? And Leilani? Leilani's practically a kid. If I left, she'd fall right back into the same sort of trouble we fished her out of last year."

Keahi clicked his tongue in disagreement. "Give the girl some credit, boss. She's cleaned herself up real good in the last few months, especially now that she's seeing Sam. She'd land on her feet."

"No." Dane shook his head. "I'm not taking the easy way out. We've got a good product, Keahi, and you know it. We just need some capital to get it out there."

"And what about this Miss Reid? You gonna kick her out?"

Dane leaned back in his chair and grimaced.

"I don't think I can. She paid for her week in advance, and we can't afford to refund her deposit."

He chewed the inside of his cheek to prevent himself from voicing the rest of his thought aloud. Ophelia Reid was a pleasant addition to the inn with her honey-blond hair and startling green eyes. All the more reason, however, to keep his guard up around her. The inn and plantation's rising debt left him vulnerable to whatever tactics Ms. Reid possessed.

"Do you know who her mother is?" Dane looked over his shoulder and made a dramatic pretense of shuddering. "Lillian Reid, founder and executive CEO for Reid Recruiting. That woman is merciless in her pursuits, and I'm sure she raised her daughter in the same manner."

Dane felt a twinge of guilt after uttering these words. Ophelia may have been a headhunter, but he hadn't sensed she was as ruthless as her mother. Then again, perhaps her lean form and pretty face had swayed him more than he wanted to admit.

"You know her mother?" Keahi questioned.

"Mostly by reputation. I met her a time or two at various fund-raisers, though." He shrugged. "She had sharp teeth, as I recall. Like a vampire. And they say she runs her firm with the same sort of bloodthirsty fierceness."

Keahi clicked his tongue. "Maybe you gotta feel sorry for this girl, then. With a mother like that?" He shook his head. "Maybe she's just doing what she has to, coming here and making you this offer."

Dane clenched his jaw before unhinging it to speak. "It doesn't matter. I'm not accepting any contract. Ophelia Reid is wasting her time."

Keahi sighed. "Then you best run those numbers again, boss. Because unless you can start pulling in a whole lot of customers like this Miss Reid, you might have to."

CHAPTER TWO

AN HOUR AFTER her arrival at the inn, Ophelia lay in the center of an enormous bed, eyes fixed on the circling ceiling fan. Dane had brought her bags up from the car, and now they rested on the floor as she counted the rotations of the fan blades above her, willing her weariness to ease her into slumber.

She had drawn the suite's shades, dimmed the lights and turned on her traveling white-noise machine, but the chatter in her brain wouldn't allow for rest. Rolling onto her side, she closed her eyes and focused on her breathing, instead. In. Out. In. Out. In…

It was no good. She was too distracted by the task at hand.

You can do this, Ophelia. You can do it.

She had made this her mantra for the past forty-eight hours—ever since her mother had drawn Ophelia into her private office and commissioned her with this task. Even now, recalling the conversation, Ophelia felt her stomach churning anxiously.

She had just finished wrapping up negotiations for a CFO in an investment group when her assistant, Holly, had stuck her head through the door.

She'd looked up with a grin. "Dinner at Le Petite Renard to celebrate? It's on me."

The fact that her assistant didn't jump at this invitation was Ophelia's first clue something was up.

"Your mother's back from her meeting with Bianca Towers."

Ophelia's relaxed posture tightened up at Holly's warning tone. She waited.

"She wants to see you in her private office." Holly paused and then added, "Now."

Ophelia swallowed and instantly rose to her feet.

She, of all the people in this city, knew better than to keep Lillian Reid waiting. Quickly, she headed out into the main office area of her floor. She brushed by Holly on her way, catching her commiserating glance before moving toward the elevators.

The digital reading blipped all too slowly as she counted the floors until the elevator car reached her. She nodded politely at her coworkers, stepped inside and asked for the senior-executive floor.

Her mother's floor.

Was it her imagination, or were they nudging and sharing glances behind her? It felt as if several sets of eyes were drilling pointed stares into her shoulder blades. She squared her posture and kept her expression impassive.

The wait for the elevator had been far longer than the ride. As the doors pinged open, Ophelia barely resisted the urge to chew her lip with nervousness. She tried to keep her face professionally neutral as she stepped toward the reception desk and was waved through to the inner sanctum of Reid Recruiting Agency.

She caved to insecurity as she passed the black marble awards wall and paused to try and assess herself in the shiny reflection of a plaque.

Everything was perfect, every blond hair in place. She straightened her spine, just as her comportment lessons had instilled in her, and smoothed the designer suit that hugged her thin, five-foot-nine-inch frame. She tried to smile.

Nothing happened.

Her eyes were blinking rapidly, a sign of her distress. This would not do. Lillian expected a placid pool, no matter what sort of emotions raged underneath. Emotional displays were for lesser people. The face you presented to the world must be…flawless.

Ophelia slid her eyes closed, willing a neatness of composure. When she opened them again, the hunted look was still evident.

She prayed her mother would not notice.

Knowing she had wasted precious seconds on this perusal, she hurried toward the glass doors and greeted Tamara, her mother's assistant.

"You can go on in, Ophelia," Tamara offered. The other woman's tone sounded almost pitying.

Ophelia swallowed as she approached her mother's door and knocked briefly before sticking her head inside.

"Ms. Reid? You wanted to see me?"

Lillian Reid had strict rules about how her daughter addressed her. While "Mother" was appropriate at family events and in the privacy of the home, when in the office or among business associates, only Ms. Reid would do.

"Ophelia. Come in." Lillian made a pointed show of studying her wristwatch, though she made no remark on the length of time it had taken Ophelia to reach the top floor.

Ophelia remained composed as she crossed the room and waited behind the Parisian leather chairs reserved for those summoned to sit across the desk from Lillian. She knew better than to sit immediately. Lillian enjoyed issuing commands, even ones so small as when you might seat yourself.

Lillian lifted her gaze from her watch, looked at her daughter and after a pause, gestured toward one of the chairs.

"You may take a seat."

Ophelia gracefully brushed a hand beneath her skirt as she did. She folded one leg over the other, her spine straight and several inches away from the seat's back. Just as she had been taught.

She did not speak, knowing Lillian preferred to take the lead in such meetings. Her mother took longer than usual, however, to voice her wishes, and so Ophelia did her best not to fidget, not even to shift her weight from one side of the chair to the other.

Lillian Reid stared down at her desk for an inordinate length of time, her eyes sharply assessing the spotless surface. The silence lingered for so long that Ophelia felt an unusual concern rise within her.

Swallowing, she broke the rules with a soft murmur. "Mother?"

It was the wrong move. Lillian's hawklike gaze shot upward and caught her in its sights.

"Ms. Reid," she firmly declared.

Ophelia dropped her head in shame. "I apologize, Ms. Reid."

Her poise proved flawless in nearly every situation she found herself thrust into, but one moment beneath her mother's—Ms. Reid's—sharp stare, and she felt reduced to a humiliated child.

Though she ignored the apology, the exchange at least shook Lillian from her silent reverie. She smoothed her short, faded blond hair, a display of tension from her that Ophelia rarely witnessed, and then folded her neatly manicured hands before her.

"We have a situation," she announced, her voice matter-of-fact.

Not trusting herself to speak further, Ophelia waited for her mother to continue.

"I have just come from a meeting with Bianca Towers."

Ophelia prepared herself for potentially bad news. Bianca Towers was the heiress of an internationally renowned resort chain. With the recent passing of her uncle, the young socialite now possessed sole command of the Towers business and fortune.

Her reputation as a flighty party girl had caused a drop in revenue for the Towers name once she came into the seat of power, and Bianca seemed anything but happy about it.

Towers Resorts International had been employing Reid Recruiting Agency for years as their main source to fill top positions within their company. As one of Reid Recruiting's most lucrative accounts, it remained imperative they keep Bianca Towers on good terms.

This was no easy task considering the temperamental, impulsive nature of the twenty-five-year-old socialite. And if anything put Lillian Reid in a bad mood, it was schmoozing the rich.

"She wants to turn the company's image around and restore its reputation as one of the chief international resort chains."

Ophelia remained silent, letting her mother continue at her own leisure.

"She wishes to launch a major PR campaign to draw in a diverse clientele—something that holds universal appeal."

Ophelia tentatively cleared her throat. "She seems...ambitious." Ophelia wouldn't have thought that from what she'd read of the girl.

Lillian Reid did not comment on the observation. Instead, she continued, "Miss Towers believes there is only one way to make this happen."

Ophelia braced herself. Lillian rested her eyes on her daughter's. "She wants Dane Montgomery to head the creative marketing division and lead the campaign."

Ophelia swallowed. "He's retired."

Lillian rolled her eyes, and Ophelia berated herself for having pointed out the obvious.

"He's *the best*." From Lillian's tone, it was clear she was mocking the very words Bianca must have spoken in Dane's regard.

"Where is he?" Ophelia asked.

"Hawaii, if what the trades said three years ago still holds true. He gave everything up to—" she waved her hand dismissively "—grow fruit on an island or some such dull venture."

Ophelia processed this. "So, Bianca wants us to recruit Dane Montgomery for her?"

Lillian nodded. Ophelia hesitated, loath to ask the next question.

"And...if we can't?"

Her mother's piercing stare sliced into her once more. "She pulls the entire Towers Resorts International account."

Ophelia's eyes widened. "What? Everything?"

The same clipped nod.

"But that would mean—"

"Cutbacks. Layoffs." Lillian shuddered as she uttered the dire word, "*Downsizing*. These actions will be interpreted as weakness, and more clients will follow in Bianca's wake."

"We can't let that happen."

For the first time in ages, Lillian bestowed a rare smile of approval upon her daughter.

"No. We cannot." She swiveled in her desk chair, tidying a stack of paperwork. "That's why I'm sending *you* to Hawaii to recruit Dane Montgomery."

This pronouncement elicited a round of blinking from Ophelia. She fought to maintain her poise in the face of this startling statement. "You're…sending…me?"

True, she was one of Reid Recruiting's best. Yet, such a crucial assignment surely called for the cream of the crop.

Lillian tented her fingers and fixed the full weight of her considerably intimidating stare on her daughter.

"You started as an assistant at this company, following your graduation from college. You have worked your way up the ladder without any help from me. I have shown no favoritism toward you thus far, and yet you have still made it clear your wishes are to expand our offices into Paris, with you at their helm as Director of European Operations. Do you, or do you not, wish to see your dreams fulfilled?"

Ophelia swallowed, striving for the same cool demeanor her mother exhibited now. Paris. It had been her dream since she was a child, during the short years she and her mother had lived abroad in France with her father. Those had been the happiest times of her life, and it was the tragedy of her existence that they had been so fleeting. Her father, considerably older than her mother, had passed on, and Lillian Reid had returned to the States with her young daughter in tow to found the Reid Recruiting Agency. Ever since that time, Ophelia had wished for two things: to earn her mother's everlasting approval by following in her footsteps and to expand the corporation's success into the city where she had been happiest— Paris, France. Every step of her education and career had been aimed toward that one, solitary goal.

"Are you saying…if I do this, if I can convince Dane Montgomery to return to New York as the Creative Marketing Director of Towers International…you'll help me open the Paris branch?"

Lillian gave a short nod. "It's what you've always wanted, is it not? I've certainly listened to enough chatter from you about it."

Lillian rotated her chair toward the expansive window overlooking the city. "Countless others have tried to bring Montgomery out of retirement. If you succeed in procuring him for Bianca Towers, a coup like that will assure your success in an overseas venture. Our client lists will triple as everyone scrambles to sign with the agency responsible for doing the impossible—bringing Dane Montgomery back into the game."

Ophelia felt a tremble beginning deep within the center of her chest, radiating outward in a peak of adrenaline. Paris. Her dream city. Her mother was right; she had talked about this for a long time. It had been her one desire ever since she'd been old enough to understand her mother's business. She nibbled her lip as she considered the possibilities.

The offer, however, appeared to have a limited response time, and her reply must have been taking too long.

"Of course, if you feel you're not ready, not up to the task…I can send someone else, one of the senior recruiters…"

"No!"

This slip of decorum caused Lillian to glance at her.

"No," Ophelia continued in a calmer voice. "I'm capable. You know that."

Lillian nodded. "I agree. Because you see, Ophelia—" she pivoted the chair back in her daughter's direction "—only you can truly appreciate what is at stake here. Only you, as my child, know the sacrifices that have been made, the labor that has been involved in making Reid

Recruiting one of the top agencies in the field. Only you can understand."

She paused, her gray eyes calculating as she looked at her daughter. "We cannot lose that. Do you understand me? We *will not* lose that."

Lillian was right. Only Ophelia could appreciate the significance of the situation—she had to succeed at this. She had to keep Reid Recruiting on top. If she didn't do it, they were lost. And she, along with her mother, would suffer the worst of the consequences.

Should she accomplish this, however, she would be rewarded accordingly—Paris, Director of European Operations, her mother's stamp of approval. A dream fulfilled.

Ophelia had set her features with the same frosty determination her mother's had exhibited. "Yes. I understand. You can count on me, Ms. Reid."

Another rare, if somewhat deprecating, smile had been bestowed.

Now, some forty-eight hours later, and thousands of miles away from that tense scene, Ophelia could still feel the stab of her mother's grim expression. Compelled by the memory, she slung her long legs over the bed's edge and pulled herself from its soft foundation to head toward the bathroom.

Staring into the carved-wood-frame mirror, she ran her fingers over her features, picking out the items which possessed a similarity to Lillian Reid's. There were only slight resemblances—very little, other than the hair color her mother now dyed—between the two. She could have been anyone's daughter, could have belonged to anyone.

But her lips. Her mouth. This was the one characteristic linking them genetically. The soft pink lips tapering outward to a pointed edge. This was her inheritance.

She touched that feature now and willed her lips upward.

Her mother's infrequent smile stared back at her in haunting reminder.

Only you can understand.

AFTER UNPACKING HER suitcase, Ophelia stood beneath the bathroom shower for long minutes and let the warmth of the spray ease away her tension. Changing into more casual clothes, she stretched out on the bed once more and logged on to the inn's internet connection.

She spent the next few hours on her laptop in the Liliuokalani suite, clicking through websites and articles that mentioned Dane Montgomery. The research Holly had given her, along with her mother's instructions and her own memory, provided the necessary framework to form a profile of Dane's past and accomplishments. But Ophelia knew she needed to dig deeper if she was to achieve her goal.

The web was a wealth of information on the former advertising executive, highlighting awards, achievements, accolades and a sparkling career path that had sent Dane higher and higher into the echelons of the corporate world. And then, suddenly, articles dated three years previously exploded into her browser, announcing Dane's retirement and exit from business. There were dozens of speculations on the reasons: everything from a love child with some celebrity or other to a debilitating disease eating him alive. It was all fodder for the gossips, especially when Dane's official statement proved to be rather dull reasoning.

I plan to seek out new challenges in a different direction. While I value my time spent in this industry, I'm looking to find personal fulfillment at a less frenzied pace.

He was labeled everything from "certifiably insane" to "a groundbreaking genius."

In the end, Ophelia sensed he simply felt tired—a feeling she could relate to after her years climbing the ladder at Reid Recruiting. But she had worked relentlessly to prove her value, and now, finally, she would be rewarded. *If* she could drag Dane back to the world he had left behind.

With a sigh, Ophelia logged off and closed her laptop. She reached for a pillow and curled herself around it, her mind cataloging everything she'd gleaned from her research. She mentally filed away each scrap of information on Dane as she continued to form and revise her plan to recruit him. Soon, jet lag and the six-hour time difference between Hawaii and New York caught up with her. The next thing she knew, she woke to darkness outside her window and the soft sound of island crickets filtering in on the midnight air.

Sitting up in the bed, she realized she'd slept away the rest of the afternoon and all of the evening. Annoyed with this waste of hours, she swung her legs over the side of the bed and decided to see if, by chance, anyone remained awake.

Easing open the door to her room, she glanced down the hall in both directions. A soft light illuminated the stairs, so Ophelia headed that way, her feet moving soundlessly across the carpet. She had just reached the bottom step and noted all the inn's lights were off for the evening when she heard what sounded suspiciously like a motorcycle outside. She crept closer to the open windows. The echo of hushed dialogue and muted giggles drifted toward her as the motorcycle purred gently.

Leaning forward, she carefully parted two of the blinds' slats and peered out. In the pale light spilling from the front porch, Ophelia saw a girl leaning against the solid form of a young man as he remained seated on the bike.

They were murmuring affectionately, their foreheads pressed together, and Ophelia felt a sudden tug of longing. She couldn't remember Cole ever cradling her in such a way—not even in the early stages of their relationship four years ago. But then, he had never much liked public displays of affection. She suppressed a sigh and though she felt jealous of the young couple outside the inn, she experienced no such regret for ending things with Cole.

But to be held in such a way…wasn't that every girl's dream?

As the embrace lingered, Ophelia felt embarrassed for intruding. Straightening, she began to head back toward the stairs but stubbed her toe on the edge of a cabinet, causing her to hop around and bite back a string of curses. By the time she regained her balance, the front door had eased open, and the girl she'd been spying on stood before her. For a moment, they simply stared at each other in surprise.

Ophelia rubbed her opposite foot over her smarting toe. "Sorry," she apologized.

"For what?" the girl asked.

"Um…" Ophelia trailed off, reluctant to admit she'd been watching the younger woman's midnight tryst.

"Are you a guest?" The girl stepped forward, and Ophelia could only nod in acknowledgment. The younger woman's face split into a beaming smile featuring even white teeth against the backdrop of her smooth, sun-kissed complexion. "Aloha, I'm Leilani." She extended a hand. "I'm in charge of reception, events and bookings."

Though the words were spoken softly in deference to the late hour, Ophelia noted the pride in them. She relaxed at the friendly introduction.

"Ophelia Reid," she said in equally hushed tones and inserted her hand into Leilani's. "I flew in from New York this morning. I'm booked in the Liliuokalani suite for the week."

"Oh, yeah." Leilani's head bobbed, her long, dark hair swishing forward with the movement. "You booked at the last minute, right? Something about unexpected travel plans?"

Ophelia licked her lips, uncertain how much she should reveal to one of Dane's employees.

"Well, um…yes. My assistant would have been the one to make all the arrangements."

Leilani's eyes widened. "Oh. Your assistant?"

"It's a long story."

Leilani cocked her head with curiosity, studying Ophelia. "Have you eaten?" she questioned at last.

Ophelia's stomach growled right on cue. She frowned apologetically. "I fell asleep for a few hours. The time difference and all."

Leilani waved a hand as if this happened all the time.

"I suppose I could drive down to the coast," Ophelia considered. "Surely there's got to be some late-night diners open or something."

Now Leilani was shaking her head. She reached out to grab Ophelia's hand, dragging her along as she spoke in whispers. "I'm starving! We'll raid the fridge together. That way, if we get caught, I can tell them you forced me into it."

Ophelia couldn't help grinning at this girl's friendliness.

"But there's one condition." Leilani halted and turned to face her. "You can't tell my *tutu* or Dane that I got in so late."

"Tutu?"

"My grandmother," Leilani explained.

"Oh." Ophelia considered her. "Are you breaking your curfew? I did that a time or two myself back in high school." Never any more than that, though. She dared not risk it and upset her mother.

"I'm almost nineteen," Leilani said, "but after everything that happened last year, I still get treated like I'm a toddler sometimes. Especially by my *tutu*."

Leilani released Ophelia's hand and led her through a doorway, flicking on lights to reveal the interior of the inn's kitchen. When Leilani began speaking once more, her voice was soft but not nearly so hushed as before.

"Dane's not so bad—he trusts me. But *Tutu* still worries."

"Your grandmother…er, your *tutu,* is…" Ophelia prompted.

"Oh, Pele. The housekeeper and cook? You probably met her already. You'd remember if you had."

Ophelia grimaced at the recollection of the short, feisty woman. "Yes. I know what you mean."

Leilani nodded, her expression serious despite the humor in Ophelia's tone. "I got into some pretty bad stuff a year ago. I cleaned up my act but grandmas…you know how they are."

Ophelia bit her lip and didn't say anything.

Her paternal grandparents had been gone long before she was born, and she had never gotten to spend much time with her maternal ones before they passed away during her college years. Her mother had avoided visits with them as much as possible.

Leilani seemed not to notice Ophelia's silence as she turned and opened the fridge door to begin rummaging inside.

"Do you like *huli huli* chicken?" she asked from within the recesses of the refrigerator.

"I'm sorry—what?"

Leilani emerged holding several containers. "*Huli huli* chicken?"

"I don't know what that is."

"Oh, um…I guess it's sort of like barbecue chicken but with ginger, soy sauce, brown sugar, you know."

Another rumble in Ophelia's stomach settled the matter for her. "I'd love to try it."

Leilani nodded with a grin and continued to pull containers from the fridge, announcing their contents as she placed them on the kitchen island.

"Mango bread, *huli huli* chicken, steamed rice with pineapple, roasted sweet potatoes…"

Ophelia began peeling lids off the dishes. "Sounds like a feast."

"*Tutu* may be a little prickly sometimes, but her food is pure sweetness."

Inhaling the fragrant scents of soy, spice and sugar, Ophelia didn't argue this statement. Leilani opened cupboards and pulled forth plates and glasses. Placing them on the kitchen island, she gathered utensils and began spooning out generous helpings of the leftovers.

"How are you enjoying Hawai'i?" the younger girl asked conversationally.

Ophelia noticed she pronounced her homeland's name with the appropriate accent. It was a pleasant sound.

"It's beautiful. An island paradise. But I haven't even been here twenty-four hours, so I can't say I've experienced much."

"Except *Tutu*'s hospitality?" Leilani smirked as she slid a plate of food into the microwave above the stove to heat it.

"Is she always so…"

"Outspoken? Usually." Leilani shrugged. "But she's been touchy lately. Things are… tense."

Ophelia straightened with interest. "Oh?"

"Yeah. The inn and plantation are experiencing financial issues. When Danc bought the property, it had fallen into pretty bad disrepair. He sank all of his savings into the renovations and roasting equipment, and he hasn't been able to recoup his investment."

Ophelia mulled over this new information. "Any new venture takes time to turn a profit," she remarked.

"That's what Dane tells *Tutu* to keep her from worrying. But it's not hard to tell that he's worried, too."

The microwave emitted a series of beeps, and Leilani swapped out one plate for another. She turned to face Ophelia once more.

"So you should feel good, knowing your stay here contributes to a worthy cause." She winked pleasantly, and Ophelia felt the sting of guilt.

"It's a lovely inn, and I'm happy my stay will provide a bit of income. Only…"

Leilani placed the first warmed plate of food on the table and gestured for Ophelia to take a seat. Carrying her glass and a set of flatware with her, she settled at the teak table.

"Only?"

"Only, I'm afraid you've been nothing but sweet and open with me, and you'll likely not appreciate my reasons for coming here in the first place."

Leilani considered her for several seconds, and Ophelia left the plate of food untouched as they stared at each other. Eventually, the microwave's beeping broke the silence.

"You're one of them, aren't you?" Leilani made no move toward the microwave.

"Them?"

"From Dane's past. From New York."

"No, not exactly. I mean, yes, I'm from New York. But I just met your boss this morning. I knew him by his reputation in the corporate world, but we never laid eyes on each other before today."

Leilani cocked her head, studying. "Then you're one of those recruiters."

Ophelia dipped her head in acknowledgment. "How many have there been? Before me?"

Leilani shrugged carelessly before turning toward the microwave. "Enough to become an annoyance." She turned back and studied Ophelia. "None as pretty as you, though."

Ophelia blushed, but Leilani turned back toward the microwave without commenting further. Removing her own warmed plate, she joined Ophelia at the table, settling comfortably across from her. Ophelia toyed awkwardly with her silverware, not wanting to appear rude by diving straight into the food. Her mother had instilled that habit in her long ago.

Leilani noted her fidgeting and grinned, putting her at ease once more. "Go ahead. *Tutu's* a much better cook than conversationalist—I promise."

Offering a small smile in return, Ophelia took up her fork and speared a chunk of roasted sweet potato. The starchy morsel melted on her tongue, a tangy ginger glaze causing her taste buds to tingle happily. She quickly forked another bite and then a third into her mouth before moving on to the crisp, smoky, soy skin of the *huli huli* chicken. After a long stretch of minutes and more bites that included the doughy, honeyed mango bread and fragrantly steamed rice with pineapple, Ophelia paused to take a breath. At some point while she ate, Leilani had filled her glass with lime-spiked water. She took a long sip before shrugging apologetically.

"I must have been hungrier than I realized."

Leilani beamed at her. "It's good to see a city girl eat like that. Most of the other recruiters who came turned up their noses at our food. It offended *Tutu* immensely."

"It's their loss," Ophelia assured as she peeled another savory section of chicken from the bone and popped it into her mouth.

"*Tutu*'s going to end up loving you."

Ophelia wrinkled her nose with skepticism. "I somewhat doubt that, but…" She paused. "Thank you. For not getting upset about why I'm here."

Leilani licked her fingers and leaned back in her chair. "You're just doing your job."

"That's a very positive outlook. I hardly imagine other recruiters were welcomed so generously."

"Dane's a grown man. He knew what he was doing when he left the mainland, and he knows what he's doing here. No one can change that, except him. *Tutu* doesn't give others enough credit to make their own decisions."

Ophelia reached for a napkin from the stack in the middle of the table. She wiped her fingers with it before placing it next to her plate. "Is that why you were sneaking in tonight? She doesn't trust you?"

"It's more complicated than that. *Tutu* has been responsible for me for years. And she had good reason to worry for a long time. But things are different now. *I'm* different. And she hasn't been able to see that."

"She seems like a woman who could be pretty stubborn...." Ophelia thought about her own mother's rigid standards and dropped her eyes to toy with the remains of her rice, pushing the grains into a tidy pile in the corner of her plate. "But I'm sure she loves you. She seems like someone who would love fiercely."

When she looked back up, Leilani nodded. "She is! She's been there for me through a lot.

I just wish she'd give me some credit for how much I've changed."

Ophelia tried redirecting the subject. "Who was it that brought you home tonight, if you don't mind my asking?"

Leilani's eyes sparkled at this question. "My boyfriend, Sam. We've been seeing each other for three months now. Dane's even been giving him odd jobs around the plantation. I think it kinda drives *Tutu* crazy, having him around so much." Leilani giggled at this.

"So do you have a boyfriend?" she asked.

Ophelia started at this unexpected question. "Um…"

"You're not wearing a wedding ring." Leilani pointed out the obvious.

"No. I, er, recently got out of a long-term relationship."

"Oh, I'm sorry to hear that."

But even as she said the words, Ophelia noticed the younger girl smiling.

She raised her glass of water. "Then here's to your week of island adventures."

Ophelia thought it a strange toast, but she clinked her glass next to Leilani's and then took a sip.

"I'm glad you're here," Leilani said. "It will be good for Dane."

Ophelia couldn't be sure what Leilani meant by that and decided perhaps it was safer not to ask.

DANE WAITED RATHER anxiously for Ophelia Reid to appear in the inn's dining room the following morning. Keahi filled a large plate with stacks of golden macadamia nut waffles slathered in coconut syrup while Pele listened to Leilani chattering about her time kayaking at Keala-kekua Bay the day before. Dane sipped from his coffee and made occasional attempts to read the newspaper, but with each slight noise, he would glance up, expecting to see Ophelia enter the room.

He attributed this edginess to Ms. Reid's agenda—the last thing he wished to deal with was a pushy recruiter making the same offers he'd heard dozens of times in the past three years. But deep down, he had the uneasy feeling that Ophelia's proposal wasn't the only reason his gaze kept wandering to the dining room doorway.

He was sending just such a glance toward the entry when she finally appeared. The sight of her caused a tingling of interest along his nerves, but he forced himself to greet her casually with an offhand, "Good morning."

He noted with a frown that she was not much more suitably dressed than the day before. Her pale green button-down shirt and knee-length black skirt flattered her figure immensely but reinforced the impression of her professional image. Dane didn't much like the reminder, even if he did admire the long length of her calves as she crossed the room.

He forced himself to look away, returning to his papers, though he couldn't find where he'd left off in the article he'd been reading. He finally placed the page aside and looked up, catching Ophelia's eye. She offered a friendly smile, which ignited a warmth in his stomach. He found it a difficult endeavor to tear his gaze away from her.

"Are those waffles?" she questioned as she pulled out a chair.

"Macadamia nut," Keahi offered around a mouthful of food. He shoved the platter her way before introducing himself. "I'm Keahi, the boss's right-hand man." He stood and reached across the table to offer the hand he had just mentioned.

She took it before seating herself across from Leilani and to Dane's right. "Pleased to meet you. I'm Ophelia."

"Keahi is my plantation manager," Dane felt the need to elaborate.

"Would you like some sausage?" Leilani extended the plate.

Ophelia nodded and took a link. "Everything looks delicious, Pele."

Pele didn't utter a sound of acknowledgment but moved around the table to begin mounding several spoonfuls of fresh fruit onto Ophelia's plate.

"*Tutu* loves to cook. It's part of her nurturing spirit," Leilani informed.

Dane cocked his head in curiosity. "Ophelia, you haven't met Leilani yet, have you?"

Both girls flushed with what looked like guilt to him. He studied them more closely.

"Have you?" he pressed.

"Of course not," Ophelia spoke up and then reached across the table to extend her hand. "Leilani, you must be in charge of reception and bookings. You probably spoke to my assistant, Holly, on the phone on Friday."

"Miss Reid, of course."

"Please, call me Ophelia."

They looked way too conspiratorial for two people who had just met. He glanced at Pele, but she was busy pouring Ophelia a glass of juice and didn't notice the exchange. And then, as one, the two younger women turned to look at him. He had the strangest feeling of being left out of something, and he didn't much like it. When he gave no reaction, they turned back to each other.

"And what are your plans for your stay, Ophelia? I believe your assistant said you were on a business trip?" Leilani questioned.

"Yes, I'm actually here to present your boss with an offer to return to the mainland. As the Creative Marketing Director of Towers Resorts International."

"Towers Resorts? Aren't they opening a resort in Waikiki?" Keahi questioned.

Ophelia nodded in acknowledgment. "Yes, among a few others. It's part of an ongoing expansion project. However, Bianca Towers, who inherited the company following her uncle's death, is striving for a new image, and she'd like your boss to lead the way for her."

"He's retired," Pele flatly informed.

Dane said nothing and waited for Ophelia's response.

"I understand, but your boss was the best the business world has seen in terms of innovation and success in the advertising and marketing field. It's why he still receives offers, even three years into his retirement."

She slid a glance his way, but he refused to react to this praise. He had heard the same drivel spouted endlessly for years—it failed to penetrate anymore. He was proud of his previous successes, but he felt driven by his newest challenge—cultivating coffee. Ophelia spoke of his old life, and he was only interested in the new.

Leilani, however, looked at him with a curious gaze. "Is that true? Were you really as good as she says?"

He reached for his coffee. "Headhunters exaggerate."

"Recruiters," Ophelia corrected, and he felt gratified by the way her jaw tightened on the word, "focus on potential."

"Well, *my* potential has been refocused. Here. To this plantation."

She met his gaze with a determined one of her own. "Perhaps you'd like to hear the terms of the proposal before you dismiss it out of hand?"

"After breakfast," Dane relented, knowing he'd have to at least look at the offer. She wouldn't give up until he did, and they might as well get the formalities out of the way so he could focus on running his plantation. "Deal," Ophelia declared, the one word causing him to cringe as if it indicated he'd agreed to the contract.

Ophelia must have noticed his reaction because she frowned. "My suite is beautiful," she said, as if this one compliment could make up for her being here.

"Ms. Reid—"

"Ophelia," she again corrected.

"Ophelia," he repeated with a nod in her direction, "is staying in the Liliuokalani suite."

"Without a husband," Pele tacked on as she settled into her own seat.

"I believe Lili-uo-kalani," Ophelia pronounced the name with care, "was a forward-thinking lady, was she not? Surely she would approve of a single woman renting a suite that bears her name."

Pele clucked her tongue. "What do you know of Liliuokalani?"

Ophelia's grin seemed slightly smug, Dane thought. "I know she reigned as Hawaii's last sovereign before the monarchy was overthrown around the turn of the previous century. She became queen following her brother's death. David Kalakaua—am I saying that right?— who had named her his successor when he had no children to inherit the throne. A terrible injustice, the way she was imprisoned in Iolani Palace for a year and then later forced to abdicate. It is a fitting name for such a lovely suite, by the way."

Dane stared at Ophelia following this unexpected flow of information. His gaze shifted to find Pele's eyes narrowed to slits but then she gave a nod of approval. "You should eat more. You're too skinny."

Pele moved to pile another stack of waffles onto Ophelia's plate. She nudged the syrup within easy reach. Dane eyed Ophelia again until she glanced his way, and then he arched his eyebrow in question at her newfound knowledge.

"I looked it up," she confessed as she unfolded her napkin and smoothed it across her lap. "Your free Wi-Fi amenity is quite good here."

He found himself fascinated by her confident demeanor, and the way she licked her lips before cutting into a section of waffle. The movements held him mesmerized, the length of her fingers, the curve of her wrist...until Keahi cleared his throat, and Dane shook himself back to awareness.

Ophelia didn't seem to notice his distraction. "I only managed a brief glance at the property on my way in yesterday. Tell me more about the coffee plantation."

Dane hesitated, uncertain why a recruiting headhunter wished to know about his life here unless she planned to use it in her arguments somehow. The air around the table grew thick with tension as he waited, studying Ophelia's face. She remained turned toward him, her expression open and genuinely curious. He could feel the rest of his staff waiting for him to respond.

"There are fifteen acres, and about 2,500 coffee trees. We also have an orchard with mangoes, papayas, bananas and coconuts. Most of the fruit you're served here at the inn is harvested from the plantation. We sit at an elevation of 1,200 feet above Kealakekua Bay, but we're a short drive to some of the best attractions you'll find anywhere, including snorkeling, swimming, historic spots, shopping and tours."

"Yes, your brochure was most impressive," she noted, and Dane frowned, realizing he had repeated most of what was already in their literature.

"So, why coffee?" Ophelia questioned as she speared a bite of sausage. "Why Hawaii?"

"Why not?" he countered. "Coffee is one of the world's most sought-after commodities, and Hawaii is paradise."

"But don't you ever miss the city?" she pressed.

He leveled his gaze on her. "The concrete, the press of people, the exhaust fumes?"

"The accessibility, the high-rises, the adrenaline?"

"Didn't we agree we'd negotiate *after* breakfast?"

To his consternation, he felt that same
warmth spreading through his stomach as Ophelia Reid grinned brightly at him and didn't say
another word.

CHAPTER THREE

AFTER FINISHING HER proposal outlining the generous offer from Towers Resorts International, Ophelia was gratified to witness a slight break in Dane's composure. He leaned back in his chair on the lanai and eyed her carefully.

"Those are some impressively decadent figures. Color me flattered. But I have to disagree on my worth—my skills hardly do such a number justice."

"Bianca Towers would disagree. She feels you're worth every penny of that price."

"Ms. Towers is a spoiled brat, from what I've read," Dane commented.

"Ms. Towers is quite concerned with the future image of Towers Resorts International. Her uncle's passing and her subsequent inheritance of the company have created a media furor."

"I noticed," Dane dryly remarked. "Those photos of her, passed out drunk in the back of that rock star's limo, were really in poor taste, even for the paparazzi."

"Mmm, exactly. She needs a solid team behind her, to reestablish her company as a worldwide mecca of luxury and refinement."

"And Ms. Towers feels she needs *me* to accomplish this?"

Ophelia leaned forward in her own seat and cocked her head. "Come now, Dane, don't be modest. How many companies was it that you turned around during your time in the corporate spotlight?"

He scowled at her, but she would not be deterred.

"Take the case of the Heston Group alone. They were on the verge of bankruptcy from bad investments and poor media relations, and you stepped in at the last minute, raising them from the ashes and placing them within the top three companies in their field. *Time* magazine did an entire feature on it."

"I don't do that kind of work anymore," he insisted. "And there are plenty of others who do. Go dangle your enormous salaries in front of one of them." In his agitation, he stood and began pacing in front of the patio's railing.

"Bianca has been very specific," Ophelia smoothly returned. "She wants you. Only your skills and knowledge will do."

"Has no one ever told her she can't have everything she wants?"

Ophelia felt her lips turn upward of their own

volition. "I rather doubt it," she couldn't resist remarking.

He looked at her directly then, in such a way that Ophelia's heart began to pound in her chest, and she was forced to turn her attention elsewhere before she began to blush. She focused her gaze on the garden below and savored the breeze, breathing deeply of the fecund scents of greenery and soil.

"Have you ever tasted Kona coffee, Ophelia?" Dane questioned, drawing her attention back to him.

He leaned against the lanai rail, his gaze intent on her. "No," she confessed. "Though I've heard it is incomparable."

"The remarkable thing about Kona coffee is how each farm's beans lend a different layer to the flavor profile. While some Konas are nutty with a faint caramel flavor, others are slightly sweeter with berry notes. In general, all Kona coffees have a bright but mellow acidity to them with a full, almost buttery body."

"You must have a gourmet's palate," she said.

Dane shrugged off this remark. "Not especially. But what I find interesting about coffee is the same thing I find interesting about people—the diverse layers of flavor, or purpose. Some are more complex than others with notes so varied and subtle that it takes true effort to define them."

She held his eye as he studied her. "And you're still trying to figure out mine, is that it?"

He didn't respond, and the silence was broken when Pele entered the lanai carrying a tray with a white carafe, two demitasse cups and a plate of candied fruits and chocolate-covered macadamia nuts.

Dane took the tray from Pele and thanked her. She lingered, head cocked as she watched the two of them, until Dane pointedly cleared his throat.

"Thank you, Pele."

With a shrug, she turned and headed back inside.

"Here." Dane poured them each a demitasse cup of rich, dark coffee and passed one her way.

She leaned her nose into the fragrant beverage and noted the faintest scents of berry and cocoa. Blowing first on the liquid, she took a small sip and was rewarded with a satisfying explosion of tart fruitiness and mellow cocoa flavor along her tongue. She allowed the full body of the brew to linger in her mouth before it slid down her throat. Greedily, she took another steaming sip

"It's fantastic," she admitted. "Easily the best cup of coffee I've ever tasted."

He grinned proudly. "I knew you'd think so. It's our own beans, roasted right here on the plantation."

His pleased expression reminded her of a little boy who had been praised for a job well done. She took another sip. "Impressive."

She reached for one of the chocolate macadamia nuts. The delicate milk chocolate against the nutty flavor of the treat only served to highlight the Kona roast's cocoa notes even further.

"I assume this little exercise is meant to demonstrate for me the allure of island life?"

"The point of this little exercise was to demonstrate the quality of the product. Coffee is the second-most-traded commodity in the world, next to oil, and Kona is one of the most lucrative beans. Why should I give that up, along with paradise, to return to a city that never held much appeal for me and a career I left behind?"

As much as she hated to play the card Leilani had handed her the evening before, she knew she had to use it. "Because you're drowning in debt, and the very best coffee beans in the world can't save you if you don't have the capital to properly distribute them."

He sat in what she assumed was stunned silence. Ophelia placed her demitasse cup back on the tray.

"With all due respect, I think it takes more

than a good cup of coffee to turn down an offer such as the one Bianca Towers has made you."

She could tell by the hardening of his jaw that her words had only served to anger him.

"How do you know about the plantation's financial situation?"

Ophelia held her breath for a second before releasing it. "Like you said, I've done my homework."

He glared at her, and she felt every ounce of the pressure he must be under.

"Let me make you another offer," she said. "My firm will pay you $10,000 in addition to my reservation at the inn if you'll be my personal guide for this week. It will give you the opportunity to show off your paradise here, and it will allow me the chance to highlight all the benefits of Ms. Towers's offer to you."

The glare dissolved, replaced by wariness. She could tell he hadn't expected this change in tactics.

"That seems somewhat…desperate."

Ophelia attempted to keep her expression neutral. "Perhaps we're both a little desperate, hmm? Why not see if it can work to our advantage?"

She had always known Danc Montgomery would be the toughest recruitment of her career. But she had the feeling that if she could just spend enough time with him, get to know him, find some sort of compromise to their situations...

"Fine."

She knew that this time, her face revealed her surprise. "Fine? I mean...you'll do it?"

"For $10,000, I'll be your personal tour guide...for *this week only*." He rose to his feet. "But let me warn you, Ms. Reid, that others with more experience than you have tried many times over the past three years to lure me back."

"I'm well aware of that."

He paused, seeming to consider her. "What makes you think you'll have a better chance than they did?"

She met his gaze with determination. "I don't know that I do," she confessed, "but I have to try."

He straightened at this, and did she imagine it, or was there just the slightest hint of respect in his gaze?

"Then let the games begin."

FOLLOWING HER PRELIMINARY negotiations with Dane, Ophelia excused herself, heading to her room so she could check in back home. She stared at her cell phone for a long time before she finally decided to send her mother an email instead. It would be much less stressful than attempting to fill in the details by phone.

She opened up her laptop and typed a short missive.

To: Lillian Reid <lillian.reid@reidrecruiting.com>
From: Ophelia Reid <ophelia.reid@reidrecruiting.com>
Subject: Dane Montgomery

Ms. Reid,
Things are progressing naturally concerning Dane Montgomery, with the expected resistance to our offer. As we discussed, I have offered him the additional monetary incentive in exchange for his time, and he has agreed to the terms. I will continue to outline the benefits regarding his acceptance of this contract and will keep you apprised of any developments.

Sincerely,
Ophelia

She considered adding something of a more personal nature, even going so far as to type *PS The weather is lovely,* followed by *We should visit here together one day,* and then she immediately deleted such trite words, knowing what her mother would think of them.

She sent off the email and closed her laptop, hesitating as she considered calling Cole to see how he was doing. A sense of obligation prompted her to reach for her phone. She took note of the time difference, opened her speed-dial list and tapped Cole's name. She drew a breath and held it as the line rang once, twice, three and then four times before her ex-boyfriend finally answered.

"Hello, Fee."

She cringed at Cole's nickname for her.

"Ophelia," she corrected.

"Right. Of course. Sorry."

He sounded truly contrite, and guilt washed over her. She quickly brushed it aside.

"How's paradise?" he asked.

"It's lovely," she said, and realized she was nervously tapping her index finger on her laptop. She cleared her throat and pushed the computer from her lap.

"Have you convinced Montgomery to accept the contract yet?"

She felt a twinge of irritation. "I've barely been here twenty-four hours. It's not the easiest recruitment ever, you know."

"So I take it that's a no?"

His voice held a hint of amusement, and she found her irritation rising.

"If you were here—"

"I'm not." He cut her off.

This sudden interruption gave her pause. She couldn't fault him for being touchy, not after she'd broken things off between them.

"I'm sure you'll convince him eventually," he said. This generous nod to her recruiting abilities sharpened her guilt even further, but she reminded herself of the reason she'd broken up with Cole in the first place.

"I'll certainly do my best."

The silence between them was strained.

"Cole—"

"Ophelia—"

They both stopped.

"Are you sure you know what you're doing, Fee?" She didn't correct him a second time about the nickname. She already knew to what he referred.

"It's all I've ever wanted, Cole. It's the only thing I've ever asked of you—that you be willing to move to Paris so I could oversee the European branch when the time came. I know that it's a big commitment, but every time we discussed it, you said you'd be willing to go with me when the time came. Now it's finally coming to pass, and you're backing out of your end of the bargain."

"Don't forget that the entire deal hinges on you bringing Montgomery out of retirement. You just pointed out that it's not the easiest recruitment, by far."

"It changes nothing about you and me, though. I asked you to choose. I told you what it came down to—Paris with me or New York without me. You made it quite clear what you preferred."

"I asked for some time to think about it—I didn't know I was writing us off forever by wanting a chance to consider my options."

"I want to be more than an option for you," she stated. "Besides, has anything changed since I left? Have you decided I'm worth it, after all?"

The soft static of the line spoke volumes even when Cole said nothing. She scoffed slightly.

"Paris is everything to me. Everything," she reiterated.

"Everything?" His voice was wounded when he finally spoke.

She sighed with weariness and leaned over to rest her forehead in the palm of her hand. "Cole, please. You have always known how important this is to me."

"But you'd be leaving everything familiar behind. Including your mother."

A strangled laugh escaped her throat. "I could finally prove myself to her."

"Prove yourself? To your own mother? Ophelia, that's not necessary. Surely you know that."

She couldn't explain it to him. She wondered if he had ever understood, if he had ever even paid attention to what passed for a mother-daughter relationship between her and Lillian Reid.

Her lack of a reply must have compelled him to speak further. "Ophelia, be reasonable. We're talking about our future."

She felt a twist of pity for him. "Cole, I don't think we have a future."

Another minute of silence stretched out between them.

"And what's your plan if you don't succeed? If you can't convince Montgomery to return?"

The thought left a weight of apprehension in her stomach. She couldn't fail her mother like that. She couldn't fail herself and her dreams.

"I'll figure it out. There's no need to concern yourself."

"Of course not. Why would I do that?" His words were laced with resentment.

She felt herself bristle. "Right. No need to expect your support or anything."

They sighed at the same time.

"Well, I just wanted to check in," she said.

"Yeah. Thanks for that. And good luck with Montgomery. You're probably going to need it."

She resisted the urge to grind her teeth together.

"Right. Take care, Cole."

"You, too."

As she ended the call, she marveled at the two of them, how awkwardness outweighed any heartbreak they might have experienced. She wondered if their entire relationship had been based on convenience and expectation rather than love. For her part, she felt only frustration.

Placing these thoughts aside and trying not to let Cole's words get to her, she began preparing for her tour with Dane.

When Ophelia reappeared on the first floor of the inn to meet up with her host, she found Leilani waiting for her instead. The younger girl appeared awkward and uncomfortable as she shifted from one sandaled foot to the other and tugged on the hem of her coral-colored T-shirt.

"Dane's a little preoccupied right now, so he

asked if I could give you a tour of the plantation in his place."

Ophelia clenched her jaw. Her assignment here was difficult enough, given Dane's stubborn recalcitrance, but to have him renege on their arrangement so soon rankled thoroughly. Her mother had not advised her to throw away money needlessly. The $10,000 incentive was meant to anchor Ophelia to Dane's side, allowing her time to get to know the man and continually illustrate the benefits of his return.

But seeing Leilani's discomfort, she didn't feel she could take out her annoyance on the younger woman. She forced herself to relax.

"Well, he'll just have to make it up to me later, won't he? At least it will give us some girl time together, right?"

Leilani's fidgeting eased as a look of relief bloomed on her pretty face. She nodded enthusiastically. "Come on. I'll show you around."

"Surely you can appreciate my situation, Dane."

Dane clenched his jaw to keep from arguing. After all, Kenneth Masters had been generous enough in loaning Dane money to continue operations some months ago…if only Dane had realized the motives behind Masters's scheme before he had accepted. Now, the other man was suddenly revising the terms and requesting payment in full within the week.

"It's been a difficult year for all of us. You know how hard it is to compete with the larger estates."

Dane still said nothing. It was rumored that Masters imported cheaper, inferior coffee beans from other regions, mixing them with his own crop of Kona in order to offer "quality Kona coffee" at a significantly lower rate of sale than his fellow farmers could provide. No one had dared to pursue an investigation on Masters, however, and Dane hadn't learned about these illegal practices until after his deal with his shady neighbor had already been struck. It had unfortunately not occurred to Dane before this that perhaps Masters's motivations in loaning him the sum went beyond the simple profit he would make on their interest terms.

Dane continued to dig his shovel into the dirt as he formed holes for a new crop of coffee trees. After he felt he had the right depth, he tossed in some fertilizer consisting of macadamia husks, coffee cherry pulp and other various greens and compostable materials.

When he finally looked back up from his task, he saw Masters frowning at him critically. He wondered if the man disapproved of his tenacity in planting more trees when his farm was on the verge of bankruptcy.

"I thought we had agreed to six months on the loan," Dane finally said as he wiped the sweat from his forehead with the back of his arm.

"Well, as I've said, it's been a difficult year."

Dane sighed and leaned his weight wearily against the support of his shovel. "You know I was waiting until I harvest to pay you back the first installment."

"I hate to put you in a tough place, Dane. I know you've been trying your best with this plantation. Perhaps your reach has exceeded your grasp, hmm? Coffee trees aren't the same as corporate marketing. I have our contract in writing. There is a clause that states I can call in the loan at any time. My lawyer has all the necessary paperwork."

Dane held Masters's gaze until the other man looked away. He then straightened, took his shovel and began driving his spade into the earth once more, directing all his anger into the movement. He knew the clause Masters had mentioned. He hadn't noticed it until the deal was already done. At the time, he'd been distracted—another recruiter had shown up on his doorstep, this one more obnoxious than most. Coupled with his growing concerns over the farm's finances, he had been sloppy in his final review of the loan contract with Masters. The clause had not appeared until the last revision of the document, and he'd overlooked it in his haste to finalize the deal. When he had found the clause later, he'd hoped it was merely a formality. Now, he knew better. And he was angry at both himself for his carelessness and Masters for his underhanded trickery.

"Maybe we can come to some other sort of arrangement?" Masters suggested.

"I'm sure you already have something in mind," Dane remarked as he continued forcing his shovel into the soil, sweat beading on his brow.

"Why not a partnership? I'll provide the funds to carry you until the harvest, and in turn, you use your reputation and business contacts on the mainland to advance our joined operations."

Dane stopped digging but gripped the shovel handle tightly. "What was that?" He turned slowly, every line of his body tense at Masters's suggestion. "We could do *what?*"

Masters didn't even have the grace to look abashed. If anything, his smirk seemed even more pronounced than when he had first arrived and sought Dane out, forcing him to forego his afternoon tour with Ophelia and leaving his guest in Leilani's hands. He was sure Ms. Reid had been anything but happy about the handoff. But now, his pesky recruiter lingered in the corner of his mind. The $10,000 incentive would go a long way in repaying his loan to Masters, even if the other debts still piled up in the interim.

"Come now, Dane. We both know this is a tremendous undertaking for you, especially given your background."

"I was raised on a farm," Dane pointed out. "In the Midwest. I'm not a stranger to the manual labor or the long hours."

"Perhaps during your boyhood…" Masters trailed off. "But now? So many years later?" He clicked his tongue. "You're in over your head, man. If you're half the genius they claim, surely you can already see that."

Dane only knew one thing—success was a lot of hard work and a healthy helping of luck. The hard work wasn't the problem—he just hadn't stumbled into the luck bit yet.

"Why not let me help you out? By merging your name with mine, we could go far, Montgomery. Especially given your reputation in the corporate world—why not use that to our advantage?"

In that moment, Dane wanted very much to command Masters to leave his property, but he knew that such a reaction would gain him nothing but the satisfaction of Masters's indignation. It seemed everyone wanted a piece of his past and reputation, wishing to use his previous successes to their own benefit. He kept silent following Masters's suggestion, considering the best response to buy him more time without surrendering to the other man's demands. He was just thinking how desperately he needed some sort of miracle when he raised his head and saw Ophelia Reid striding toward them.

THOUGH OPHELIA HAD found Leilani to be an excellent guide, Dane's absence had chafed more and more as they'd continued her tour of the plantation. Granted, the rows of coffee trees laden with green orbs waiting to ripen into red coffee cherries had proved an impressive sight, but Ophelia had continued to calculate the minutes as lost opportunities to speak with Dane personally. Still, she'd occasionally found herself absorbed by Leilani's descriptions of wet processing, which resulted in a Kona coffee's clean, bright acidity, and the technique of sun drying the beans on decks called *hoshidanas*. She'd found herself asking questions and then clarifying each step of coffee cultivation, harvesting, processing, roasting, packaging and finally, distribution.

And despite her irritation over Dane's disappearing act, she had to admit his small operation was pretty impressive. She and Leilani had emerged from the plantation's roasting room and begun walking back through the orchards as Leilani summarized the seasons on the plantation and the cycle of life on a coffee farm. But Ophelia had begun tuning out the words as she'd once more wondered exactly where Dane had hidden himself away.

Had that been his intention, to simply hide from her throughout the remainder of her stay? Clearly, his word meant nothing if he planned to avoid her, hoping she would go away. What about the $10,000 incentive? And if he thought, for even one second, that she would lack determination then he had certainly underestimated her!

The longer she'd thought about it, the higher her anger had risen so that by the time she and Leilani had rounded the corner of a row of coffee tree saplings, she had worked herself into an internal lather of righteous indignation.

And when she'd seen Dane Montgomery, standing at ease with a shovel in his hand, she'd muttered a triumphant, "Aha!" under her breath and barreled toward him.

She sensed Leilani's gasp and the girl's struggle to keep up with her, but she kept up a clipped pace down the row of trees until she came abreast of her quarry.

"We had a deal."

"Ms. Reid—"

"Ophelia," she snapped. "And you broke our bargain."

Dane cleared his throat. "I apologize if you misunderstood—"

"Misunderstood?" She placed one hand on her hip. "*Misunderstood?* I hardly think I'm the one in need of clarification here."

She noticed Dane's jaw tighten. He seemed to have something to say, but she sensed he was desperately trying to hold his tongue. Then she became aware of the man beside Dane—a deeply tanned, silver-bearded gentleman who put Ophelia in mind of Long John Silver from the book *Treasure Island.*

"I don't believe we've met," the would-be pirate announced. "Kenneth Masters." He extended a hand. "Dane's neighbor."

Ophelia stuck her hand into his automatically. "Ophelia Reid, executive recruiter. From New York."

"Ahhhh." Masters's face lit up with what seemed to be approval. "So you've come to make an attempt at whisking Mr. Montgomery back to the mainland."

"No one is *whisking* me anywhere," Dane remarked.

Leilani came into Ophelia's line of vision, but she didn't look at her. She hoped she hadn't gotten the younger woman in trouble, but she wasn't about to let Dane off the hook.

"Mr. Montgomery and I had an appointment. He agreed to give me a tour this afternoon." She decided not to mention the particulars of their arrangement. "But he apparently has a different agenda."

"I'm afraid that's my fault," Masters apologized. "Dane was not expecting my visit today, but it could not be put off. We had an important matter to discuss."

Ophelia hesitated at this, her gaze shifting to Dane. She had never seen such tension in a man, tightly clenching his fist around the shovel's handle, the veins in his arm standing in sharp relief along the lines of muscle. She wondered what it would be like to be cradled in the safety of that strong embrace. Blinking, she looked back at Masters and shoved the thought aside.

"I—" She stopped. "Is that true?" she asked.

Masters nodded. "Perhaps you could help us come to some sort of agreement on the subject."

"Masters," Dane's tone was filled with warning, but Ophelia found herself curious. She suddenly realized the strain within the immediate atmosphere was not the direct result of her out-burst against Dane. He had already been tense when she'd come upon this scene.

"Oh, Montgomery, why not get her input? After all, if she's offering you some sort of con-tract, that could be a benefit to us all."

Ophelia had been manipulated enough by her mother to see Masters's tactics for what they were. Still, she waited. Dane made a noise of disgust, but he didn't stop Masters from elab-orating.

"I'm afraid Dane owes me a tidy sum of money—a loan I issued to him recently. Cer-tain circumstances have forced me to call in the debt earlier than anticipated, but of course, Dane is not yet prepared to pay it. I'm suggest-ing a partnership, which would pair his name with my own resources. Of course, his contacts and reputation in the corporate world would help elevate our joint venture. Wouldn't you agree?"

Ophelia stared at Masters. He stood, smil-ing amicably, and beneath the thin veneer of his pleasantness, she noted a flicker of smug conquest. He had Dane right where he wanted him, and the man was hard-pressed to keep from gloating. Ophelia felt a shudder of disgust run through her.

Shifting her gaze, she saw Leilani eyeing her

with sympathy while Dane looked off into the distance, as if he couldn't bear to witness this conversation.

She turned back to Masters, who continued to wait patiently, his grin growing more cocky and self-satisfied by the second.

"You're suggesting you take over his operation and gain the benefit of his name and reputation?"

"That's correct—a solution to satisfy everyone involved. Even you might benefit, should Dane decide to return to New York—he could promote our business there at the same time he accepts your client's offer."

Ophelia shook he head. "I'm afraid I have to disagree with you."

Masters's cheery smugness dissolved, his sneer faltering. "Excuse me?"

"It seems this scheme benefits you more than anyone else. Hardly a fair trade for a small loan of such short terms. And on the contrary, the proposal I'm offering would allow Dane the benefit of a substantial bonus, meaning he could easily clear any debt to you. No point in giving up his farm before harvesting his crops." She waited a beat before speaking again. "Wouldn't you agree?"

She found the sour twist to Masters's mouth strangely gratifying. Risking a quick glance at

Dane, she noted him watching her intently, his expression unreadable.

"Well." This single word from Masters's lips drew her attention back to him. "You'll hardly convince Montgomery to return to the mainland with such faulty logic."

The man suddenly seemed eager to leave.

"Dane, I'll stop by again in a few days' time. Unless, of course, you prefer to phone me with your decision sooner." He cleared his throat and bowed to Ophelia. "Best of luck to you, then, Miss Reid."

"Nice meeting you," she answered, but the compliment was not returned as the man strode away.

The atmosphere felt slightly lighter after Masters's departure, but Ophelia still recognized tension in the air as she faced Dane. She knew her outburst had done little to endear him to the object of her mission.

"I apologize for speaking so hastily concerning our agreement. I didn't realize you were dealing with important plantation matters."

Dane continued to eye her carefully, as if he couldn't quite make up his mind about what had just happened.

"The problem with you and your kind, Ms. Reid, is that you never stop to consider the world is not revolving around you and what you want."

Ophelia stiffened but bit her tongue to keep from offering a sharp reply. As she paused to rein in her temper, Leilani spoke up.

"I'm sure Dane still wants to honor your agreement. Right, boss?" Leilani nudged Dane's arm, seeming to remind him of his position in this situation.

In spite of her frustration with the man, she felt a sort of pity as his shoulders sagged. He sighed, his voice simply weary. "Right. Fine."

"How about if you and Ophelia join us for the bonfire tonight? Sam and some of our friends are having one on the beach. It'll be fun, and maybe it'll make up for this afternoon."

Ophelia hesitated. The entire day had already been a mess of conflict and misunderstandings. She couldn't imagine spending an entire evening in Dane Montgomery's presence, given his current mood. And although she knew it was part of her assignment, she felt disinclined to continue pursuing negotiations with him just now.

But to her surprise, Dane agreed to Leilani's suggestion.

"All right. If it will make up for my absence this afternoon." He turned to Ophelia, and she couldn't be sure if he was resigned or merely reserved on the matter. "Miss Reid...*Ophelia.* Would you like to join us this evening for a bonfire?"

And despite her own reservations, she answered with a polite nod.

"I would love to."

CHAPTER FOUR

OPHELIA COULDN'T KEEP from smiling as Leilani's boyfriend, Sam, continued to demonstrate the steps of the hula to her. Their friends gathered around the golden circle cast by the bonfire's light, alternating between shouts of encouragement for Ophelia and playful teasing toward Sam.

"You have no rhythm, brah! You've got to move your hips more!" one of Sam's friends called out.

"That's it, Ophelia! You were born to hula, girl!"

Despite the compliments, Ophelia knew the group was being kind. Her awkward movements couldn't compare to the elegant demonstrations Leilani and her friends had offered earlier. In fact, she suspected Sam's goofy flailing beside her was merely to draw attention away from her own lack of grace. It didn't bother her, though. Sam and Leilani, along with their friends, had been so warm and welcoming that she felt completely at ease among them. She had sustained mild teasing about her attire—after all, practicing the hula in business-casual pants and blouse hardly embraced the laid-back spirit of the islands. But she had endured the ribbing good-naturedly and wondered whether her professional dress had any sort of influence on Dane's decision, anyway.

As Sam segued into the next part of the hula, she held up her hands. "I think Sam and I have embarrassed ourselves enough for one night."

There were several calls of disappointment, but Ophelia shook her head. "You've all been a terrific audience." She bent at the waist and then straightened, flashing them a grin. Sam grabbed her hand and tugged her down into another brief bow.

"Ophelia and I are available for private parties, if any of you are interested. Our rates are negotiable."

This elicited another round of banter as Ophelia laughed and stole away from the center of the circle to settle herself on a blanket near Dane. She sensed him watching her for several seconds before he finally moved from his own blanket and onto hers. He passed her a bowl of pineapple and papaya chunks, and she fished a cube of ripe, golden fruit from the dish.

"Thanks," she said before popping it into her mouth. She enjoyed the juicy explosion of sweet and tart on her tongue. She was beginning to realize that tropical fruits tasted even more delicious when eaten on the same island where they were grown.

"You're a fast learner," Dane finally remarked, after she had chewed and swallowed her bite of pineapple.

She couldn't help laughing softly. "I don't think I'll be entering any hula competitions anytime soon."

"You weren't bad," he replied.

She made a face. "But not that good. You can say it."

He didn't. In fact, he didn't say anything at all. She slid a glance toward him out of the corner of her eye and saw that his gaze stretched out over the ocean. Another set of guys had taken Sam and Ophelia's place in the circle, and they took turns mimicking Sam's antics of a few minutes before.

"Do you hang out with these guys much? They seem like a lot of fun."

Dane's attention pulled from the water and back toward the others, fondness touching his features. "Sometimes. They're more Leilani and Sam's friends than mine, but they're a good crowd. They've been kind to Leilani, taking her under their wing."

"Leilani mentioned she was in some trouble last year. Nothing too serious, I hope? She seems like too sweet of a girl to be into anything very bad."

"Bad crowd, poor decisions." He gave a little shrug. "I don't think it's what she wanted—she was just trying to find a place for herself."

Ophelia hesitated. "I guess she's not the only one. Hawaii seems like a good choice to find a place for yourself." She looked at him pointedly after this observation, but he didn't rise to the bait.

She finally released a small sigh and followed his line of sight out over the ocean, observing the lip of foam-tipped waves as they ran up the shoreline and then receded with precise regularity. Moonlight silvered the water's surface, creating beautiful shades of metallic-blue, which complemented the dusky cobalt of the twilight sky. Ophelia tried to memorize the sight, knowing she would never witness anything like it back in New York.

"Why did you do that today? With Masters?"

The soft question startled Ophelia as she turned her attention back to the man beside her.

"Do what?"

He didn't immediately reply as he kept his stare fastened on her face. She forced herself to keep meeting his eyes, despite the uncomfortable directness of his gaze. The bonfire's light illuminated his features in a soft bronze glow, and she was able to truly appreciate the strong length of his stubble-dusted jaw, the chiseled lines and planes of his face and the piercing awareness of his deep, blue eyes. No wonder he had captivated the corporate world so completely. In addition to his immense intelligence and skill, he was handsome enough to compete with the very best Hollywood itself had to offer.

She felt a rapidly growing consciousness of his proximity and the heat that radiated as much from him as from the fire several feet away.

"I confess that I can't quite figure you out, Ophelia Reid."

She blinked. "Oh? Well, perhaps recruiters are more complex than you give us credit for."

A corner of his lip twitched, but he shook his head in denial at this statement. "No, I don't think so. It's just that you're…more subtle than the rest of them."

This caused her to laugh. "I never thought of subtle as one of my strong suits." She shrugged. "I'm not as aggressive as some, but I try not to be manipulative, either." Looking away, she tried to explain herself without putting him off. "I like what I do because I believe I'm helping people in some way. I enjoy placing others in their dream roles and careers so that they can achieve some sort of fulfillment in their everyday lives."

"And that, in turn, fulfills *you*. Is that what you're saying?"

She watched as the others in the group pulled out a ball and began tossing it around. "Sure. Of course. It's a noble endeavor, wouldn't you agree?"

He scoffed lightly, and her eyes snapped back to him. He, too, had turned his attention to the game the others were playing so that his eyes mercifully rested elsewhere. "Helping others fulfill their dreams seems like an easy way to keep from living your own."

She felt a flare of indignation at this remark but bit her cheek to prevent herself from responding in kind. His words were an attempt to goad her into an outburst, she was sure of it. She would not let him have the satisfaction. After all, a lifetime spent beneath Lillian Reid's caustic remarks had taught her the value of silence in the face of criticism.

"You're offended," he stated.

She clamped down harder on her cheek until she could formulate a proper response. "Not at all. I understand your prejudices may prevent you from seeing a clear picture of my life."

Or in other words, she thought, *You don't know me. Stop acting like you do.*

His genuine laughter caused her to relax a bit. "Maybe you're right," he admitted. "But how do you justify what you're doing here, with me?"

She frowned. "What do you mean?"

"What if I don't *want* you to place me in my 'dream role,' as you put it. What if I'm perfectly happy and fulfilled right here, in my current everyday life?"

She looked away again, unable to form an immediate response to this question. She spotted Leilani in the midst of her friends. Sam's arm rested protectively around her shoulders, and Ophelia felt a strange twinge of jealousy. Not for Sam, who was handsome enough but far too young for Ophelia's interest, but rather for the ease the two young lovers clearly felt around each other.

"Did I touch a nerve?"

Dane's voice drew her attention back.

"Of course not," she replied. "It's only that your situation is unique. Your high profile has made you a target—a trophy of sorts. Everyone wants to be the person who brings you back because then, perhaps some of your greatness will rub off on them."

He grunted with what sounded like annoyance. "You really do enjoy flattering me, don't you, Miss Reid?"

Something inside her shifted at these words. She rolled her eyes. "Hardly. Thus far, *Mr. Montgomery,* you have proven to be rather unworthy of flattery. You have been rude to the point of caustic, and your behavior seems to be based solely on your prejudice for my profession. You don't even know me, so I hardly think you have the right to judge me."

Dane's eyebrows had shot up during this little speech, and from her peripheral vision, she noted a few stares turning their way.

"Furthermore, concerning my remarks that you seem so intent on labeling as 'flattery,' might I remind you that for all your so-called brilliance in the corporate world, your latest venture is on the verge of bankruptcy. If you find my conversation to be obsequious, I can assure you that I am not attempting to ingratiate myself with you. In fact, if your coffee plantation fails, I may be the last recruiter you ever see. So enjoy skewing my words while you can. You may never get another chance to do so."

With that, she stood to her feet, noticed that every one of Sam and Leilani's friends had fallen silent and felt a rush of embarrassment. Turning on her heel, she stomped off down the beach, cursing her inappropriate clothes and wondering how she was going to explain her failure to her mother.

The farther she walked, the more distressed she became. She rarely lost her temper in such a manner—she had long ago taught herself to remain composed in every situation. Lillian demanded it. And now, on only her second day, she had allowed Dane Montgomery's ego to get the better of her. Stupid! She could just imagine her mother's cold disapproval when she returned to New York several days early and without Dane. Paris would remain a distant dream on the horizon. Cole would be sickeningly sympathetic. She might even face demotion.

She was just considering whether her mother would actually fire her over this failure when she heard footsteps pounding on the sand behind her. Looking over her shoulder, she realized that in her distress, she had walked quite a distance down the beach. But the figure coming up on her was the last she had expected to see—Dane Montgomery slowed to a walk as she stopped in her tracks.

"You didn't need to run off," he said.

Somehow, this statement ruffled her feathers all over again. "You can't tell me what to do— I'm not one of your inn's staff." It sounded ridiculously petulant, even to her own ears.

But to her surprise, Dane chuckled. "Thank

God for that. I have no idea what I'd do with you if you were."

She blinked. "Are you insulting me? Because I really don't think—"

"Not at all," Dane hastened to say. "On the contrary…I may have had that speech coming." He considered. "Well, maybe not all of it. After all, *you're* the one who came here trying to drag me back to a life I left behind. And you have to admit that you really aren't taking my 'no' very well. Besides, throwing money at the situation is pretty insulting in itself, wouldn't you agree?"

Ophelia narrowed her eyes. "If this is an apology, I've heard better."

He sighed elaborately and ran a hand through his hair. The moonlight cast his face in softly sad lines, the sharp cut of his frown standing out in stark contrast. Ophelia felt a sudden and unexpected tug of sympathy for him. How many times must he tell the world to leave him alone before they listened? No wonder his reception of her had been cool. She should feel fortunate he hadn't been outright hostile, given the constant intrusions to his private life, especially considering all he faced with his current financial situation.

"We've gotten off to an abominable start, haven't we?" she remarked.

He looked startled as he shifted his eyes her way. "To put it mildly," he replied with the faintest twitch of his lips.

She drew a breath. "I know it must be difficult for you," she conceded, "with strangers prying into your life every couple of months and attempting to pull you in a different direction."

He said nothing, but she noticed he had gone very still, his eyes intent on her.

"I'm not your enemy, Dane. What you do with your life is your own choice. But please try to accept that I'm in a difficult position, as well. Perhaps we could just call a truce and try to see the next few days out in peace?"

He remained wary, still eyeing her carefully. "And at the end of it? What will you do if I still don't want to go back?"

She didn't answer him immediately, considering everything she would lose if he didn't return with her. The weight of that responsibility rested heavily on her shoulders, but she forced herself to lift them into a casual shrug. "We'll worry about that when my time here is through."

He continued to size her up, and the longer he studied her, the more grateful she was for the twilight so that it could camouflage the blush she knew must be staining her cheeks.

"You never answered my question," he finally said. "On why you spoke up for me today with Masters."

She swallowed, shifting her gaze from the intensity of his to look out over the diamond-cut waves glittering in the moonlight.

"Because…" She drew in a breath and then released it. "Because no one should be forced into giving up on their dreams."

She looked back to find his head cocked, his expression much softer than she'd seen it at any point during her trip thus far.

"Do you speak from experience, Ms. Reid?"

She tried to shift the subject away from her. "Why not apply for a loan with a local bank and clear your debt to Masters that way?"

His frown deepened. "I tried that—it seems Masters isn't the only one who doubts that my corporate skills will carry a venture such as coffee farming."

"And using the plantation as collateral?"

"The market is already saturated with properties, what with the state of the economy. Apparently, I'm a high risk."

Now it was her turn to frown. It sounded as if Dane Montgomery had truly found himself with his back against the wall.

He paused before bowing slightly and gesturing toward the bonfire some distance behind them. "Would you like to return to the party?"

With a nod of acknowledgment, Ophelia stepped past him and began heading back the way she'd come. As she passed Dane, however, she noted a different glint in his eye, a spark of kindled interest.

She only hoped it could work in her favor during this upcoming week.

DANE WATCHED OPHELIA step ahead of him down the beach on their way back to the bonfire. He found himself distracted by the golden sheen of her hair, rich as burnished gold in the tropical luminescence. He considered her statement that no one should have to give up on their dreams. These mysterious words had woken a curiosity in him. What were Ophelia Reid's dreams? He'd never considered such a question of all the other recruiters who had come before her.

But then, none of the others had possessed her unique charm, either. How many would have shot Masters down in such a manner, especially when the man's suggestion of a partnership supported Ophelia's goals? Accepting the Towers job held the possibility to give both this recruiter and his neighbor exactly what they wanted. But Ophelia hadn't played Masters's game. Instead, she had taken Dane's side even if it wasn't in line with her quest.

He had to confess that such a move was either highly calculated on her part or revealed a depth of character he hadn't seen in some time—perhaps ever. The thought appealed to him, and he found himself wondering just what kind of person Ophelia Reid was—cool and calculating as her mother's own reputation suggested or was there something softer and more understanding in her nature? He knew it was best to keep his guard up where his inn's guest was concerned.

Coupled with his growing financial concerns surrounding the plantation, Ophelia Reid's presence was more than a little dangerous to his endeavors. He couldn't deny the attraction he felt toward her, and the uncertainty of his future made her proposal more tempting than he would like. Yet he did not want to give up on his dreams here in Hawaii. Nor did he wish for his awareness of Ophelia Reid to be heightened. Doubt and desire were a dangerous mix.

Just then, Ophelia glanced over her shoulder, catching his eye as they approached the bonfire, its fiery light illuminating her from behind with a soft glow. She cast him a friendly smile, as if to seal their truce, and he found his breath caught in his chest at the sight.

He swallowed and attempted a neutral expression in response.

Ophelia Reid might be dangerous, indeed.

THE FOLLOWING MORNING when Ophelia came downstairs, she found Dane already waiting for her. He was dressed casually, in khaki slacks and a plain black T-shirt. Ophelia couldn't help noticing how well the dark shirt complemented his island-bronzed skin, revealing the cords of muscle in his forearms. It was only when his arms lifted and crossed over his chest that she realized she'd been staring at them.

"Good morning," he greeted, and she fought a flush as she tore her gaze away from his physique and to his face.

"G-good morning." Her glance flickered from his bemused expression and toward the dining room.

"Am I...late for breakfast?"

"Not at all. I was actually thinking we could eat breakfast on the way."

"On the way?"

"To Honaunau. As part of our arrangement," he prompted.

She broke into a smile as understanding dawned. "You're taking me sightseeing."

He gave a short nod and then his eyes dropped, inching slowly up from her designer shoes, past her slacks, over her button-down shirt and back to her face, which she knew must be bright red, considering how hot it felt after his intense perusal.

"Did you pack anything other than business suits for this trip?" Disapproval colored his tone, and she chafed at the sound.

"My travel plans were a bit unexpected," she defended. "I didn't have time to shop for anything more appropriate."

He stared at her in disbelief. "You mean you don't have a pair of shorts or jeans in your entire wardrobe?"

She frowned, imagining what her mother would think, seeing her daughter sporting shorts. Even as a teenager, Lillian's dress code for her daughter hadn't permitted anything quite so casual.

"I…I…" She was at a loss.

"Please tell me you at least have a swimsuit along."

"Of course!" She latched on to this. "It's upstairs. In my suitcase." She didn't feel the need to explain the suit belonged to Holly, who had insisted she bring it along. Ophelia had emphasized the business nature of this trip, but Holly had told her she never knew when it might come in handy. She made a mental reminder to buy Holly something extremely nice for Christmas.

"And what about the rest of your attire?" Dane pressed. "Did you bring anything that could be worn outside of the office?"

She ground her teeth together and glared, not bothering to answer.

"Ah. All right, then."

She found his amusement infuriating.

"Leilani is in the office with Keahi. Let's ask her if she has anything that might fit you."

The idea of sharing Leilani's clothes alarmed Ophelia initially. She had visions of herself in cutoff jean shorts and midriff-baring tops such as the one the younger girl had been wearing the first night she and Ophelia had met. But Leilani's tastes proved to be far more diverse than simple weekend attire. Within thirty minutes, Ophelia emerged downstairs once more, sporting olive-green capris and a crisp, white camp-style shirt. She had brushed her hair up into a ponytail, its ends swishing against her neck as she landed on the bottom step.

Something about the casual dress and the feel of her hair off her face left her delightfully buoyant and carefree. She couldn't remember the last time she had experienced such a feeling.

She decided her effervescent emotions must

have been evident in her expression because when Dane looked up from where he'd been leaning over the receptionist desk, his jaw slackened in seeming surprise.

Approaching the reception area, she cast a glance down at her borrowed outfit. "Will this do?"

Dane made a noise, deep in his throat, which caused her eyes to jerk back up. He snapped his mouth closed and coughed. "Um, sure... that will do just fine."

His gaze swept over her once more. "Leilani didn't have any shoes in your size?"

Ophelia curled her toes beneath her self-consciously and held up the pair of shoes she'd been holding. "She gave me some flip-flops that are too big for her."

"That'll work." Dane's face had retreated back into casual passivity. "Are you ready to go?"

She nodded.

"Then let's head out."

OPHELIA DIDN'T CHATTER endlessly throughout the drive as Dane feared she might. She seemed content to look out the window, asking the occasional question about the highway along the coast in between bites of the banana muffins and sips of the Kona coffee Pele had provided.

He found himself hard-pressed to keep his eyes on the road as he navigated his Jeep down the mountain and toward the coast. The morning breeze filled the interior of the cab, teasing his senses with the fresh scents of island dew, warm banana muffins and the floral notes of Ophelia's shampoo. He had noticed its pleasant smell when he'd held the passenger-side door open for her as they'd prepared to leave the plantation. Now, it wafted under his nose, causing him to work doubly hard in focusing on the road before them.

"So where are we headed?" Ophelia finally asked as she brushed muffin crumbs from her lap.

Dane's stare rose from her hands to her inquisitive gaze. She seemed truly interested in the day's outing, he realized. On some level, he had assumed her desire to tour the area was feigned, and this dawning recognition of her genuine anticipation warmed him until he actually felt a smile stealing its way across his mouth.

"Pu'uhonua O Hōnaunau," he answered.

"Now say it three times fast," she said.

He laughed, pleased at her quick response. *"Pu'uhonua O Hōnaunau,"* he repeated, "means Place of Refuge at Hōnaunau."

"Okay, so what is it, then, this Place of Refuge?"

"It stood as a safe haven for ancient Hawaiians. It could be used in times of war as a sanctuary for either side of the conflict. The old native religion was filled with all these laws, and to violate one of those sacred commandments often meant death. The Hawaiians called it breaking *kapu*."

Dane had been looking at the road in front of him, but he stole a glance away now to see Ophelia's eyes trained on his face. She appeared engrossed in his words, and he felt a swell of gratification as he turned his attention back to the highway.

"If someone broke *kapu,* the act rendered them a criminal, and the only way to escape execution was if they could swim the shark-infested waters of Honaunau Bay and reach the walls of the temple grounds before their pursuers caught up with them. If they managed that, the priests would take them in and feed them, sheltering them in the *heiau,* the temple, for a couple days so they could be kept under the protection of the gods, who were the spirits of ancient chiefs."

Dane slid another quick glance at Ophelia and saw her absorbing this explanation. "What happened if their pursuers came after them into the temple?"

He shook his head. "It was forbidden to spill blood within the boundaries of the *Pu'uhonua O Hōnaunau*. The refugees couldn't be touched as long as they remained there."

"And once they left?"

"Supposedly, the protection of the gods went with them. Although I'm sure not every story had a happy ending."

Dane rounded a curve as he sensed Ophelia shifting in her seat. "Like Esmeralda in *The Hunchback of Notre Dame,* when she claims sanctuary in the cathedral to escape Frollo."

He glanced her way. "You're a fan of the classics?"

"Not the classics, per se. I grew up in Paris. I've been to Notre Dame several times. Hugo's novel was a favorite obsession of mine as a teenager."

Dane searched his memory, trying to recall any references he had heard of Lillian Reid having ties in Paris. He could recall none.

"I assumed you were born and raised in New York," he commented.

From the corner of his eye, he saw her shrug. "My father was French but much older than my mother. We lived there until his death when I was seven. That's when my mother returned with me to the States and opened the recruiting agency."

He sensed that her casual response blanketed a much deeper story but chose not to pursue it. Yet.

"Do you speak French, then?" he asked.

She responded by rattling off a long string of words in lyrical French and then shrugged. "I'm fluent. I spent summers in Paris as a teenager, staying with my cousins."

He recognized the nostalgia in her voice. "It sounds like you miss it."

She was silent for a long stretch.

"It's the only place I ever felt really at home. Like the Place of Refuge, it was my sanctuary."

She grew quiet once more, and though Dane wished to question her further, he didn't know how to broach the subject. But he recognized that something unspoken weighed on her, some burden she hadn't shared aloud.

He longed to learn what she had kept hidden, but just then, they arrived at the Place of Refuge, and his opportunity passed.

He determined that before the day was out, he would discover more about Ophelia's need for a sanctuary.

CHAPTER FIVE

OPHELIA BREATHED A sigh of relief as Dane pulled into the parking lot of *Pu'uhonua O Hōnaunau*. Their conversation had been trespassing on dangerously familiar ground, and she wasn't sure how much personal information she should share with Dane.

Not that she didn't want to share with him. She found him amazingly easy to talk to, but she barely knew this man, and her objective here did not include creating any real intimacy between them—only gaining his trust and confidence so she could steer him toward the right decision.

She put these thoughts aside, however, as she exited the vehicle and followed Dane to the entrance. By the time they paid the admission fee and entered the Refuge area, her attention was fully refocused by the historic views around her. She took in the sight of the wall bordering the Place of Refuge. It was an impressive display of the boundaries guarding the sanctuary.

"It's made of lava rock," Dane informed as

he stood beside her. "Something like twelve feet high and seventeen feet thick. It's over one thousand feet long."

"Amazing to think this was all done before the invention of modern machinery. It must have taken forever to assemble."

"Well, if you think this is impressive, wait until you see the *ki'i* statues guarding the temple that overlooks the cove. They're a fierce sight to behold. I can't imagine swimming the bay only to encounter such monstrous images."

"Like the gargoyles of Notre Dame," she observed.

His eyes lit up. "Exactly!"

The animation in Dane's voice tugged at Ophelia somewhere deep inside. He loved this place—the islands with their rich history, beloved traditions and warm people. They drew him in the same way Paris had always drawn her. Just then, something in Ophelia shifted, and as she watched Dane, still highlighting the significance of sanctuary within the walls of the Refuge, she suddenly felt a kinship with him take root in her. Perhaps their dreams differed a bit, but this mutual passion for a place of belonging drew her a little closer to understanding his intense reaction to interlopers.

She waited until he paused for breath before speaking once more. "Well, then, give me the grand tour of the place. It sounds like you're the best guide I could have."

He positively beamed at these words, and before she quite realized it was happening, his palm was resting in the small of her back, gently guiding her along the wooden walkway toward the beach. At first, her muscles tensed at his touch, and then she gradually relaxed, even leaning in toward him to catch his every word as his voice fell hushed with reverence.

It was the sacredness of the spot, she realized. The other tourists were equally soft in their conversations, immersed in the tranquility of the Refuge. Dane led her toward the beach where a young man worked at carving a log of koa wood into an outrigger canoe. Other tourists gathered around to watch until a little girl exclaimed and drew their attention several yards away to the presence of two sea turtles slowly making their way up the shore.

Ophelia and Dane observed their steady progress for a bit before moving on toward the temple, which Dane pronounced as *Hale o Keawe heiau* in Hawaiian. He whispered in her ear that the bones of twenty-three ancient chiefs were once housed in the structure, and it was their ancestral power that gave the temple its honors of asylum.

"The Refuge wasn't just for those who broke

kapu, either," Dane elaborated. "When war broke out, it was neutral territory for anyone who sought safety within its walls. Your enemies could not come past the white *tapa* streamers. If you made it past those lines, you were safe. For the time being."

He turned his head in her direction, and she was confronted with the intense stare of his blue eyes before jerking back, realizing how close she had been leaning in toward him. He cleared his throat and looked away while she fought the blush she knew must be rising in her cheeks.

Before she could say anything to dispel the awkwardness, a group of performers began filing out onto the platform before the *heiau*. They were dressed in full ancient tribal regalia complete with colorful feathered capes and headdresses that gave the impression of tropical birds. The women wore long-flowing grass skirts and swaths of fabric across their chests in colors of turquoise-blue and lava-red. Their thick, dark hair reached down their backs to touch the base of their hips as they began to rotate slowly into the beginnings of the hula dance.

Two of the men began singing in soft cadences of the Hawaiian tongue, their voices growing louder as they progressed and the women's hips undulating in time to the music. As it had been since she and Dane arrived, the atmosphere remained reverent, the grounds bathed in hushed respect for the holiness of the place. Ophelia relaxed once more as she observed the graceful swaying of the dancers' hips, the fluid movement of their arms as they weaved them through the air. She felt rather envious of their elegant, easy gestures, their arms gliding through the movements in an expression of culture and tradition.

As the hula dance concluded, the small crowd of tourists dispersed, and Dane led her away farther down the beach. They strolled in silence for a few minutes, and Ophelia breathed in the clean, crisp scent of the salty air.

"This place is amazing," Ophelia confessed, turning her attention to Dane and finding him watching her closely. "How reassuring to have such a safe haven—the opportunity to escape your mistakes by seeking refuge here."

"After swimming past the sharks in the bay and finding your way over the lava-rock flats of the shore," Dane reminded her.

She rolled her eyes. "Well, there's *that,* yes." She paused. "But it had to be a comfort of sorts, didn't it? To know that if you messed up and broke *kapu* or if someone had it out for you… you could always try to reach this place and be sheltered from whatever pursued you. To have a refuge like that, in the midst of any crisis—the Hawaiians were brilliant to think it up."

She thought maybe Dane would laugh at this, but he nodded seriously. "I always liked the idea of a clean slate—coming here and having your sin absolved, for whatever law you'd broken. It makes the thought of slipping up a little less…dramatic."

She nudged him slightly. "Dane Montgomery? Make mistakes? I don't believe it."

The teasing tone in her voice caused him to smile but only slightly. "When the world puts you on a pedestal, one mistake is a very long way to fall."

This statement sobered her. "Is that why you left? Stopped doing what you did? Were you afraid you'd take a fall?"

He shrugged and looked out over the water. "I stopped because…I didn't enjoy it anymore. Any of it. I had no one to tell me the truth, to bounce ideas off without receiving some sort of worshipful response. The challenges became the same, day in and day out, and the people who surrounded me…they were all the same, too."

He looked at her, and she felt a swell of sympathy.

"I left because it wasn't worth it anymore."

She knew now was the time to highlight all the reasons he should return, under this particular assignment. She considered saying how Towers Resorts International was a unique situation, requiring his specific skills and how he'd be working among those who challenged his vision, as well as complemented it....

But seeing the weary expression on Dane's face, the haggard look in his eyes when he talked about his life before this one—the words died before they could reach her lips.

Dane began walking along the shore, just beyond reach of the waves stretching across it. Ophelia followed.

"So how about you?" he asked. "What made you decide to follow in your mother's footsteps?"

Ophelia hesitated, but when Dane looked back at her, she shrugged. "I never really considered doing anything else. Except..."

"Except?"

"For photography. I used to love taking pictures, and I had this crazy dream to become a Parisian photographer, live in an artist's studio and sell postcards of the Eiffel Tower featuring my own photos." She laughed softly to dispel the regret in her words. "But Ms. Reid, um... Mother soon convinced me of the impossibility of such a plan."

Dane didn't reply immediately, but they walked side by side in the direction of the visitor's center.

"Were you any good?" he asked at last.

"I won a few awards in high school, took photographs for the school newspaper. That sort of thing."

"So is that what you were referring to, concerning the conversation with Masters? When you said no one should be bullied into giving up on their dream?"

She frowned. "Something like that, I guess."

She was relieved when Dane didn't pursue the topic further.

Instead, he suggested they head the short distance to Honaunau Bay to do some snorkeling. The idea both intrigued and intimidated her. She had been raised in the city, after all, and most of her underwater adventures had taken place at her mother's upscale gym. When she told Dane this after arriving at the bay, he laughed and thrust a mask into her hands.

She turned her back as she slipped out of her borrowed outfit to reveal the swimsuit beneath. Though she was grateful for Holly's insistence in offering her a suit, she wished her assistant's tastes were a bit more modest. The bikini left little to the imagination.

Her fears were confirmed as she turned and

caught Dane drinking in an eyeful of her figure. To his credit, he quickly turned away and directed her toward the gear he had brought.

She and Dane settled on the lava-rock flats fronting the bay to don their snorkeling equipment before stepping into the waves. She had been reluctant when they first entered the bay and more than a little distracted by the sight of Dane's chiseled chest and shoulders as he treaded water beside her. His instructions had been simple enough on how to clear the snorkel's tube and comfortably position the mask and mouthpiece to look at her reassuringly.

Her hesitation must have been evident on her face because Dane removed his own mask and mouthpiece to smile at her.

"You'll be fine, Ophelia. I'm right here, okay? It's only a depth of about ten feet this close to shore, and I'll be right next to you the entire time."

She nodded and suddenly relaxed, as if her body simply needed the reassurance that Dane wasn't going anywhere. He repositioned his snorkel and mask and waited until she gave a nod before leading the way and ducking into the water ahead of her. With a deep breath, she followed.

For an hour, they explored the underwater landscape of Honaunau Bay, and Dane kept his word, always staying near enough that she could reach out and touch him, if necessary. Gradually, she relaxed so completely that the experience became one of wonder rather than worry. She frequently swept her hand through the water to brush Dane, drawing his attention to her latest discovery: a unique formation of coral, the flick of a tang's tale, the slithering departure of a moray eel, and the ever-present sea turtles gliding through the water with a grace they simply could not replicate on land.

Ophelia and Dane surfaced repeatedly to purge their snorkel tubes but did little speaking before returning underwater. Finally, they looked at each other and with unspoken, mutual agreement, surfaced and swam for the shore. Dane helped Ophelia stand and guided her back to a shelf of lava rock where she could sit and catch her breath.

"That was…*amazing!*" she gushed. "Did you see how close the turtles came? They swam right by me! One even brushed my arm!"

Dane grinned as he shook the water out of his hair. "I noticed. I was there."

She laughed and reached up a hand to wring the water from her own hair. "Oh, of course. You must be used to this by now."

"What? Never. It's a new experience every time I do something like this. You never know what you'll see. Of course—" he eyed her "—it's fun seeing it for the first time through someone else's eyes. Besides, you did pretty good for a city girl."

His words were teasing, but she felt a flush of pleasure nonetheless. "Thanks. Guess those lessons at Mother's gym paid off."

His laughter warmed her even more.

"So…you grew up in Paris?" he asked.

She spread her palms across the sun-warmed surface of the rock beneath them, letting the heat soak into her water-wrinkled fingers. "Until I was seven," she reminded.

"Right, when your father died."

"Mmm."

He leaned back, his weight leveraged by his arms as he supported himself on the stone plateau. "That must have been difficult, losing your father so young."

She released a sigh. "It was a long time ago."

"Did you miss it? When you moved back to the States?"

Ophelia wasn't sure why she didn't mind these questions from him. Generally, she shied away from speaking about her childhood, her father's death and the bitter changes in her mother's personality once she moved them to New York. Perhaps it was the water, which had washed away her inhibitions, or the comforting warmth of the sun, heating the rocks beneath her, but she felt completely at ease as she answered him.

"I missed it so much that it became my dream to move back there one day. I've never wanted anything as much as I've wanted to return there for good. It was home. No place since has ever felt so inviting to me."

"I take it your mother didn't feel the same way?"

Ophelia cringed involuntarily. "It was more difficult for her. She had lost her husband, was saddled with a young daughter to raise. I don't think she saw beyond the basic need to provide for us after my father died."

"Your father had no means in place in the event of his death?"

"Some," she confessed. "Enough for the initial capital to get Reid Recruiting off the ground. My mother worked very hard to see that it paid off."

She tilted her head back, allowing the sun to saturate her skin and send waves of warmth across her body. After a time, she realized Dane had fallen silent. She opened her eyes and turned her head to find him studying her intently. She felt the first twinge of self-consciousness since she had begun speaking.

His stare lingered for a moment longer before he turned his attention away.

"It must be difficult," he ventured after a brief silence, "to live in her shadow."

"Not so much her shadow as her very aura."

"Mmm." His silence following this nettled her, so that she looked at him.

"Don't pretend to know what it's like. I bet your parents are wonderful people—a mom who baked apple pies and welcomed you home from school, and a father who worked hard but took the time to help you with your homework at night."

"You're not that far off," he agreed. "But my father's gone now. He died of a massive heart attack two years ago."

"Oh. I'm sorry to hear that." She felt a swell of sympathy for his loss, especially so soon after his retirement. She wondered if his father had ever had the chance to visit the inn and plantation to see what his son was trying to accomplish. "And your mother?"

"I tried to convince her to move here after his death, but she didn't want to leave her life in Ohio behind. My sister lives about two hours from her, so she keeps an eye on things. Mom loves having her grandkids visit, and yes, it just so happens that her specialty is apple pie."

Ophelia felt a swell of resentment, perhaps

even jealousy. "My mother's just not that kind of woman. It doesn't mean she doesn't love me or anything like that. She does. I know she does." Ophelia hated how defensive she sounded.

"I never said she didn't." Dane paused. "It must have been difficult for her, raising you alone." He paused again, then said, "So how about dating? Anyone special?"

"Not…currently."

He raised an eyebrow with interest. "I sense a story."

"No, no story." She spoke a little too quickly, and his second eyebrow rose. "Okay, well, there was someone, but we recently…decided to take a break."

"We? A mutual parting?"

"Um…"

He rose up from where he'd been leaning on the rocks. She did the same.

"Was it a long-term relationship?"

"Four years."

He whistled low. "So why the *break,* as you called it?"

"It's complicated."

He folded his arms across his chest, and she forced herself not to stare at the sight. "Come on, I'm curious."

"I'm sure you are." She made a face.

He unfolded his arms and held up his hands in surrender. "Sorry. It's obviously a sore subject."

She looked away.

"Did you love him?" he asked.

She felt a tug of something like…disappointment. "Like I said, it's complicated."

"When isn't love complicated?"

Her eyes jerked to his. "And what about you? There was a long list of high-profile dates during your time, but you never stayed with anyone for long. Has someone here in Hawaii captured your attention? Is that why you're so adamant about staying on the island?"

He shrugged noncommittally, and Ophelia felt another twinge of disappointment. His vague response led her to believe that maybe there was a special someone in his life, and to her chagrin, she found the thought upsetting.

"I'm sorry. I guess it's not really my business, either."

They sat in silence for a long time after that, watching the tourists in the bay and listening to the roar of surf. Ophelia found herself surprised that she wasn't really uncomfortable in the quiet between them. Despite the awkwardness of their conversation, she continued to feel at ease around Dane.

She was marveling at this when Dane finally spoke up once more.

"There's no one special in my life."

She had her legs drawn up to her chest with her arms resting upon them. Now she turned and laid her cheek against her arm, waiting for him to look her way.

When he did, she felt her stomach somersault inside her.

"I've dated a lot of great women. I just never found one that I still wanted to be waking up to thirty, forty, fifty years down the road."

She felt a swell of relief and hated that her emotions seemed to be reacting with no consideration for the part of her that knew attraction to Dane Montgomery was a bad idea.

"I have plans...to move to Paris," she confessed. "Cole doesn't want to join me. We argued about it— He always told me he'd come with me, when the time came. But now that I'm moving forward with the plan, he doesn't want to leave New York."

"Ah."

"Yeah. So...I told him I thought it would be better if we weren't together for a while."

She swiveled her head away from Dane and looked out over the ocean once more. "The truth is, I'm not sure if I love him or not. After four years…shouldn't a person be more certain?"

Dane didn't respond, so she shrugged.

"I don't suppose hearing about my love life was what you had in mind when you agreed to take me sightseeing."

"I don't mind." There was something in his tone, some catch of interest that drew her eyes back to his. He was studying her with that same intensity she had witnessed on and off throughout their morning together. She couldn't be sure what he was thinking, but the heat in his stare warmed her more thoroughly than the Hawaiian sun.

She cleared her throat and straightened up. "Okay, then, what's next on the agenda?"

Dane shook his head slightly, as though clearing it of whatever thoughts had been distracting him as he watched her. "Well, in keeping with the theme of sanctuary, there's a church you might be interested in seeing."

She cocked her head. "A church? Sounds like an odd tourist hotspot."

He grinned. "Don't judge it just yet. Come on, let's head back to the Jeep."

AT THE ENTRANCE of the St. Benedict Roman Catholic church, Dane gestured for Ophelia to precede him.

He couldn't help inhaling quickly as she passed by, breathing in the faded scent of her shampoo along with salt water and sun. She had swept her blond hair back into a ponytail again, following their morning swim, and as she walked by, he noticed glittering crystals of sand sprinkled throughout the strands.

He followed behind her into the church, smiling with gratification as he heard her intake of breath.

"I've never seen so much color in a church," she breathed.

They strolled down the center aisle together, Ophelia's neck arching to take in the Gothic nave-inspired ceiling with its vibrant tropical hues conveying water, sand and palm trees. As they moved farther into the room, her head dropped to swivel right then left then right again as she took in the artwork covering the church's walls. Images of saints and Biblical tales were reenacted throughout the murals and frescoes.

"The painting was done by a Belgian priest, Father Velghe, in 1899," Dane said.

Ophelia moved down one of the pews to inspect a mural. "What kind of paint is it?" she asked, reaching out a hand to slide her fingers down the wood.

"Simple house paint," Dane answered. "He

did it for his parishioners, many of whom couldn't read—"

"—but they could understand the Biblical stories in pictures," she finished. "Smart fellow, this Father Velghe."

Ophelia moved out of the pew toward the next painting. Dane followed a few steps behind, more interested in her reactions to the artwork than in the paintings themselves. He had made several visits to the painted church since he had moved to Hawaii. At times, the building hummed with parishioners, clergy or tourists. Other days, it rested still and serene, like now. It gave him the perfect opportunity to observe Ophelia while she directed her attention elsewhere.

He was still processing some of what he'd learned during their morning together. The history of her childhood and relationship with her mother had quickly drawn them into an emotional intimacy he hadn't expected. And to his consternation, he had to admit that for a headhunter, he found Ophelia Reid rather…likable.

More than that, he confessed to himself, he realized he was attracted to her—and not just for her tall, trim figure and observant green eyes. He enjoyed talking with her and found himself simultaneously surprised and pleased by how understanding she appeared to be of his situation in Hawaii—his desire to retire from corporate life and his resentment at the continuing intrusions of his former career. During their time at the Place of Refuge and snorkeling in the bay, he'd experienced Hawaii anew through her eyes, thrilling at her pleasure in the culture and history of his island home.

He watched as she moved down another pew, her fingers gliding absently across the wooden back. Her hands were slim and finely boned with long, tapered fingers and neatly manicured nails painted in pale shades of opalescent pink. Her index finger showed slight wear, the nail polish chipped at the edges, and he found himself strangely intrigued by this minor detail.

It looked almost as if she had been chewing at the tip of her nail—a sign of nervousness, perhaps? He hadn't seen her lose her composure, other than when she had challenged him at the bonfire...but perhaps the pressure of her assignment weighed on her. After all, a $10,000 incentive spoke of some desperation on Lillian Reid's part.

What had the dragon lady said to her daughter before sending her off to the islands in an attempt to secure a contract with him? Did Ophelia feel the strain of those who had come before her and failed to convince him to return? If she did, she possessed a masterful ability at hiding it. She seemed easygoing and professional, confident enough to take on the challenge of his recruitment.... He wondered if there were any doubts beneath her steady facade.

The sound of Ophelia's throat clearing drew his attention back to her face. She stood watching him with a curious expression, and he smiled as though his careful study of her had been purely intentional.

"What do you think?" he asked.

She ran her fingers through the ends of her hair. A nervous gesture? He imagined his staring had disconcerted her a bit. Cracks in her composure. He liked the thought.

"I love it," she admitted, her eyes sweeping over the vaulted ceiling once more. "It's an unmatched combination of Hawaiian culture and European imagery."

"Well said." He nodded with approval. "I thought, with your photographer's eye, you might have an appreciation for it."

She nodded, still eyeing several of the frescoes. "I wish I had brought a camera along. I'd love to take a few photographs."

Before he could respond, he felt his cell phone vibrate with a call. Removing it from the pocket of his jeans, he checked the caller ID and saw Leilani's name. He touched the screen to answer and brought it to his ear.

"Hi, Leilani, what's up?"

The sound of Leilani's sniffles brought him to attention.

"Leilani?"

"Dane, you have to come to Kona Community Hospital's emergency room."

He felt a stab of panic deep in his abdomen. "What happened?"

"It's Keahi. He's hurt."

"What happened?"

"There was so much blood. Just please hurry!"

Dane stood stunned for a moment. His face must have paled considerably because the next thing he knew, he felt Ophelia's hand touching his arm.

"Dane? Is everything okay?"

"Are you with him now?" Dane asked, ignoring Ophelia's question.

"I came outside to call you—cell phones aren't allowed in the E.R."

"What happened?" he repeated.

"He was doing some maintenance on the pulper. The next thing we knew, he came into the kitchen dripping blood."

Dane drew a breath. "Okay, go back inside

and stay with him, Leilani. I'll be there as soon as I can."

As Dane ended the call, he was already heading for the door with Ophelia close on his heels.

CHAPTER SIX

"I'M SORRY, BOSS."

Keahi uttered those words for the fifth time since Dane had been ushered into his friend's bay in the E.R., and just as he had the previous five times, Dane offered the same reply.

"It's okay, Keahi. I don't blame you."

"It happened by accident," Keahi reiterated. "I was doing maintenance on the pulper, and it tipped the wrong way. I tried to grab it, to hold it upright, but it cut into me." Keahi waved his freshly bandaged arm. The doctor had informed Dane that the four-and-a-half-inch laceration had required twenty-two stitches. "I should have called up Sam to help me."

Dane watched as Keahi picked restlessly at the perimeter of his bandage.

"I'm really sorry, boss. It was an accident."

Dane sighed. "Would you stop that?"

"Sorry."

"I meant stop apologizing in general. And stop poking at your dressing unless you're trying to get that pretty nurse to come back in here and redo her handiwork."

Keahi broke into a grin, and Dane felt a flood of relief. "She said I put on a brave face while she stitched everything up. I'm going to ask for her number when she comes back."

Dane shook his head. "Maybe this entire situation will work to your advantage, after all."

Keahi leaned back on the hospital bed with a sigh. "You know me, brah. I never waste an opportunity with the ladies."

This pronouncement elicited a soft chuckle from Dane that slowly faded. His gaze flickered around the curtained cubicle, observing the various machines and instruments. He felt relieved that Keahi's wound hadn't been more serious, though he knew his friend would be stuck in the office instead of out on the grounds until he healed. Guilt at the thought gnawed at the corners of Dane's stomach. "Keahi?" He looked back at his friend. "I think I'm the one who should be apologizing to you."

Keahi straightened. "Why's that?"

"I should have been there today. I never should have been wasting my time with some New York recruiter."

Keahi clicked his tongue in disapproval. "It was for a good cause, remember? That pretty lady is paying you ten grand to 'waste your time' with her as you put it."

"I'm not sure it's worth it." His feeling of responsibility cut far deeper than Keahi's wound. He was just grateful the damage to his friend's arm hadn't been worse.

"Dane."

He turned to see Keahi's round face leveled with seriousness. "This is not your fault."

He wished he possessed the same certainty on that score. Before he could reply, the curtains of the bay rattled as the nurse reentered the room.

"Mr. Inoa, your family just arrived." She turned to Dane. "I'm sorry, but there's only one visitor allowed per patient in the E.R."

"Sure thing." Dane straightened. "I'll head back out to the waiting room and send in someone else."

Keahi was grinning brightly at the pretty young nurse. "No hurry, brah."

Dane suppressed the urge to roll his eyes. "How much longer do you think he'll be here?" he asked the nurse.

"As soon as we process the paperwork, we'll be giving Mr. Inoa—"

"Call me Keahi, sweetheart."

The nurse paused at this interruption before

continuing. "Final instructions before discharging him."

Dane offered his thanks as the nurse directed him back to the waiting room. As he was leaving, he heard Keahi ask if his injury would require at-home visitation. He only wished he could have heard the nurse's reply before he moved out of earshot. Upon reaching the waiting room, he was greeted by Keahi's parents, who drew him into a hug.

"Pele called us," Mrs. Inoa explained as she released Dane. "Is it a serious injury?"

Dane shook his head. "It's a deep laceration, and he'll have to refrain from any heavy lifting with that arm until it heals, but he's going to be fine. He'll likely have an impressive scar, though."

Mr. Inoa chuckled, the sound tinged with relief. "He'll probably find some way to use that to impress the ladies. I can't wait to hear what stories he will come up with to explain how he received such a wound."

Mrs. Inoa ignored her husband's amusement and looked to Dane once more. "Can we see him?"

"Only one visitor is allowed with him at a time."

"You go," Mr. Inoa said to his wife. "I will keep Dane company."

After directing Keahi's mother to the E.R., Dane faced Mr. Inoa. "I'm sorry, sir."

Mr. Inoa's expression revealed his surprise. "Whatever for?"

Dane had to look away. "I wasn't there when the accident happened. I should have been."

When Mr. Inoa didn't respond, Dane raised his eyes. The older man frowned in confusion.

"I was out sightseeing." Saying the words out loud only served to deepen the shame Dane felt.

"With the recruiter?"

"Keahi told you about her?"

Mr. Inoa shrugged. "He said another recruiter had arrived, this one much prettier than the others." He paused. "No one will judge you harshly, Dane, should you decide to return to the life you left behind."

"No," Dane emphasized. "I have no plans to do that. But it's because of her that I wasn't with Keahi today, helping with the pulper maintenance."

"Because of her?"

"Yes. Because she offered a monetary incentive if I agreed to show her around the island."

"Ah. I see. And you're feeling guilty that you accepted her offer."

"I feel guilty that I wasn't there when Keahi needed me," Dane corrected.

Mr. Inoa studied him for several long, uncomfortable seconds. He finally shook his head. "No. That's not what's bothering you."

"Excuse me?"

"Where is she?" Mr. Inoa asked by way of reply. He glanced over his shoulder, his eyes roaming the waiting room. "I assume she came to the hospital with you?"

"I insisted that she and Leilani head back to the inn together."

Mr. Inoa's gaze swiveled back around to study him. "What's her name?"

"The recruiter? Ophelia Reid. Why?"

To Dane's discomfort, Mr. Inoa didn't answer but rather continued to study him.

"You like this one," he finally pronounced.

Dane immediately scoffed and turned away, glancing around to see if anyone had overheard Mr. Inoa's traitorous observation.

"You like her," Mr. Inoa repeated, this time more softly, "and you feel guilty that you were enjoying your time with her when Keahi got hurt."

Dane lifted his head to stare at Keahi's father. He tried to convey with his expression that Mr. Inoa should abandon this line of thought.

"The plantation is ultimately my responsibility, as is the equipment. Now the pulper will need repairs, and I don't have the money for it.

If I'd been there to help Keahi, this never would have happened."

Mr. Inoa seemed unfazed by this. "Bring her to the café tomorrow."

"What?"

"Bring this recruiter woman to the café in Holualoa tomorrow. I would like to meet her."

"Um…can I ask why?"

"I'm curious about her."

Dane's doubt must have showed because Mr. Inoa offered up a suggestion. "Perhaps this one should see what all you'd be leaving behind if you left here—not just the plantation and scenery but everyone who cares about you."

This unexpectedly touched Dane. "Okay," he said. "I'll think about it."

"I DON'T EXPECT you to understand. But it's imperative that Dane Montgomery comes to work for me."

Lillian Reid kept her face impassive and didn't correct Bianca's assumption—she understood more than the girl realized. Instead, she watched as her young client speared an olive from her chef's salad and brought it to her lips. She resisted the urge to look around the establishment to see which of her rivals might be having lunch at this same restaurant. She had chosen it specifically because it was a place her fellow recruiters and clients frequented, aiming to show that Bianca Towers remained on her list of exclusive, high-profile clientele. She wanted them all to see that Reid Recruiting still held the Towers account.

"He's the forbidden fruit, the executive no one else has managed to procure. I can certainly understand how that must hold some sort of allure," she offered.

Bianca put down her fork with a frown, a small indentation forming between her brows. Lillian envied the girl's smooth features, still unlined and fresh. How young she seemed. Young and perhaps a touch naive. She should have left these decisions to her board of directors and spent her days shopping and her evenings in clubs…or however she had been misspending her youth before her uncle's death and the transfer of the family business to her name.

"No, that's not it." Her client's words were firm, but Lillian suppressed a sigh. The girl had illusions about Dane Montgomery—that bringing him back to New York would redefine her as a serious businesswoman. Lillian felt hard-pressed to keep from pointing out that Bianca's own reputation had preceded her to the boardrooms of Towers International. The young woman had been known for extravagant indulgences and celebrity bad-boy relationships. Her belief that Montgomery could somehow repair her image aggravated Lillian. The girl's tenacious insistence on bringing him back threatened serious repercussions for Lillian's own business.

"Bianca, there are plenty of other talented executives in this field—"

"No."

Lillian plastered a false smile on her face and then focused on her own salad for a full ten seconds, allowing her annoyance to fester and flame as she stabbed a bit of lettuce, cut it three times and then brought a tiny leaf to her lips. By the time she swallowed, she had regained control of her irritation.

"And if he refuses to come out of retirement for you? Will you consider someone else then?"

"I *told* you," Bianca insisted, "it has to be him. If not, I'm pulling our account."

Lillian gritted her teeth as she tried to remain calm. "I'm not sure that would help your situation. Such rash action might be deemed flighty or uninformed—exactly the sort of perceptions you're trying to shed."

Bianca's jaw clenched, and Lillian knew she had gone too far.

"Listen, Lillian, I like you because the way you built your business, all on your own, is something I admire. But I'm not as inexperienced as you and my board seem to think. I studied my family's company for years, and I learned a lot from my father growing up before he died and the business passed to my uncle. And it was my uncle who kept me out of the Towers offices so that he could run things the way he wanted. I rebelled at that, tried to tarnish our family's name out of hurt and anger. It was selfish and stupid. But it's my turn now, and I'm tired of being treated like a child."

She ripped her napkin off her lap and began balling it up.

"I want Dane Montgomery. I've read all about him—my father always spoke of him as brilliantly talented. He's the one to help me re-establish my image and the identity of my family's company. If I can't have him…then you can't have the Towers account."

And with that, the girl stood and strode away from the table, leaving Lillian fuming and hoping that Ophelia was doing everything she could to convince Dane Montgomery to return.

THEY ALL HOVERED around Keahi the morning after his accident. Pele kept scooping extra helpings of eggs onto his breakfast plate, Leilani refilled his coffee cup half a dozen times and even Ophelia continually asked if there was anything she could get him. Dane watched the entire scene with a mixture of amusement and shame, silently chastising himself every time he saw Keahi move his bandaged arm and flinch with discomfort.

Following breakfast, Keahi insisted on joining Dane outside so they could ascertain the damage to the pulper after yesterday's accident. Dane was relieved when they determined the repairs would be minimal, and Keahi suggested they call Sam, who had a gift for fixing machinery, to take a look at it free of charge.

After putting in a call to Sam, who said he could be by later that morning, Dane hung around, reluctant to leave his friend again after what had occurred. The two returned to the office where Dane insisted on moving everything within easy reach for Keahi, from the stapler to the rolling file drawer. At last, his friend held up his uninjured arm.

"Boss, you do realize my arm was just cut, not amputated, don't you?"

Dane felt a twinge of embarrassment. "I'm just trying to help you out."

Keahi grunted. "I get it, brah, you feel bad. But I can't do my job if you're playing nurse-maid."

Dane frowned. "I wasn't—"

"Shouldn't you be busy showing our pretty guest around the island?"

Dane found he had to suppress a cringe at this. As much as he'd enjoyed his time with Ophelia Reid the day before, it didn't make up for the fact that he hadn't been here when he was needed. It was another reminder that he belonged on his plantation and not back in New York.

"I'm not leaving, Keahi. I don't see the point in indulging a recruiter's whims when my plan is to stay right here."

Keahi rolled his eyes. "Brah, if she's paying you $10,000 for the week, I don't care if you sail to the moon with her. Just fulfill your end of the bargain."

Dane clicked his tongue. "Are you trying to get rid of me?"

Keahi met his gaze. "Yes. I need to get some work done, and if I wanted to be fussed over, I'd have invited my mother to visit."

Dane couldn't help grinning. "Actually, your father suggested I take Ophelia to Holualoa so they could meet her."

Keahi threw his one good arm up in the air in a gesture of relief. "Perfect plan! Take her. Go."

"But shouldn't I—"

"Go."

DANE FOUND OPHELIA on the lanai, curled up on one of the chairs and looking out over the garden. Her expression was troubled, her lovely features marred by sadness. He felt a fleeting regret for leaving her to her own devices all morning.

"Hi," he greeted as he stepped onto the lanai.

She stirred, unfolding her long legs from where they were curled beneath her.

"Hey," she replied. "How's Keahi faring?"

Dane made a face. "He called me a nurse-maid."

"He's lucky to have such a good friend."

Dane didn't respond to this statement, changing the subject, instead. "Are you ready for a bit more touring?"

She visibly perked up at this suggestion. "But I thought…with Keahi…"

"He insists he's fine, and that we carry on with our arrangement."

"Oh. Well. Dane, I understand if you have to temporarily suspend our agreement, due to unforeseen plantation business."

Dane held up a hand to stop her. "A deal's a deal. Let's go."

ON THE DRIVE to Holualoa, Dane gave Ophelia an overview of the village community.

"The town is situated on the incline of a dormant volcano—Hualalai, which is a perfect setting for the nearby coffee farms growing Kona beans. The village itself is filled with coffee shops and artists' studios."

"It sounds exactly like the sort of place I'd love to photograph," Ophelia said in a wistful tone.

Dane went on to describe several of the cafés and art galleries before he realized the Jeep's fuel gauge was resting near the *E*. Flicking on his turn signal, he pulled into a station to fill up the tank.

While Ophelia waited in the vehicle, Dane headed inside the convenience store and moved toward a display of tourist-inspired impulse buys that included overpriced sunglasses, high-SPF sunblock and—just what he had been looking for—several disposable cameras.

He ripped one off the rack and headed to the counter, laying down bills for the fuel as well as his purchase. He hurried back out of the store, offering a rushed "Mahalo" by way of thanks.

He tried to remain casual but he knew he grinned like a little boy as he approached the vehicle and saw Ophelia in the passenger seat, eyes closed and humming snatches of some song he couldn't name beneath her breath. Her eyes flew open as he touched his door's handle, and she looked at him with a happy grin. The sun from the previous day's swim had bronzed her pale skin to a faint golden brown, setting off her green eyes and the honey tints in her hair. The look suited her, he decided with just the faintest of ripples stirring in his stomach.

He climbed inside the Jeep and handed her his purchase. "Here. This is for you."

She frowned, first at the camera, and then at him. "What is this for?" she asked.

"I know you've been wishing you had a camera to take photos while you're here. I figured a cheap disposable is better than nothing."

She stared at him for so long that he began to wonder if his impromptu gift had offended her somehow.

"Never mind." He reached to take it back, slightly embarrassed. "You're probably used to high-end equipment. You can get better photos off a smartphone than with these."

As his hand wrapped around the camera, his fingers brushed hers, and she jumped. But she didn't let go.

"No, wait."

He froze, their hands still touching.

"Thank you. It's…" She drew a breath and looked away. "It was very nice of you."

Her mumbled response left him uneasy. "I just thought—"

"Really." She looked at him, and he could

see her pleasure was genuine. "No one has ever done anything like that for me before. It's a lovely gesture."

Her eyes met his, and he felt his heart jerk involuntarily in response.

"Thank you," she repeated.

He turned his attention to starting the Jeep in order to keep from falling into her soft, green gaze.

AS THEY REACHED the Holualoa village, Ophelia sat up straighter to drink in the sight of the artistic enclave, her interest piqued by the quaint, beautiful shops and galleries. She glanced at Dane as he explained that Keahi's parents had invited them to stop by for a visit.

"They manage the Ho'okipa Café," he said. "I try to make it a point to stop in every time I'm in the area."

"Oh, that's kind of you," she remarked.

He gave a little shrug as he navigated the Jeep off the main street. "It's partly guilt, I think. It's only due to the family's misfortune that Keahi ended up working for me."

Ophelia frowned. "What happened?"

"Keahi was raised on a coffee farm that his family had owned for generations. His father got sick several years ago with a rare form of cancer. Keahi's mother learned about a new treatment on the mainland, but because it was still in the trial stages, insurance wouldn't pay for it." Dane turned his face toward the driver's-side window for an instant and then looked back at Ophelia. "They sold the coffee farm and all their holdings to pay for the trip and treatments."

Ophelia swallowed. "Wow," she murmured. "That's love."

Dane glanced at her for a few seconds longer before turning his eyes back to the street. "The good news is that the treatments worked wonders. The cancer is in remission, and now Mr. and Mrs. Inoa manage the café here for a businessman based out of Waikiki. Keahi says selling the farm was worth every penny."

This story left a knot in Ophelia's throat. She considered her own pressures regarding the family business and how her mother had pressed upon her the need to right their precarious situation. What would Lillian Reid have done in a similar predicament? Ophelia had a feeling her mother would have chosen to go down with the ship rather than sell it off for salvation.

She shuddered and put away these gloomy thoughts.

"And Keahi doesn't mind working for a plantation that's not his own?"

Dane hesitated. "I've talked about eventually bringing him on as a partner. But considering the state of things…" He trailed off, and Ophelia felt bad for the reminder of Dane's shaky financial condition, especially considering yesterday's unfortunate accident.

The conversation halted awkwardly after that, and Dane parked the Jeep in silence. They exited the vehicle, and Ophelia carefully stowed her disposable camera in her bag before Dane came around and opened the door for her. She stepped outside and followed his lead to a modestly-sized café featuring a charming exterior with vintage signage and weathered antique tables on display. Inside, the café felt pleasantly cool with a breeze flowing freely from the many open windows and rotating ceiling fans. A plaque on the wall explained that *Ho'okipa* was Hawaiian for hospitality, and that this was the aim of the Ho'okipa Café toward their patrons. The floors were a worn hardwood, and each table displayed mosaic images of island flowers: hibiscus, plumeria, red ginger. Smooth koa boards with tribal designs etched along the front made up the base of the coffee bar while its surface was a sturdy, shining marble. Several customers were scattered through the small shop, their soft conversations blending with the relaxing strains of island music coming from the speakers. The scent of freshly pressed coffee and baked goods made Ophelia's mouth water.

Dane directed her to the bar where handwritten chalkboard displays announced the day's offerings: Kona coffee by the cup along with several choices of iced teas and other beverages, paninis with distinctive island flavors such as pulled pork and gruyère with a mango-pineapple salsa and teriyaki chicken with sweet Maui onion, and desserts that ranged from banana pudding with freshly whipped cream to coconut cheesecake.

She had just turned to Dane to comment on the cozy elegance of the place when a voice greeted them.

"Dane, aloha!"

An older gentleman approached with outstretched arms. His frame was broad and solid, but he looked too thin for a man of such wide proportions. Ophelia noted he had Keahi's features, but his own were weathered with time and age.

"Aloha, Mr. Inoa," Dane returned the salutation.

"We just spoke with Keahi. He says he's feeling fine this morning, that his arm hardly bothers him."

Dane sighed. "I hope that's true. It seemed

to pain him a bit this morning when he would move it."

"That's to be expected," Mr. Inoa said and then cast a glance toward Ophelia.

Dane cleared his throat and gestured toward her. "This is Ophelia Reid, a guest of the inn. Ophelia, this is Keahi's father, Makana Inoa."

Mr. Inoa swept her hand into his, pumping it with a firm grip that belied the lack of weight on his large frame.

"Keahi told us all about it. A recruiter, aren't you, Miss Reid?"

Ophelia wondered if Keahi had been generous or critical in his explanation of her to his parents. He'd been extremely congenial to her in their encounters at the inn, but perhaps his hospitality skills exceeded his boss's on the matter of recruiters.

"Please, call me Ophelia," she insisted. "And yes, I've come from New York to negotiate Dane's possible return."

"Miss Reid is overly optimistic in her thinking," Dane stated as she felt him tense beside her and shift slightly away.

She tried to stifle her disappointment in the subtle gesture and focused her attention back on Mr. Inoa. "This is a lovely café, Mr. Inoa. Dane tells me you and your wife are the managers?"

Mr. Inoa nodded. "There is a wealthy businessman in Waikiki—he does not have the time to be in Holualoa every day, so Nani and I run the café in his absence."

"You must have a lot of knowledge about coffee after your years of farming."

Mr. Inoa smiled, and Ophelia thought it was a touch wistful. "It was a hard life but a good one. To defeat the cancer, though, that is better. I could not have done it and continued to farm."

His words moved Ophelia. "Your family must love you very much to have helped you with such a struggle."

"I am blessed," Mr. Inoa agreed.

"Dane, there you are. I just hung up the phone with Keahi."

Ophelia turned to see an older woman with Polynesian features and graying hair approaching them.

She drew Dane into her arms, and Ophelia caught his pleased smile.

"Keahi had to practically shoo me out the door today. He called me a nursemaid, if you can believe it."

Ophelia frowned, feeling a twinge of contrition for tearing Dane away from his friend so soon after the accident.

"Then you must be Miss Reid." Mrs. Inoa turned to her.

"Please, call me Ophelia. And you must be Mrs. Inoa."

To Ophelia's surprise, the other woman drew her into a hug, as well. She allowed herself to be embraced, breathing in the faint fragrance of matcha as Mrs. Inoa enveloped her.

"Keahi told us you were staying at the Okina Inn. Welcome to Hawai'i."

Much as Leilani had pronounced it, the name of her native state rolled off Mrs. Inoa's tongue in the traditional cadence with a hard *v* sound placed where the *w* was typically written.

"Thank you." For whatever reason, Ophelia found herself near tears as Mrs. Inoa released her. It took her a minute to realize it was because she could not remember the last time she had been hugged so genuinely. Certainly not by her mother. Lillian Reid abhorred overt demonstrations of affection. Even Cole was often uncomfortable with public displays of emotion.

"Come, you must sit."

Mrs. Inoa ushered the two of them to a table while Mr. Inoa turned to address another couple who had entered the café. Ophelia and Dane each took a seat.

"What can I get for you? A cup of Kona? Or perhaps something cooler, such as an iced tea? We have several varieties of Ceylon tea blended with either passion fruit, pineapple or coconut."

"That sounds wonderful. I'll have the passion fruit tea, please."

"And a cup of Kona for me, thanks," Dane put in. "Do you think we could try those paninis on the menu?"

"Of course. I will put your order in right away."

"And if you and Mr. Inoa have time, we'd love for you to join us."

Mrs. Inoa glanced at Ophelia, seemingly uncertain if she felt the same way as Dane. Ophelia nodded at her. "Yes, I'd love to get the chance to hear more about your family. You must have quite a history with the island."

These words caused Mrs. Inoa to beam proudly. "I will see if the staff needs any assistance or if they are all right without us for a few minutes."

She moved away, and Ophelia turned her head to find Dane watching her once more. She attempted a smile, but the mood between them felt awkward.

"The Inoas seem like lovely people," she commented, wanting to ease the tension she felt between them. Did he think she was only interested in spending time with him because of her recruitment agenda? The thought disappointed her, though she couldn't understand why it should.

Dane gave a short nod in reply to her words but stayed silent. Ophelia concentrated on keeping herself from fidgeting by counting the tiles in the mosaic pattern on the tabletop before them. This practice had always served her well as a child at dull dinner parties where one hint of boredom would earn her a chastising glance from her mother. She simply trained herself to count something as a distraction—silverware, patterns in the wallpaper, designs in a table-cloth…

"You said you were working this assignment without commission."

Ophelia looked up as he spoke, thrown by his sudden choice of topic. She found herself caught in the directness of his gaze. "But surely there's something in it for you, if I agree to return."

Ophelia leaned back in her seat and measured her answer. After a moment's consideration, she saw no reason to keep it a secret from him.

"If you sign, Reid Recruiting will open another office in Europe, in Paris," she clarified, "and I'll become Director of European Operations."

Following this admission, Dane remained frozen, and then he let out a low whistle. "So there really *is* a lot riding on this for you. Paris. Your dream city."

This observation both thrilled and discouraged her—his tone held a slight edge, but she was pleased he had immediately noted how much living in Paris meant to her.

"And if I don't agree to sign with Towers Resorts?"

She took in the rigid tension of his posture and felt some of her own buoyancy dissipate. "I suppose it won't concern you at that point, will it?"

"Touché." He leaned back, folding his arms over his chest. "Lillian Reid doesn't seem like the sort to take failure lightly."

Ophelia's jaw clenched. "My mother may appear harsh to others, but she has her reasons."

"I'm sure she does. I doubt her life has been easy, what with losing her husband at such a young age and finding herself with a daughter to raise on her own. She must have worked very hard to get where she is, and I don't suppose she'd like to lose what she's gained without a very hard fight."

These words surprised Ophelia. "That's… true."

"So I'm sure she's the type of woman who can appreciate how someone else might feel the same—having fought so hard to remove myself from the corporate environment and establish myself here in Hawaii, I don't plan to leave."

She flushed more deeply at how he had turned the conversation on its head. Before she could think of a response, Mr. and Mrs. Inoa approached, each carrying a platter with drinks and plates of paninis and intriguingly bright purple chips which Mrs. Inoa explained were taro chips, sliced and fried from the starchy root vegetable that grew on the island. They settled everything on the table, and Ophelia and Dane abandoned their conversation as they shifted to make room, forcing their chairs closer together by necessity.

They spent the next hour eating and chatting with the Inoas, and Ophelia felt her tensions dissolve in the presence of island hospitality. Mr. and Mrs. Inoa were as easygoing and kind as their son, and Ophelia found herself relieved that they had joined their table when they had. Even Dane's edginess thawed over the lunch until he was laughing and sharing much as he had been the day before. The sound of his pleasure sparked something deep inside her being, warming her and drawing out her own laughter, as well.

At one point, Dane caught her eye, his grin broadening, following an anecdote Mr. Inoa had shared about Keahi and his brothers. His gaze held hers, and she felt herself drawn to him in a way she had never experienced with anyone else before. For one brief instant she felt as if she…belonged. She held the feeling close until Dane eventually looked away as Mr. Inoa launched into another story. But she savored the sensation, even after it had left, and wondered what sort of magic the islands possessed to cause such happiness, no matter how fleeting.

IT WAS OBVIOUS to Dane that Ophelia had charmed Mr. Inoa. Her lilting laughter at his stories and the prodding questions that she asked must have appealed to the older man's storytelling abilities. By the time they finished lunch, Mr. Inoa had offered to show Ophelia some of his pencil sketches of the local flora and fauna. Ophelia seemed genuinely interested, even eager, to take a look, and Dane found himself marveling at how different she was from every other recruiter he had encountered before.

Mrs. Inoa checked on the staff—the café had filled with patrons for the lunch hour as the four of them had talked—and returned shortly after Mr. Inoa and Ophelia had excused themselves to look over Mr. Inoa's sketch collection.

Dane drained the last of his Kona as Mrs.

Inoa resumed her seat, automatically reaching for the carafe to refill his mug.

"This Ophelia, she seems like a very nice woman. Very interested in the culture and history of the islands," Mrs. Inoa remarked.

Dane said nothing. What was there to say? Ophelia *was* very nice. More than that, he found her easy to talk to and fun to be around. But that changed nothing about her true motives for being in Hawaii.

Mrs. Inoa studied him closely, and he pretended not to notice as he fiddled with his coffee mug.

"You are worried," she noted, and he forced himself to meet her eyes, hoping his expression remained neutral.

"Now, why would I be worried?"

Mrs. Inoa clucked her tongue. "Have you forgotten that I have been where you are? Facing the struggle of keeping a coffee plantation running without the necessary funds?"

He couldn't meet her gaze after that— He looked away, his own eyes roaming over the customers scattered throughout the café.

"There is no shame in it, Dane."

He took a swig of his coffee, barely tasting it. "There is for me," he murmured. "I've never failed to accomplish something I set out to do."

"And you haven't failed at this," Mrs. Inoa reminded him. "You must simply find another way."

His stare swiveled back to hers as if of its own volition. "If anyone should know the impossibility of that…it's you."

She scoffed slightly and poured herself another cup of Kona from the carafe. "I did not fail at what I set out to do."

He waited for her to elaborate.

"I set out to save my husband, not my plantation. A sacrifice had to be made to ensure my success. Selling the coffee farm provided the money for my husband's treatments. It was not a failure, to lose the plantation."

He frowned with chagrin. "I never thought of it quite like that."

She clicked her tongue once more. "You must consider what it is you want, Dane Montgomery. Is it the plantation? Or something else?"

His frown only deepened at these questions.

"What else could I possibly want?"

Her gaze slid in the direction Mr. Inoa and Ophelia had departed. He felt his own eyes widen after another second passed.

"Mrs. Inoa, I'm not sure I appreciate what you're implying."

Her look was bemused as she sipped from

her mug. "You like this woman. Ophelia Reid. You cannot hide it."

He grunted and leaned back in his seat, feeling rather petulant at this forthright observation.

"I do like her. She's not quite as pushy as the others. But she's still one of *them*."

Mrs. Inoa shook her head. "You are so bitter, for one so young. I think it has less to do with *them* and more to do with your own fears."

"I'm not afraid—"

"But you are, dear boy. You are afraid you made a mistake in coming here. As much as you love it, you worry that you cannot see it through. The recruiters are only a reminder of what you may lose. They remind you of your own possible shortcomings and precarious situation. It is not fair to blame them all for your own choices—especially not this girl."

Her words left a sour taste in his mouth. "You do realize that if I accept her offer, I'll be leaving the island—that Keahi may be out of a job."

Mrs. Inoa waved a hand in dismissal. "It will hardly come to that. On the contrary, if you accept, Keahi can run the plantation in your absence, and you will have the necessary income to keep it afloat."

He remained silent at this.

"At times, a sacrifice must be made to see something through," Mrs. Inoa pointed out. "The only question that remains…is what will your sacrifice be?"

DANE AND OPHELIA departed the Ho'okipa Café amid hugs and well wishes from their hosts. Ophelia felt the warm glow of an afternoon spent with friends, and before leaving, she insisted Dane pose with the Inoas for a photo with her disposable camera.

They spent the remainder of the afternoon touring the studios and galleries of Holualoa's art district, taking in sculptures, paintings, photography, artisanal crafts and more. By the time they exited the last shop, Ophelia felt both inspired and awed by the abundance of local talent.

She noted that Dane had been pleasant but slightly preoccupied throughout the remainder of their day together, and as they climbed into the Jeep to head back to the inn, she felt a twinge of guilt for how her sightseeing had taken him away from more pressing duties at the plantation.

"Dane, I should… I want to…" She drew a breath, steadying herself. "Thank you for taking the time to show me around today. I really had a lot of fun."

He slid a glance her way. "Wasn't it all part of our arrangement?"

She felt a keen stab of disappointment. "Oh. Of course. Yes. But…with Keahi, and yesterday…" She stopped before she said something she'd regret. "I appreciate you holding to your end of the bargain, given how difficult this week has been for you." But it had been more than just that for her. Somehow, over the course of their time together, Ophelia had thought that she and Dane might have grown a little closer—moved beyond the roles of recruiter and candidate, even if only by a small margin. Apparently, Dane didn't feel the same, and now her cheeks began to flame with embarrassment.

"I just appreciate how, er, thorough you were in fulfilling your duty."

She caught the flicker of a grin at the corner of his mouth. "I had a lot of fun, too."

Then, to her utter astonishment, he winked, and she felt her heart speed up in her chest. Ophelia looked out her window, trying to still the rapid tripping of her heartbeat, and focused on the horizon, a golden strip with lines of pink fire at the edges. They drove in silence for a few miles until Dane put on his flashers and pulled the Jeep off the road and onto a stretch of gravel.

"Come on," he said.

"Where are we going?"

"We're going to catch the sunset. It happens fast in Hawaii."

He climbed out of the vehicle, and Ophelia followed, coming to stand beside him as the sun began sinking rapidly in the distance.

"It's a clear sky," he observed. "Maybe you'll see the green flash, if you're lucky."

"Green flash?"

He looked her way. "It's a natural phenomenon here—somewhat rare but not impossible to witness. In that split second after the sun disappears into the horizon, an emerald-green spark can flash. It's easy to miss, but you also have to be careful not to watch for it too closely because your own eyes will create a green retinal burn by staring at the sun, so you have to look at just the right time to catch it."

"Sounds complicated."

"It's worth it." He held her stare for a little longer and then looked back at the horizon. "Look for it when I tell you but not before."

Ophelia did as he told her and kept her gaze focused elsewhere, finally settling it on the man himself. She studied the angle of his jaw with its light dusting of scruff, the length of his neck before the line dropped to his broad shoulders.

"Ophelia?"

"Hmm?" she responded distractedly.

"Do you think I could be happy, working for Bianca Towers?"

As his words registered, she felt her mouth open in disbelief.

"Now. Look now."

She automatically turned her head in time to see the sun's last brilliant light before it dipped beyond view, and then, in that brief second of its disappearance, an ethereal green glow winked at her in the dusk before burning out.

"I saw it! Dane! Did you see?"

"I did."

"I saw the green flash!" She gasped with joy. "It was there!"

She laughed in utter delight before turning her attention back to the man beside her. "I saw it flash!"

But she realized Dane wasn't looking at the horizon—he was watching her. She felt a shiver stretch over her from head to toe at the expression in his eyes.

He inched closer, and she leaned in as though it were the most natural thing in the world. His hands came up to rest against the sides of her neck, his thumbs running back and forth along her jaw.

His face was so close that she could count the lashes rimming the warm blue pools of his eyes. He had a few freckles scattered across the bridge of his nose, and his lips were parted ever so slightly, his breath faintly raspy as he stared down at her.

Her stomach felt lodged into her chest, and her heart beat wildly against the confines of her rib cage. Her skin tingled with a thousand pinpricks of awareness—the brush of his elbows against her forearms, his fingertips kneading lightly into her hair, the slightly rough touch of his palms along her jaw.

He held her for so long that she closed her eyes, wanting to remember this feeling of security, of safety in his arms.

Then he kissed her, and her lips came alive under his, moving slowly and without urgency. She trembled and reached her arms around his waist, both for support and to draw him nearer. She didn't know how long they stood, locked together like that, as the sunset dissipated, and the world shifted toward evening.

At last, they pulled apart and looked into each other's eyes.

"You were right," he murmured.

She was finding it hard to regain her equilibrium after what had just happened. Her blood sang in her veins, and her mouth kept willfully attempting to turn upward.

"About what?" she breathed.

He ran his palm over her cheek, and she felt herself turning into it.

"I really shouldn't have underestimated you when you first arrived on my doorstep."

She tugged him close and planted another soft kiss on his lips before answering him.

"I told you so."

CHAPTER SEVEN

LILLIAN REID RETURNED her office phone to its cradle, resisting the urge to slam it down in frustration. She loathed spending time reassuring her clients. She had built this business from the ground up, a forerunner in her field. Hadn't she earned the right to a little trust on their part? The situation with Bianca Towers would be resolved shortly. Ophelia would come through. She had not groomed her daughter for any less. But tackling a recruit such as Dane Montgomery for a client as glamorous as Bianca was bound to draw attention. She supposed she should be grateful that her company's name was on everyone's lips. Even if most of the chatter was concerning whether this recruitment would skyrocket her firm to international success or plummet them into eventual bankruptcy.

Considering this potential outcome caused her to shudder. She had not come this far to see her business face downsizing. With the economy's turn, she'd worked harder than ever and had kept the Reid Recruiting name at the top of the nation's list of reputable, successful executive search firms. Landing Montgomery would solidify that reputation and allow her to expand into Paris, with her own daughter at the operation's helm. With her contacts and background in France, such a move would push her firm into the sphere of international business and increase the overall net worth of her company.

She pushed back from her desk and stood, moving to look out over the Manhattan skyline. She had labored to ensure Ophelia's future. It was why Cole was such a perfect match for her daughter. He was one of the best recruiters she'd ever seen, and with him at Ophelia's side, Lillian could rest assured that her business would continue to thrive under the couple's leadership. That is, once the two of them reconciled.

Of course, turning over the reins wouldn't happen for many years to come. She had no intention of retiring early to some tropical paradise like Montgomery had done. The very thought elicited another shudder.

She checked her watch. It was shortly after 6:00 a.m. in Hawaii. Her daughter would be awake by now, certainly. She knew better than to stay abed with so much at stake.

Lifting the phone's receiver once more, she dialed Ophelia's cell phone number and waited for it to ring.

OPHELIA HAD JUST stepped out of the shower when she heard her phone vibrating insistently. She'd been restless for most of the night, her dreams filled with memories of Dane's arms around her and his lips on hers. She'd been awake long before the dawn, lying in bed and basking in the thought of the day ahead, wondering what it would be like to spend the hours in Dane's company.

The phone's vibrations distracted her from these thoughts as she wrapped her towel more tightly around herself and rushed to see who was calling. She was reaching for the phone when she saw the name flashing across the screen.

Lillian Reid.

Her mother's office line. Some of her joy evaporated at this. Her mother was likely calling for an update on her progress, but she wasn't sure what sort of headway she'd made. She and Dane had spent a wonderful day together yesterday, ended it with a kiss, but that didn't mean he was any closer to accepting the Towers proposal. She knew the call would be routed to voice mail after another ring so she drew a short breath and answered the call.

"Good morning, Ms. Reid."

"I appreciate the sentiment, Ophelia, but it's past noon here."

"Oh, of course. The time difference. I'd forgotten."

"It's understandable."

There was an uncomfortable pause, and Ophelia wished, for probably the millionth time, that she and her mother could find something more to say to each other at intervals like these.

"I was calling to check on your progress."

"Certainly. I'm sorry I haven't checked in more frequently."

"As long as you've made inroads with Montgomery, it's all right."

Ophelia didn't respond, and she could sense her mother's disappointment.

"You have been promoting your purpose there, haven't you, Ophelia?"

"Absolutely, Ms. Reid," she hastened to assure. "But of course, he's not the easiest man to convince."

"No," her mother slowly agreed. "But you have more at stake than anybody. So I trust you've been appropriately motivated."

Ophelia wasn't sure how to respond to that,

but in typical fashion, her mother immediately sensed her reluctance.

"Ophelia, what is going on over there?"

She suddenly felt like a teenager again, fearful of getting caught sneaking in past curfew. "I've been doing my best to convince Dane to sign the contract."

But her earlier hesitation had already raised Lillian's suspicions. "And how have you been doing that?"

Ophelia swallowed. "As I said in my email, I offered Dane the additional incentive, and he's been acting as my tour guide."

"You've been sightseeing?"

"Yes." Wasn't that what the tour-guide incentive had implied?

"And what have you been seeing?"

Ophelia seated herself in the chair by her room's desk and drew her knees up to her chest. The open window let in the morning's trade winds, and she felt gooseflesh rising along her bare shoulders. "Oh, this and that." She felt protective of the time she'd spent with Dane, not willing to share it with anyone, least of all her mother.

"Hmm. Is he any closer to signing than he was when you arrived?"

Ophelia felt compelled to answer honestly. "I don't know."

Her mother sighed, and she heard the weariness in it. A twinge of guilt imposed itself on her. She knew what was at stake here and recognized that her mother was counting on her to see things through.

"What if I can't get him to agree?" she asked, her voice a whisper, though she knew there was no one to overhear.

"That is not an option."

"I know, but—"

"He will sign that contract. He must."

Ophelia ran a hand through the damp tendrils of her hair, pulling them over her shoulder to toy with the ends. "But he likes his life here. The islands are amazing, and the people are so welcoming. You should see the sunsets. There's this thing called a green flash—"

"Green flash? Ophelia, have you been reading comic books?"

She figured the question was rhetorical and chose not to answer it.

"If I didn't know you better, I'd think you were charmed by this man and his life there. It's fortunate we both know how much you want to move to Paris."

"Yes," Ophelia quickly replied. "Paris is all I've ever wanted." She had said the words so often that they slipped easily from her mouth now.

"I know. So keep your focus, dear. Think

about Paris and everything waiting for you after Montgomery signs that contract."

It was not a suggestion but a command. Ophelia had worked for her mother long enough to know the difference.

"Yes, Ms. Reid. I'll do my best."

"I never thought otherwise."

Ophelia didn't believe her.

AFTER HANGING UP the phone in frustration for the second time that morning, Lillian felt the sharp pain of a headache radiating toward her temples. She feared Montgomery had gained the upper hand in the negotiations, and Ophelia, tenderhearted as she could be, had succumbed to his charm. The man was a master of perceptions—wasn't that all that advertising was, perception?

Reaching toward her phone once more, she pressed the button for her assistant's line. Tamara's voice was temperate and professional as she answered, one of the reasons Lillian had first hired her five years earlier. She had served as a PA to some movie director, Lillian could no longer remember whom, for years before moving to the East Coast and applying for the job of her assistant—a role that had seen a rotation of individuals over the previous ten years. Tamara was the longest-lasting secretary she'd ever had, and though she wouldn't have admitted it to most people, she was grateful for her.

"Tamara, page Cole for me and tell him I need to see him immediately in my office."

"Yes, Ms. Reid."

Lillian couldn't sit still after this summons, and she stood to pace as she waited for Cole's arrival. Perhaps she had been unwise to send her daughter to Montgomery's island paradise. She had thought that Ophelia's goals would keep her firmly focused on her task. She suspected, however, that their recruit had somehow turned the tables and enchanted Ophelia with the idea of island life. It was the very thing Lillian had worked for years to safeguard against. She wanted Ophelia to be secure, to be happy. She would not have wished for her the life that Lillian had led. Her marriage to Marcel had been like something from a fairy tale—falling in love at a young age while vacationing with friends in Europe, marrying a man over twice her age and moving to Paris. But the dream had eventually turned to ash, as most fairy tales do.

Mothers never tell you about that, she mused. Her own mother had been critical of her marriage, disdaining the idea of her marrying someone foreign and so much older, as well. But her mother hadn't told her how things would end—that Marcel would die while she was still so young, that she would be left with a widow's inheritance that could not sustain her and a young daughter forever. She had returned to the States and invested the money in starting up her business, and then she had worked harder than anyone could have imagined to make that business a success. All so her own daughter would never have her dreams crushed as Lillian's had been.

She had determined not to do her daughter the disservice so many other mothers had done their children. She'd made certain Ophelia was smarter than the rest of them, more determined. When her daughter had named Paris as a childhood dream, Lillian had helped her fashion it into a goal. She'd given her something to work for so that she wouldn't have to rely on love to feel fulfilled.

Why did everyone laud fairy tales for their happy endings? Did they forget all the death, cruelty and loss in between? She would not have wished a fairy tale on anyone, least of all her own child.

A knock sounded on the door, distracting her from these musings. She turned to see Cole standing outside the glass, and she waved him inside. Placing aside her thoughts, she returned to the business of being her company's leader once more. She moved back to her desk and gestured for Cole to take the seat before it.

"Thank you for coming in on such short notice, Cole. I hope I'm not keeping you from anything important."

"It's no problem, Lillian. I was just getting ready to step out for lunch."

They settled themselves, and for just a moment, she allowed herself the opportunity to study him. Cole was one of her strongest assets at Reid Recruiting—charming, tenacious and successful. The perfect match for Ophelia, and yet, she was aware her daughter had ended things with him.

"Have you spoken to Ophelia since she left for Hawaii?"

Cole shifted uncomfortably in his chair. "Briefly, on the day of her arrival."

"She called you?"

He nodded. Lillian had received an email that same day. It was a good sign that Ophelia had taken the time to call him.

"I've just spoken to her, and I have some… concerns."

Cole straightened attentively. "What kind of concerns?"

"I fear she's become too wrapped up in the extracurricular side of her assignment. She seems to be enjoying herself."

She watched as Cole frowned, trying to read the emotions that moved across his face. Did it pain him, the idea of Ophelia spending time with another man? She found it difficult to tell.

"I don't think it would be wrong for her to have a good time."

He didn't say so, but his tense shoulders suggested he wasn't much in favor of the idea.

"I suppose not, but my fear is that she's lost her focus. It is a recruitment that requires concentration. Her surroundings might detract from that."

"You mean the islands?"

"Exactly. That, and her host."

"Montgomery?"

She knew she had his full attention now. "The man did not reach the heights that he did without possessing certain skills. I worry that he's managed to sidetrack Ophelia. She needs our help."

Cole's expression darkened, and she could see his mind working through the implications of what she'd just suggested.

"What did you have in mind?"

WHEN OPHELIA DESCENDED the stairs, she encountered Dane at the reception area. She couldn't tell if he was really looking over reservations, as he seemed to be, or whether he had been waiting for her to make an appearance. Either way, his face lit up when he saw her, and she felt her nerve endings tingle all over again in memory of their kiss the night before.

"Good morning," he greeted.

"Good morning," she returned, keeping her tone casual.

"I was looking over our literature for local sightseeing adventures, trying to get some ideas for today." He held up a few pamphlets that Leilani must keep on file for guests. So he hadn't been waiting for her, after all. At least, not in the way she had assumed.

She steeled herself and affected what she hoped was a professional demeanor. "I actually thought it might be more interesting if we stayed around the plantation today."

Her tone, or perhaps her expression, caused his smile to fade somewhat. "Oh? You've changed your mind about seeing the tourist hotspots?"

"Not precisely. But I'm more curious about what your day-to-day life is like, on a coffee farm."

"Ah."

Something in that simple sound caused a tug of sadness in her. Had he hoped for something more from her? As much as she liked Dane, she had to remember why she had come. Paris, her future, hung in the balance. She could not afford to see Dane any differently than she had twenty-four hours ago.

Besides, witnessing the daily tasks of his business might give her some insight, leverage if necessary, on how to lure him back to New York and the position with Towers Resorts.

"It's obviously important to you." Ophelia found her voice softening to a more intimate level. "I'd love to see it through your eyes."

He studied her for a few seconds, and she forced herself to hold his gaze, wondering what he must be thinking. Was he wounded by her words? Flattered?

After another minute, he gathered the sight-seeing brochures together and pushed them to the side of the desk. "Sure. But I have to warn you, you might find it a little dull. Island life is not as fast-paced as New York. Especially when it comes to coffee farming."

He wasn't quite meeting her eyes. "That's okay," she assured. "I want to see what you do here. Really." And she meant it.

So they grabbed a bite to eat in the dining room where Leilani, Keahi and Pele were gathered for breakfast. After she inquired about his arm, Ophelia and Keahi found themselves in a conversation about his life growing up on a rural coffee farm and his relationship with his parents. He seemed to harbor no regrets about the dreams his family had lost—their farm and livelihood. The repayment of his father's health was more than enough for what they had given up, he said. Ophelia marveled at this outlook and found a deeper appreciation for Keahi and the Inoas in the process.

As she and Keahi chatted, she overheard snippets of Leilani pleading with Dane to convince Pele to let her spend more time with Sam. She couldn't catch everything that was being said, given her absorption in her own conversation, but she heard enough to recognize that Dane seemed to mediate between grandmother and granddaughter pretty well. Had that skill come from his time as an executive? Or was he a natural-born arbitrator?

As breakfast finished, Dane doled out instructions for the day—there were two reservations arriving at the inn the following week, so Pele would be in charge of preparing the rooms and stocking the kitchen with necessities. Leilani would assemble the welcome packets and assist her grandmother while Keahi reviewed past-due invoices and called their creditors to buy more time.

Keahi slid a glance toward Ophelia, as if hesitant to speak in front of her.

"Keahi?" Dane prompted.

"Um…yeah, boss. There are a couple bills

that just won't wait any longer. I can't buy us any more extensions."

"Do we have any revenue free to pay something on them?"

He hesitated again. "A bit, but I was saving that for payroll." He swiped a glance around the table, at Leilani and Pele.

"I can wait to be paid," Leilani spoke up.

Pele pursed her lips, saying nothing.

Dane sighed.

"What if we halve the payroll for now and catch up the rest in another week?"

Pele shook her head. "Pay Keahi and Leilani. I have everything I need right here."

Ophelia was touched by this declaration from the gruff housekeeper. For all her bluster, Ophelia had the sense that Pele loved Dane and her job at the Okina Inn.

"It's not fair to do that to you, Pele," Dane said.

"Who needs fair?" Pele fired back. "Are *you* taking a paycheck?"

Dane said nothing.

"When was the last time you *did* get paid?"

Ophelia's gaze swiveled in curiosity from Pele to Dane, who glanced in her direction and then quickly away. Perhaps she should excuse herself. She doubted he wanted her to hear these particulars of his business, but then again, her mother would want her to exploit this opportunity for all its worth.

"Keahi can tell us," Pele reminded.

"Too long," Keahi returned. "He hasn't taken any pay in over two months."

"And you haven't taken any pay in three weeks. Plus, I don't have a family to support," Dane pointed out. "Like Pele said, everything I need is right here."

The older woman nodded in approval. "Then I don't take any pay, either."

"What about the money for my stay?" Ophelia found herself speaking up and felt a twinge of uncertainty as four sets of eyes turned toward her.

"Your deposit was already spent," Leilani softly pointed out.

"But there's the $10,000 that comes with Dane's agreement to show me around. I can call New York, see that the money is wired immediately instead of at the end of my stay."

Keahi leaned his large frame back in the chair and ran his palm over his chin thoughtfully. "That would certainly buy some time with the creditors."

"But not with Masters," Dane reminded.

Ophelia felt a cloud of gloom settle over the table.

"See what you can do with what we have,

Keahi. If you can't make it work, then maybe Ophelia can have that money sent."

"Sure thing, boss."

Dane rose to his feet. "I'll leave you all to it. Ophelia's going to accompany me around the plantation today, so if you need anything, we'll be in and out."

They each rose to get on with their tasks, and Ophelia followed Dane as he led the way out the door.

HOURS LATER, DANE raised an arm to wipe at the sweat on his brow before checking the reading on the pH meter. Satisfied with the numbers, he glanced down at Ophelia, who sat on the ground, up to her elbows in compost and mud. She had been asking him questions all morning, mentioning different things she had learned from her tour with Leilani, and he found himself growing ever more expansive in his replies. He rambled on about planting, harvesting, processing and roasting, along with expounding on a description of bean flavor profiles that surely would have sent most women running for the coast. But Ophelia remained engaged in the conversation, interrupting occasionally to ask for clarification on some points. He found her interest intriguing, except that he couldn't be certain whether she remained absorbed for her own sake or because it might benefit her assignment here.

It felt as though he had talked more in the past three hours than he had in the past three years, and Ophelia seemed to be listening to most of it. Even once the more physical work began—checking the plants for pests and fungus, hauling fertilizer and making sure the seedlings were receiving the proper drainage, she continued to respond to his descriptions of coffee farming and ask appropriate questions. He found himself looking her way more often than he should, studying the fall of blond tendrils across her perspiring forehead, the streaks of dirt staining her slender arms and the sparkle of her smile when she would look up and reply to something he'd said.

He didn't think he had ever met a woman more beautiful, even covered in grime, as Ophelia Reid looked right now. Turning away, he attempted to refocus on the chores. Ophelia may have been pleasantly interested in the work they were doing, but her mood earlier in the day belied something else. Neither of them had discussed their kiss from the evening before, and he could not deny he had felt some disappointment at her return to the business at hand that morning. She had certainly responded to his kiss last night. But now…

"Tell me again—how many coffee cherries does it take to produce one pound of beans?"

His train of thought halted as she glanced his way, a smudge of soil streaking across her cheek so that he was highly tempted to lean across the coffee plant between them and wipe it away.

"About four thousand," he answered.

"And that's two trees?"

"Roughly."

"That's a lot of work for one pound of coffee. I don't think I'll ever take my morning cup for granted again."

She paused.

"You know, there could be a lot of opportunities, back in New York, for you to get the word out about your coffee plantation."

He felt himself tense, his fingers fumbling awkwardly with the pH monitor he was using to check the soil's acidity levels. "And when would I find the time to do that, if I was working for Bianca Towers?"

He stole a glance from beneath lowered eyelids and watched Ophelia look up at him. "You'd still have a life of your own—time to pursue your hobbies…or date."

She dropped her gaze immediately, and he wondered if she was hinting at something or if the word had just slipped out. After all, he had to remind himself, how much longer would Ophelia be in New York if he moved there? She had Paris in the offing. There would be no point in the two of them starting a relationship.

And even as the thought went through his brain, he found himself amazed that he considered Ophelia in that light. But after their kiss, he couldn't seem to think of her any other way.

"What about you?" he asked. "Why not leave your mom's company and move to Paris—or anywhere—on your own?"

She frowned. "I thought about it once or twice, in college. But this company is everything to my mother. It's the thing that kept her moving after my father's death. To leave would feel like…a betrayal. To her. To everything she worked for."

He settled himself down on the ground beside her, still holding the pH monitor. "I understand that. It's the same feeling I get when I think about leaving this place—a betrayal of the people who work for me. A betrayal of myself. I don't quit easily."

"But it wouldn't be quitting," she countered. "If anything, it would be a sacrifice to save your dreams here. The signing bonus you'll receive from Towers Resorts would make a significant dent in your debts. It would buy you enough time to harvest and sell your crops."

"Ophelia—"

"Listen, Dane. Please." Her hand had come to rest on his, and every nerve ending in his fingers thrilled at the soft touch of her skin against his own. "I'm not going to pretend it wouldn't be hard to leave the islands behind. This place is—" she looked around her before turning her eyes back to his "—charming. But what will you do if this plantation fails? What will happen to Keahi, Leilani, Pele? How will you have helped them, if you can't get it back on its feet? Do you have any other recourse? Any other way to save this dream, than making this sacrifice?"

He stared at her, both resentful and grateful at the candor of her words. She didn't flinch away from his gaze.

"I'm not sure I'm ready to go back," he finally confessed.

"Don't forget who you are," she countered. "I think you'd relish the challenge of refining the Towers Resorts image. After all, you may have hated the corporate life, but you couldn't have hated the work you did. Not all of it."

"No," he admitted. "The work wasn't entirely the problem."

"Then why not try a comeback?"

He looked at her earnest face, the curve of her cheek with the streak of dirt along it. Unable to resist any longer, he reached out and cupped her jaw in his hands, rubbing the pad of his thumb along her skin. Was it his imagination, or did she tilt her head into his hand?

"Would you stick around? If I came back?"

A measure of sadness entered her eyes.

"Never mind." He removed his hand from her cheek. "You have your own dreams to pursue. I wouldn't want to get in the way of that." He dropped his head, unable to look at her anymore. "It's just that, if I agreed, I think it would be easier…if you were there."

She made a soft noise, deep in her throat, drawing his eyes back to hers. He wondered if, somewhere deep down, she wanted him to ask her to stay. For him.

But that was impossible. They had just met, and she had held her own dreams since she was a child. He could understand that, even admire it. And as he had said, he wouldn't get in the way of it.

"Dane…" She still gripped his other hand, her fingers tightening further. "It isn't failure to leave. It might just be a necessary sacrifice to save your dream."

He thought of Mrs. Inoa's words to him. *What will your sacrifice be?*

"I'll think about it and give you an answer by the end of the week."

These words seemed to startle her. Perhaps she had thought he was too stubborn to give in. Or maybe she had doubted her own powers of persuasion. After all, no recruiter before this had gotten him to seriously consider an offer. Then again, no recruiter had come at a time when he was so desperate for a solution.

"I believe your mother's even more calculating than I thought."

"Why do you say that?" she asked.

"Because…of all the recruiters she could have sent…she chose you."

And then, because he couldn't see any reason not to, he leaned in and kissed her once more.

CHAPTER EIGHT

THE NEXT MORNING, Ophelia lay in her bed at the inn, staring at the ceiling and enjoying the morning breeze redolent with tropical scents, as it wafted through her window. Her mind was consumed with one single thought.

Dane Montgomery.

He hadn't agreed to the Towers Resorts offer, but he had conceded to think on it. And then he had kissed her. Again.

Her stomach fizzed with delight, and she turned onto her side, drawing her legs up over her torso, as if to contain the giddiness rolling through her. She had tried telling herself that her happiness was born of the possible success in her assignment—the distinct satisfaction of completing the task her mother had given her.

But she knew that wasn't true. No other recruitment, no matter how important, had ever made her feel this way. It had nothing to do with the contract and everything to do with how Dane had looked at her yesterday afternoon during their time working the plantation.

But she couldn't get too caught up in viewing Dane in a romantic light. It simply wasn't an option, given their situations. She should be focusing on the final push to get Dane to sign the contract and then setting her sights on Paris.

That's what she *should* be doing. And yet, the butterflies in her stomach protested mightily and kept her from maintaining focus.

Throwing off the covers, she decided to shift her nervous energy into getting ready for the day. She showered and dressed and then did her makeup and hair with methodical, exaggerated care. She told herself it was an exercise in restraining her emotions, but deep down, she knew she also wanted to look her very best when she descended the stairway of the inn and entered the dining room.

Applying a final swipe of mascara to her lashes, she stood back and surveyed her appearance. She had opted for the most casual outfit in her wardrobe—a plain, turquoise, button-down shirt and khaki slacks. The aquatic-blue set off her newly tanned skin and blond hair to a flattering degree. She tested a few looks in the mirror before drawing a breath and heading for the door.

When she reached the dining room, she entered and found Dane's eyes instantly on her. While the others were engaged in conversation,

Dane sat silent, fingers wrapped around his coffee mug and gaze trained on the door. She watched him straighten with interest at her arrival, a smile tugging at his lips. She felt gratified by this reaction and responded with a grin of her own, feeling the same giddiness she had experienced upon waking this morning gallop through her midsection once more.

As she moved farther into the room, Keahi and Leilani paused to say hello before resuming the conversation. Pele stood to begin moving breakfast dishes her way, but Ophelia insisted she sit back down and allow her to serve herself. Reluctantly, the other woman agreed, but Ophelia noticed her gaze moved back and forth between Dane's quiet smile and Ophelia several times.

"—luau at Masters's tonight."

Keahi's mention of Dane's rival caused Ophelia to shift her attention. "Luau?"

She noticed Dane's smile falter.

"Masters is hosting a luau this evening," Dane remarked. "We're all invited."

"All of us?"

"He named you specifically."

"Oh." She wasn't sure how to react to that. After all, she doubted she had made the most favorable of impressions on Masters during their first meeting.

"It begins at five, if you'd like to attend."

"You're all going?" Ophelia asked as she sliced into a section of ham.

"Unfortunately." Leilani's voice held a tinge of annoyance. "Treat your enemies like your friends…"

"He's not the enemy," Dane softly chastised. "And it would be in bad form to snub our most influential neighbor."

Leilani sighed. "But you know how he makes his money, Dane!"

Ophelia looked at Dane with renewed interest. "How does Masters make his money?"

Dane met her eyes quickly and then looked away.

"He imports *robusta* beans from other countries and then mixes them in with his own Kona ones. That way, he's still selling Kona coffee, but it's of an inferior quality—which he doesn't advertise when he sells off his product at cut-rate prices to unsuspecting tourists."

Ophelia's jaw dropped. "But…that's just *wrong*."

"And illegal," Keahi added. "But so far, no one's been able to catch him at it."

"Is he under investigation?" Ophelia pressed.

"He's greased all the right wheels to avoid any formal inquiries."

Ophelia felt a swell of sympathy for Dane. His financial issues went far deeper than she had realized. How could he compete with such underhanded business practices? It made the future of the Okina Inn and Plantation appear grim, indeed.

"Well, slimy as he is, I'd love to attend a luau," Ophelia remarked, as much by way of conversation as to break the silence that had descended over the table. "It would be the perfect end to a wonderful week."

This observation only served to entrench the silence deeper. Dane wouldn't meet her eyes, and Pele frowned severely. Keahi sighed, and Leilani looked miserable. Was it because she had drawn attention to the fact her stay would be ending? Were they worried about what Dane's response to her proposal might be?

She was just opening her mouth to comment further about the inn and how wonderful her week had been when the doorbell chimed from the front hall area. Ophelia noticed that the mood shifted to one of question as Dane looked to Leilani.

"Were we expecting guests today?"

"No, boss." The young girl was shaking her head. "No one is arriving until Monday."

Dane pushed back his chair as Leilani spoke and then headed for the door. The others remained for several minutes longer, the silence more portentous than Ophelia liked. She inclined her head toward the front hall area, curious. A few seconds later, she heard the low rumble of Dane's voice, and her stomach, as if tuned to the sound, flipped with happiness.

But then she recognized the voice that followed, and everything inside her went flat.

It can't be. Mother wouldn't...

She tried to remain still and composed, tried to listen objectively to the conversation in the front hall. But when it became impossible to make out the words, she pushed back from the table, her breakfast abandoned, and moved toward the door.

She sensed the others perking up with interest behind her, but she didn't pause to see if they followed. She made her way past the reception area and stepped toward the entryway, unable to see the new arrival past Dane's height and broad shoulders. The conversation at the entrance paused, and a palpable silence hung in the air.

As she moved forward and around Dane, she felt her stomach drop, this time not with pleasure but disbelief.

Cole stood in the doorway.

DANE DIDN'T HAVE to look at Ophelia to feel her stiffen beside him.

"Miss Reid, I was unaware your colleague

would be joining you." He turned his head in time to see her jerk with surprise. Was it his more formal use of her name? Or simply shock at seeing the man she had claimed to be her ex-boyfriend arrive on the doorstep?

He waited for her to turn her head, to meet his gaze, and when she didn't, he felt a twinge of disappointment. Had this been a calculated move, this second recruiter's arrival in Hawaii? Or was Ophelia as stunned as Dane himself felt?

"Cole, what are you doing here?"

Dane noted agitation in her voice but said nothing.

"Hello, Ophelia."

Ophelia didn't return the greeting.

"Come on, Fee, why should you get to have all the fun?" Cole asked. "I think this island is big enough for the two of us, don't you? And besides, I wanted to meet the legendary Dane Montgomery myself."

Dane ignored this comment as well as Cole's ingratiating grin.

"How did you get here?" Ophelia finally spoke.

"The usual travel methods—by plane and then a taxi from the airport."

"No, I mean…you don't need to be here," Ophelia stated, her words blunt.

Dane observed her distress and felt a passing tug of sympathy, but it quickly evaporated. "Perhaps I should give you two some time to confer," he offered, turning to go.

"No, we don't— I mean, I didn't..."

He kept walking until he felt her hand grasping at his arm. He turned and met her pleading green eyes.

"I didn't know he was coming, Dane. I swear that I didn't."

Dane looked from Cole's self-assured expression to Ophelia's desperate one. Then, slowly, he removed her fingers from his arm.

"I've got work to do. Feel free to use the lanai to discuss your strategies." His lips twisted bitterly before he turned, brushed by his employees hovering on the perimeter of the scene and headed for his office before his disappointment could become evident in his eyes.

OPHELIA WAS LIVID, and she made that fact known to Cole as soon as they were seated on the lanai. Or rather, while Cole sat and Ophelia paced.

"How *dare* you," she railed at him, "infringe on my assignment! This is *my* job, Cole! *Mine!* You have no business being here!"

Cole held up his hands in a gesture of surrender. "I couldn't agree more but tell that to your mother. Lillian's the one who sent me."

Cole was probably the only one of Lillian's employees who could get away with calling the CEO by her first name. Not even Ophelia had earned that privilege during her time at Reid Recruiting. But then again, Cole had always been her mother's darling. Thinking back, it was probably part of why Ophelia and he had begun dating in the first place—both wished to curry favor with the boss.

Ophelia stilled at these words and turned to stare at him. "She...what?"

Cole rested his hands on the arms of his wicker chair and looked up. "She called me into her office yesterday and said I should take the first available flight out of JFK. What exactly are you doing down here that required me to make a twelve-hour flight on the spur of the moment?"

Ophelia clenched her jaw. "I was doing just fine, until you showed up."

Cole appeared skeptical. "From the reception I just received from Dane Montgomery, that hardly seems to be the case."

Ophelia threw up her hands in exasperation. "Well, of course he wasn't happy to see you! He resents all recruiters, especially the ones who show up unannounced and ambush him! Did you do any research on the flight over? Can you possibly conceive of what we're up against?"

She knew she sounded melodramatic, but she was making a valiant effort to mask her true emotions. She didn't want Cole to see how she really felt about Dane. It would only complicate matters further.

Cole waved her concerns away. "I'm here now, Fee. You don't have to worry about it anymore."

His pet nickname for her made her peevish. "Don't call me that. My name is *Ophelia*."

He made a face. She suspected he had never much liked her given name. He had once made some remark about Ophelia being the weakest of the characters in Shakespeare's play *Hamlet*. Ophelia had dared to point out that the title figure seemed to be the worst of the cast in terms of weakness. Cole never brought the subject up again, though he still persisted in calling her "Fee" when he felt like it.

"Why did she send you?" Ophelia tried to come back to the topic at hand. "What are you supposed to do?"

"What I always do—close the sale."

Ophelia ground her teeth together, ran a hand over her forehead as she paced, and then turned to face Cole once more. "I've got this, Cole.

Your coming here is only going to make my job harder."

He made a face and rose to his feet. "Then take it up with your mother, *Ophelia*. Believe me, I wasn't that keen on bailing you out after you just threw away what we've had for four years. But I'm here. Because I care about your mother, I care about the company and, whether you believe it or not, I care about *you*. If you really want to go to Paris as badly as you say, I suggest you make use of my talents. Because you're not going to get there without them."

He turned on his heel to stalk out and nearly collided with Pele, who was carrying in a tray with a carafe and a few scones. Cole bowed slightly and exited the room as Pele turned dark, inquisitive eyes on her.

Ophelia felt her knees giving way and moved to the seat Cole had just vacated, sinking into it with a weary sigh.

"You want me to throw him out?" Pele offered as she placed the tray on the table.

Ophelia gave a short snort of laughter. "No, don't do that. He's really not so bad. And I don't think it's his fault. He probably doesn't want to be here any more than I want to have him here."

"Should I show him to your room?"

Ophelia's head snapped up at this. "*My* room? No. No, absolutely not. Cole and I will *not* be sharing a room. Do you think you could fix one up for him? I can pay for another reservation."

Pele nodded shortly. She paused, studying Ophelia.

"I'm really sorry, Pele." Ophelia felt obliged to explain. "I didn't know he was coming."

Pele gave another clipped nod before turning and leaving Ophelia alone on the lanai.

WANTING SOME PRIVACY, Ophelia slipped out of the inn, walking toward the coffee orchard before pulling her cell phone from her pocket. As she'd predicted, there were no new voice mails or any emails referring to Cole's arrival. She felt the prickling of annoyance all over again at how her mother and Cole had taken her by surprise.

She checked the time. It was early afternoon in New York, a perfect hour to catch her mother at her desk. Bringing up her speed dial, she quickly chose her mother's number before she could talk herself out of it.

The line rang a few times before Tamara, her mother's assistant, answered.

"Tamara, it's Ophelia."

"Oh, Ophelia." The other woman sounded sympathetic. "Did Cole arrive?"

"He did," Ophelia confirmed. She tried to keep her voice level with Tamara, not wanting to take out her frustrations with her mother's poor, beleaguered assistant. That may have been Lillian's tactic, but it was not one Ophelia wished to emulate.

"Could you put me through to Ms. Reid?"

There was a pause. "She's on another line. Do you want to wait?"

Ophelia felt anxiety creeping upon her already. The longer she had to wait, the worse it would become.

"Yes. I'll wait."

"Okay, hold on." There was a pause, and Ophelia couldn't be sure if Tamara debated on saying something more or was simply locating the hold button on the phone. Several seconds later, the sound of classical music filled Ophelia's ears, doing nothing to soothe her frayed emotions.

What was she thinking? She shouldn't question her mother—nobody did. The way to earning Lillian Reid's approval did not include second-guessing her choices. Such things only elicited, at best, her mother's irritation, or at worst, her contempt.

Ophelia remembered a couple of years ago when an intern, in an effort to display his brilliant reasoning, took one of Lillian's strategies and overhauled it into a new model. It might not have been so bad, showing this sort of initiative, save for one small blunder. The intern had foolishly called his revision an "update" to the original, implying that Lillian's methods were in need of refreshing.

By the end of the day, he had cleared out his desk, and as far as Ophelia knew, he had left New York for the West Coast some time later.

She began to nibble on her lower lip as the classical music dragged on. She tried to think of something that might calm her—placid pools, scenic sunsets, yoga poses. But it wasn't until her mind finally rested on the thought of Dane walking along the beach with her at the Place of Refuge that she felt a temporary reprieve from her building anxiety.

She latched on to his image in her mind's eye with the desperation of the drowning, picturing every inch of him she could conjure—his mouth with its slightly crooked lift at one side, how his jaw flexed if he found something irritating and the way his eyes crinkled at the corners when he was pleased. The tension in her shoulders loosened as she thought about how tenderly he'd kissed her the day before. Opening her eyes, she realized that somehow, she had gravitated to the very spot where they'd been working when he'd kissed her for the second time. The realization startled and then stilled her, as if her instincts understood what her conscious mind did not.

It was then that the music in her ear cut short, replaced by a brief silence.

"Ophelia? This is Ms. Reid."

Ophelia felt as if she'd been doused with cold water.

"Mother."

It was a small rebellion, she knew. But using the maternal title rather than returning the formal use of her mother's name was Ophelia's attempt to let her parent know of her unhappiness.

There was another pause.

"I take it Cole has arrived." Lillian's voice was frosty and matter-of-fact.

"Yes, he's here. It was quite a surprise when he appeared at the inn. I'm afraid it rather threw Dane for a loop."

"And you, as well, apparently."

Ophelia ground her teeth together. "This was my assignment," she protested. "Why is he here?"

"Because your efforts have not proven fruitful thus far." Ophelia could imagine her mother leaning back in her ergonomic chair, casting her gaze out the ceiling-to-floor window of her office overlooking the city.

Ophelia glanced around at her own surroundings—the rows of coffee trees, the mountain arching up behind the inn on the hill and the flawless stretch of tropical blue sky.

Somehow, this, too, felt like a rebellion against her mother. To be admiring this view while Lillian surveyed her own domain.

"We have a deadline, if you'll remember, Ophelia."

"I'm aware of that. But you cannot expect me to come here, as so many others have done before, just snap my fingers and have Dane Montgomery come to heel."

"No? But I thought you were ready for this level of responsibility."

Ophelia felt torn between stamping her foot and throwing her phone into the coffee trees. "You're asking a man to rearrange his entire life, to return to something he quite deliberately chose to leave behind. And you expect this decision to be made in the blink of an eye?"

"You've had five days, Ophelia."

Ophelia's forehead fell into her hands with weariness. "Mother…*please*." She wasn't entirely sure what she was pleading for, but she had a feeling it went beyond Cole's arrival and this assignment.

"I've told you what's at stake here, Ophelia." To her surprise, her mother's voice was slightly softer. "Bianca Towers won't budge.

She's made it clear that if you don't bring Dane back, she's pulling the account. I'm counting on you. I thought you'd be pleased to have Cole there for moral support. The two of you haven't had a vacation in such a long time."

Ophelia sighed. "Cole and I are no longer together. You know that."

"Of course, but I suppose I feel somewhat responsible. You two make such a good team, and I haven't given either of you enough downtime to allow your relationship room to grow."

Ophelia hesitated, uncertain whether this gesture was genuine or simply employed to placate her.

"For that matter," her mother continued, "it's been ages since you and I took a trip together, hasn't it?"

Ophelia felt her jaw grow slack with surprise.

"Where was it you always wanted us to go together? The Loire valley, wasn't it?"

"Yes, I wanted us to tour the castles there," Ophelia replied, dumbstruck that her mother had remembered.

"Yes, that was it. I remember you couldn't get the idea out of your head as a teenager. You were always talking about it."

Ophelia was stunned her mother remembered. As a teenager, she had been absorbed in French literature, especially stories set during the French Renaissance. She had talked of the châteaus in the Loire valley for weeks, begging her mother to take a vacation there. Lillian's disinterest in the subject, however, had finally caused her to drop it.

She hadn't known her mother remembered the idea.

"I didn't think you wanted to go."

Lillian made a noise of dismissal for this notion. "You know how difficult my schedule can be. There was never time. But perhaps, after this Towers crisis is resolved and Dane Montgomery is settled in New York, we could take a trip there, and then stay in Paris for a few days to get things set up for your move."

Ophelia felt her stomach twist with both delight and apprehension.

"You really would?"

"Of course. You're my daughter, aren't you?"

To her embarrassment, this observation caused a well of tears to rise to Ophelia's eyes. She was ashamed to admit how often she wondered if Lillian Reid forgot she had a daughter.

"I would really like that," she admitted, trying to keep her emotion from being too obvious.

"Then it's settled. I'll have Tamara begin checking flights. Send Cole my regards and do be good to him, Ophelia. He was so gracious about dropping everything to hop a flight and help you."

"Yes, I will. Thank you—" she hesitated, uncertain which title was the proper one at this point "—Ms. Reid."

She had apparently chosen correctly because she could practically feel her mother's approval radiating from the other end of the call.

"You'll let me know immediately when everything is in order."

It was a command, more than a request.

"Of course."

"Very well. I'll look forward to speaking with you again soon."

The call ended before Ophelia could say goodbye. She lowered her phone and stared at its screen, her stomach a strange tangle of emotions. She couldn't remember the last time her mother had mentioned them taking a trip together. There was the requisite Sunday brunch and the occasional dinner together, but Lillian's personal life was so consumed by maintaining her professional relationships that she never suggested she and Ophelia carve out opportunities for more.

Maybe her efforts on this assignment had renewed her mother's desire to establish a connection. It was a happy prospect for Ophelia. She craved a more intimate relationship with her mother, but it always seemed to be a possibility that was just out of her reach.

If convincing Dane to return to New York would create a mother-daughter connection with Lillian Reid then Ophelia had to see this through.

DANE WAS IN the far section of the orchard when Ophelia found him. He had meant to help Keahi in the office for a bit but after Cole Dorset's arrival, he couldn't remain at the inn. Keahi seemed to understand when he said he had to get some air, but he wondered if his friend had betrayed him when he saw Ophelia approaching through the row of coffee trees.

She had the decency to look abashed as she approached. "I didn't know Cole was coming."

He suspected that might be true. Why else would she have let him kiss her twice, had she known her ex-boyfriend was set to show up on the scene? Unless she had intended to make Cole jealous... But then, hadn't she been the one to initiate the breakup? Or perhaps her motives did include making Cole jealous, to show the other man what he'd be missing when she moved to Paris?

Dane shook his head to clear it of these thoughts. "I suppose it's really none of my business."

He could tell his tone had wounded her by the crease that appeared in between her eyebrows. It disconcerted him to realize he had recognized and cataloged this gesture. He had come to know Ophelia Reid far too well during this past week.

"He came at my mother's request."

"I'm sure he did." Dane turned to step farther into the orchard, to put more distance between them.

"I wasn't pretending when you kissed me," she said, her voice so low he barely caught it. He turned, slowly.

"It wasn't part of some recruiter's game. I know that's what you're thinking, but it wasn't. I would never behave like that to get someone's contract. I don't work that way."

And to his frustration, he suspected that this, too, might be true.

"Then why did you let me kiss you?" His voice sounded far gruffer than he intended, gravelly as lava rock.

"I—" She started and then stopped. He wondered if she was trying to come up with an excuse that might appeal to him.

"I guess because I'm…attracted to you." This admittance sent her face awash in a flush; it covered her cheekbones and spread up to her temples. To his consternation, he found it enchanting.

"That must have made your job here easier."

Again, that little indent in between her brows. He was tempted to step toward her and run the pad of his finger against it, willing it away, but he remained rooted where he stood.

"Oh, Dane. It's not like that. It never was. Can't my feelings be separate from my assignment?"

He didn't know the answer to that question. Could they?

"I don't think I can give you what you want, Ophelia." Even he wasn't entirely sure what he was referring to—the offer from Towers International…or the attraction between them?

When he looked back at her face, the flush had deepened. From anger, disappointment or embarrassment—he couldn't be certain which.

"Was it really so bad…" she murmured, "your old life?"

He sighed and looked away, unable to witness the challenge in her green eyes.

"It was…lonely."

"Lonelier than the exile you've chosen here?"

His gaze narrowed. "This is not an exile. Don't play the psychology mind games with me, Ophelia. Others better than you have tried."

This last insult caused her to take a step

backward, and he knew, by the way she looked at him, that he had won. It was a hollow victory, however, especially as he witnessed the expression on her face. What would have happened if they had met under different circumstances? What if he had known her in his previous life, back in New York? Would they have dated, eventually marrying? Would there have been children? Would he have still wanted to leave, move to Hawaii and begin anew? Perhaps Ophelia would have supported him in such an endeavor. She was loyal, that much he had learned. Perhaps his life would have been different, if he'd had her by his side.

While he had been mapping out a past that hadn't happened, Ophelia had been regaining her composure. She straightened, her chin held high. "I'm sorry you feel that way."

She cleared her throat and turned to leave before seemingly reconsidering and turning back. "You know, not everyone is out to use you, Dane. As difficult as it may seem to believe, perhaps some people—like the people who work for you—care about you just for *you*. They don't measure you by your performance or what you can accomplish for them."

"Don't bring my employees into this—"

"But they're *not* just your employees. They're your friends. They're standing behind you, putting their faith in you. And it's not because of who you were. That doesn't mean anything to them. It's because of who you *are*."

Her words stunned him. In part because he hadn't even recognized he'd placed such pressure on himself, but now that Ophelia brought it to light, he realized it was true. As much as he cared for those who surrounded him on the islands, he hadn't entirely believed they could be sticking around just for him—just because he was their friend, and they were his.

"And whether this coffee plantation succeeds or fails, they're not going to hold it against you. They know you're doing your level best to keep this thing going until you begin turning a profit. They're counting on you, but they're not condemning you." She drew a breath and then exhaled it in frustration. "You are the luckiest kind of man, Dane Montgomery. You've been given a second chance, and an opportunity to see it through, no matter how much you may dislike humbling yourself and going back to the place you left behind. But if it allows you to keep this thing going then…you should do it." She stared him down. "The recruiter in me aside…you should do it."

He could only look at her, without words after her speech.

"And don't sell yourself short—or me, either, for that matter. I liked that you kissed me. I liked kissing you back."

And before he could react to those words, Ophelia moved forward, placed both her palms against his neck and drew his face to hers, kissing him firmly but thoroughly before pulling away.

Then she turned and walked back the way she had come while he stood, staring slack-jawed and silent after her.

CHAPTER NINE

FOLLOWING HER CONFRONTATION with Dane, Ophelia returned to the inn, her lips still tingling, and found Leilani at the reception desk assembling welcome packets. She approached her young friend warily, uncertain how Leilani would react after the morning's events. It humbled her when Leilani looked up from her tasks, the younger woman's face blooming into a grin at the sight of Ophelia.

"I was afraid you were going to keep to your room for the rest of your stay," Leilani confessed.

Ophelia sighed apologetically. "I'm really sorry about…" She trailed off, uncertain how to finish that statement. There were many things she felt sorry for—Cole's intrusion, her own agenda, the inn's financial troubles.

But Leilani nodded with simple understanding. "It's not your fault."

"Maybe. Maybe not. But I never meant for things to become so complicated."

Leilani moved out from behind the desk and

laid a hand on Ophelia's arm. "They were complicated before you came, Ophelia. If anything, I think you've woken Dane up a little bit. He seemed stuck in a daze before this, and I was afraid he would never see that he needs to do something. The loan from Masters was a bad idea, but he wouldn't listen to Keahi. If you hadn't come…" She drew a breath. "You've awakened him. In more ways than one. Don't apologize for that."

Ophelia longed to know in what other ways she had *awakened* Dane, but after boldly kissing him in the orchard, she was feeling a bit too shy to ask. So she cleared her throat and changed the subject.

"Can you tell me where my colleague Cole is? I should probably see how he's settling in."

Leilani hesitated, and Ophelia felt a moment's panic. What had Cole gotten up to now?

"He's in the kitchen. With *Tutu*."

"Pele?"

Leilani nodded, and Ophelia knew she must have paled because Leilani rushed to reassure her. "She's feeding him the leftovers from breakfast. I'm afraid he charmed her with compliments."

Ophelia stared in disbelief. "He was able to charm your grandmother?"

It shouldn't surprise her. Cole could be quite

charming when he wanted something. She was more irritated that he had ingratiated himself where Ophelia had failed. She didn't feel as though Pele had warmed to her much during her stay. Though she had attributed it to her position as a recruiter, clearly Pele did not hold that role against Cole.

Leilani shrugged. "Grandmother can be a bit fickle in her affections."

"I see. Well, if you don't mind, I'm just going to check on them."

Leilani looked as though she were about to caution against such an intrusion but then she simply nodded. Before Ophelia could depart, however, she called her name.

"You're still going to the luau tonight, aren't you?"

In all the excitement, Ophelia had forgotten about the festivities at Masters's that evening. She paused, considering, and then could see no reason not to attend. She nodded, and Leilani grinned.

"Good. I can't wait for you to try the *poi*."

Ophelia didn't ask Leilani to elaborate on this cryptic comment. Instead, she headed toward the inn's kitchen.

When Ophelia entered the room, she found Cole seated at the kitchen's island, his long legs spread before him as he leaned in toward

whatever dish Pele was preparing at the stove.
Ophelia observed Pele bestowing a benevolent
expression on Cole as her ex-boyfriend beamed
with deceptively boyish charm. Her skin prickled in irritation at the sight, annoyed once more
at the idea of Cole stealing in on her assignment.

"I see Pele is introducing you to her excep-
tional cooking."

Pele looked up at Ophelia's entrance, and the
happy face she'd been wearing faded. She gave
Ophelia a nod of acknowledgment and then
turned back to stirring the pot on the stovetop.
Ophelia suppressed a sigh and wondered how
she and Pele could have gotten off on the wrong
foot so completely.

"The woman is a wonder," Cole raved and
popped a bite of breakfast ham into his mouth.

Ophelia stared, but Cole's grin was positively
devilish as he chewed the meat with seeming
glee. She decided not to point out that Cole was
a vegetarian.

And to make matters worse, her own stomach growled in jealousy at the sight of Cole's
carnivorous enjoyment, reminding her that
she'd barely had any breakfast before her morning had been interrupted.

Cole's grin grew wider at the sound, but Pele
took some mercy on her and moved from the

stove to slide a small plate with leftover ham and croissants across the island toward her.

She took the offering with a glare at her colleague and settled herself at the table a few feet away. Pele returned to her task.

"Pele here was just inviting me to the luau at the neighbor's this evening."

Ophelia suppressed a groan and forced it down her throat by swallowing a mouthful of flaky croissant. She stood to get herself a glass of water.

When she didn't comment on his remark, Cole elaborated. "She's making a...what did you call it, Pele?"

"Haupia."

"How-pee-ah," Cole imitated. Pele beamed. Ophelia nearly gagged.

"It's a coconut custard dessert, which is sliced into squares and often served at luaus," Cole informed her.

"It sounds delicious." Ophelia tried to sound upbeat, but it made little difference. Pele didn't so much as glance in her direction as she opened several cupboards until she found one containing mugs and glasses.

A silence descended over the kitchen at this point and without any more witty banter to goad her, she noted that Cole kept his gaze on

Pele, as if he couldn't bear to look Ophelia's way. She softened slightly. But only slightly.

"Cole, I wondered if I could speak to you… in private."

She glanced in Pele's direction to see how she would react to this, but it was as if the housekeeper never even heard her speak. She continued to stir the custard on the stovetop, her back to Ophelia.

Cole sighed. "If you must drag me from the company of this Polynesian goddess, then you must."

This ridiculous sentiment drew Pele's gaze up once more, and she smiled warmly in Cole's direction.

Any softening Ophelia had felt toward her ex-boyfriend was immediately displaced by annoyance.

"Fine. Follow me."

She led the way from the kitchen and back toward the reception area, not bothering to stop or glance behind her until she reached the lanai off the main entryway. As soon as Cole entered behind her, she moved around him to slide the door closed. She noted that he didn't move so she was obliged to brush against him. It felt awkward, being so close to him after their breakup. She moved away as quickly as possible and gestured for him to sit.

He shrugged and sank into one of the lanai chairs. She forced herself to take the chair beside him.

"Cole, I need you to do something for me."

"Oh, *now* you need my help?"

She didn't allow herself to become irritated by his tone. "Not exactly. I need you…to stay out of this."

He scoffed.

"I'm serious, Cole. You and I both know how delicate this situation is, and I've made real inroads with Montgomery." She tried to make herself sound as detached from Dane as possible. "He trusts me." She wasn't sure that statement was entirely true, but she had to appear confident. "I want you to leave this alone. Let me handle it. My way."

Cole stared at her, his face an inscrutable mask. She felt a wave of uncertainty. Cole could do a lot of damage to her situation here, jeopardize her position and keep Dane from returning. The idea upset her, not just because it would mean the loss of Paris but because she wasn't quite ready to part with Dane's company. Not yet. At least if he came back to New York, it would buy her a couple more weeks. But Cole couldn't know that, or things would unravel quickly.

"Tell me there's nothing going on between you and him."

Ophelia blinked, wishing she were a better liar. Her lips tingled with the memory of kissing Dane less than an hour before. "I… Why would you even think that?"

His gaze was far too direct for her liking. "Because there's been talk back at the office. That you and Montgomery…"

Ophelia's eyes slid closed. Of course, her co-workers would be gossiping about her week-long stay at Dane's plantation. It may have been an assignment, but that wouldn't prevent rumors from circulating.

"Does my mother know what's being said?"

When Cole didn't answer, she opened her eyes and found him staring at her with a wounded expression.

"Fee. How could you?"

She bristled. "How could I what? Cole, he kissed me. It wasn't as if I seduced him."

"No?" Cole stood. "Then how come you're closer to securing a contract on Dane Montgomery than anyone else in the last three years?"

She made a face. "I hardly think I'm a temptress. And I'm not even sure how close I am to getting him to return. I just know that I can't have you jeopardizing the possibility."

"Do you really think Lillian would have sent me here if she thought I'd jeopardize things? Give your mother a little credit."

That was Cole. Ever Lillian's champion. But no one played the game better than Lillian Reid herself. If she had sent Cole, she had a good reason. And what about their chat on the phone earlier? Had she meant it, about them taking a trip together? Or was it simply her way of keeping Ophelia compliant? Ophelia thought how difficult it was to doubt your own mother in such a way.

She released a sigh and sat patiently until Cole finally seated himself beside her once more.

"Cole, I appreciate your coming. I do. It must have been difficult, given our recent breakup."

He winced at the word.

"I think you being here speaks of your dedication to my mother as well as to the company—"

"But not to you."

She paused. "I'm sorry?"

He turned his eyes her way. A sweep of dark blond hair fell across his forehead, and she resisted the urge to brush it away.

"I'm here for you, too, you know."

She drew back a bit. Cole had never been one to sacrifice his own wishes for her needs.

Perhaps their breakup had opened his eyes to his own selfishness.

"I appreciate that. But it doesn't change anything…does it?"

She held his gaze, willing him to be honest with her.

"If I go to Paris…" He trailed off, and she knew she must have jerked in surprise. Cole was reconsidering Paris? For her? She couldn't think about that. She couldn't deal with anything else right now.

"I just need you to help me out here by leaving Dane alone. Let me handle it. It's my assignment—give me the chance to see it through."

"But Lillian—" He stopped abruptly, but Ophelia's suspicions immediately flared.

"What about Lillian? Did she give you specific instructions? About me? About Dane?"

He hesitated and then shook his head. He was loyal to her mother, to his very core. It was probably why Lillian doted on him so much.

"Right." She decided to let it go. "Then you'll stay away from Dane?"

He looked away quickly and then nodded, not quite meeting her eyes. She knew it was the most she would get from him.

"I'd still like to attend the luau this evening," he said.

"All right." She couldn't see the harm in it.

In fact, maybe it would fortify her to have him nearby. He was a colleague, if nothing else. And despite everything, Cole could be a pretty good coworker when it came down to it.

She stood, intending to leave, but as she walked by him, he reached out and his fingers encircled her wrist.

"Fee…"

She waited.

"When he kissed you…" There was a long pause during which Ophelia fought the blush she felt rising to her cheeks. "Did you kiss him back?"

She slowly pulled her wrist from his grasp, and then touched him lightly on the shoulder, as if in apology, before leaving the lanai.

DANE HAD TO grudgingly concede—Kenneth Masters threw a good party. From the succulent pork lifted out of the luau pit to the variety of dishes prepared by the locals, the food was mouthwatering, and the atmosphere, with its torches and island pop music, was festive and relaxed.

Dane took a sip of his punch and shared a glance with Keahi. "Masters is good at it, huh?"

Keahi made a face. "Easing his conscience over his shady business practices by hosting a luau like this twice a year?" He took a long swig of punch and then scratched at the bandage on his arm. "Oh, yeah, brah. He's a *master*."

Despite the bitterness in Keahi's words, Dane couldn't help chuckling. "Masters will get his… One day. Sooner or later, he'll slip up, and someone will finally have the evidence to shut him down."

Keahi shrugged. "I just wish it had happened months ago, long before you took that loan from him."

Dane frowned at the reminder. "Don't worry yourself with that tonight, Keahi. Just enjoy the party." His gaze scanned the crowd, sweeping over women in vibrant tropical prints and men in floral island shirts. Keahi's yellow-and-red Hawaiian shirt draping his large frame stood out in sharp contrast next to Dane's own simple outfit of teal-green shirt and khaki cargo pants.

"You searchin' for Ophelia, brah?" Keahi asked him with a sideways glance.

Dane looked his friend's way with what he hoped was an appropriate scowl. "Miss Reid isn't my concern."

But he still hoped she would show up tonight. Keahi said he'd given her and Cole instructions on how to find the entrance to Masters's property. After she had kissed him that morning, Dane had been able to think of little else.

"C'mon. It's me you're talking to. You don't need to pretend. She's a pretty lady. Smart, too."

"Are you that eager to get rid of me, ship me back to New York?" Dane attempted to infuse a degree of light teasing into his tone.

He felt Keahi's eyes on him until he turned and met his friend's gaze. "Nah. I'm just tired of all the attention you get from the ladies. I figure if I get you out of the picture, I can get a little more action."

Dane burst out laughing at this theory.

"Still," Keahi said.

"Still what?"

"If Ophelia shows up tonight…you should ask her to dance."

Dane gave a grunt of surprise that he hoped sounded like annoyance. "Her ex-boyfriend is here to perform those duties."

"What, the other recruiter?" Keahi blew a sound through his lips. "He doesn't deserve a woman like Ophelia."

"And I do?"

Keahi grinned, and to his dismay, Dane found himself smiling back. He shook his head. "You islanders need to stop sticking your nose in everyone else's business."

Keahi laughed in a low rumble. "If we did then where would we put our noses?" He began to amble away. "Just remember, boss, if the lady shows up…be nice. Ask her to dance. You never know what might happen."

Dane waved him away without replying.

OPHELIA ENTERED THE luau with Cole at her side. Her gaze swept over the scene, taking in the flickering flames of tiki torches, tables groaning beneath the weight of potluck dishes, a small stage set up with local musicians strumming island pop tunes and brightly dressed luau attendees circulating the open space behind Masters's sprawling home. She fiddled self-consciously with the belt of her coral-colored sarong sundress, on loan from Leilani.

"I love theme parties," Cole announced from beside her.

"It's not a theme party," she pointed out. "This is their culture. Don't stereotype."

"Whatever. I still love a tropical theme."

She chafed but did not respond.

"Do you think the cocktails will have tiny umbrellas in them?"

She turned to glare at him and saw he was smirking, making every effort to get under her skin.

"Remember the Gibson party in the Hamptons two summers ago?"

Her mind spun backward, recalling paper

lanterns strung along the beach and so many cocktail umbrellas that Cole had dared to ask Mrs. Gibson just whom her bulk supplier was. He convinced her that when he and Ophelia married, they'd be having a tropical theme and wanted as many cocktail umbrellas as they could find.

Ophelia's lips twitched at the memory. At the time, she had been giddy at the prospect of her and Cole marrying. But a proposal had never come, and now she wondered if he had known all along he didn't wish to be tied to her—not with her plans to move to Europe.

"Perhaps you should find Masters," she suggested, "and ask him about his umbrella supplier."

To her consternation, Cole grinned at her recollection of the event. "You'll have to introduce me to him first."

"Did I hear my name?"

Ophelia shifted with Cole to see Kenneth Masters standing before them. Stifling her annoyance at his appearance, she gestured between him and Cole. "Kenneth Masters, this is my colleague, Cole Dorset."

"Ah, you're coming in pairs now to try and negotiate Dane back to the mainland? Best of luck with that."

Cole let out an appreciative laugh as Ophelia folded her arms. She saw no reason to get chummy with Masters.

"He's a tough sell, that's for certain," Cole agreed.

"I take it you've made no progress with my recalcitrant neighbor, then?" Masters directed this question to Ophelia.

She moved her weight to her other foot and kept her arms crossed. "That's privileged information."

"Oh, come on, Fee. As Montgomery's neighbor, perhaps Masters here has some insight we're lacking."

"Please, call me Ken," Masters insisted.

Ophelia suppressed the urge to roll her eyes at Masters and Cole's instant camaraderie.

"I'm trying to convince Dane of the merits of a partnership," Masters continued, "joining his reputation on the mainland with my coffee farming experience."

"Sounds intriguing. What's your game plan?"

Ophelia looked around, desperate for an escape. She caught Leilani's eye several yards away and made a silent plea for help. Leilani abandoned Sam to weave her way through the partygoers until she reached Ophelia's side.

"Ophelia, have you tried the *poi* yet?"

"No, I haven't had a chance."

"You have to taste it! It's like a rite of passage

when you come to Hawaii. Excuse us, gentlemen." Leilani whisked Ophelia away before either man could protest. She steered Ophelia in the direction of the refreshment tables.

"Thank you," she said as Leilani grabbed them each a paper plate. "I have to confess that something about Masters makes my skin crawl."

"You and me both," Leilani commiserated. "But the *poi* wasn't just an excuse. You can't come to Hawaii without trying it."

She navigated Ophelia through tables laden with traditional Hawaiian dishes: chicken long rice with ginger and green onions, *lau lau* of steamed fish in taro leaves, *lomi* salmon with Maui onion, *poke* which looked to Ophelia like a heavily seasoned raw tuna salad and endless dishes involving sweet potato, pineapple, papaya, coconut, fish, chicken and pork.

They passed Pele manning one of the refreshment tables. The older woman greeted her granddaughter warmly, but when Ophelia stopped to say hello, Pele turned her back without responding. Ophelia frowned in disappointment and then kept moving to catch up with Leilani.

"I think your grandmother wishes I weren't here," she commented.

Leilani sighed. "I've noticed that she's been

cooler than necessary where you're concerned. Try not to take it personally."

Ophelia didn't see how she could take it otherwise. After all, Pele seemed fond enough of Cole.

"I think it's hard for her. She knows Dane has to do something in order to save the plantation, but she doesn't like the thought of him leaving. She loves him like a son. Especially since my dad passed away."

"You never talk about your parents. What happened to them?"

Leilani's eyes filled as she looked at Ophelia. "My dad died of a brain aneurysm two years ago. Totally unexpected."

"Oh, Leilani. I'm so sorry." If she hadn't been balancing her plate in her hands, she would have enveloped Leilani in a hug.

"My mom left when I was little, and when I lost my dad…well, that's when I started spending time with the wrong crowd. Dane helped *Tutu* pull me out of that, and she's been really grateful to him ever since."

"He truly cares about you and your grandmother. That's easy to see."

Leilani blinked away her tears. "It's easy to see he cares about you, too."

Ophelia looked down at her plate and chose not to respond. After all, what did it matter if

Dane might be coming to care about her? Nothing could happen between them. They were destined to be in two different places, no matter how things played out.

She followed Leilani down the line of food so that by the time they reached the dish of *poi,* Ophelia's plate was already piled high.

She took one look at the infamous *poi* and decided perhaps it was good she didn't have much room for it. The native food was a gray mass of puddinglike consistency. Ophelia frowned into its congealed depths.

"Um…are you serious about this?"

Leilani grinned from ear to ear. "You have to try it," she encouraged and promptly scooped up a spoonful, plopping it on the edge of Ophelia's plate. It looked like a blob of grayish-purple slime.

"Is it supposed to look like that?"

Leilani giggled. "Sure, it's one-finger *poi.*"

"One finger?"

The younger girl nodded. "When it's a thinner consistency, we call it three-finger *poi* because it takes three fingers to scoop it up and eat it. But most Hawaiians prefer it thicker, so that it only takes one finger to scoop and eat."

"Sounds…appetizing."

Leilani grinned. "Don't judge it until you taste it."

Ophelia remained skeptical, but in the spirit of new experiences, she knew she had to at least sample the gray glob. She was studying the quivering substance, debating whether she should attack it with a spoon, one finger or three when a voice in her ear sent shivers up and down her spine.

"It's not quite as bad as it looks."

She turned and found herself looking into the warm blue eyes of Dane Montgomery.

DANE COULDN'T HELP but be amused at Ophelia's reaction to the wobbly mass of *poi*. He'd experienced similar misgivings when he'd first tasted the pudding made of softened and mashed taro root.

Along with Leilani, he directed Ophelia toward a nearby table where she sat and stared at the item on her plate. As soon as Leilani's attention was distracted by a friend who greeted her in passing, Ophelia leaned toward him.

"Can I just use a spoon?" she questioned, an edge of desperation to her tone.

"You could," he said, "but if you want the true experience, you have to scoop it with your fingers."

She eyed him. "You first."

He laughed. "You don't trust us?"

She pursed her lips, and he found himself

laughing even harder. "All right, all right. Here, I'll show you."

Reaching over her plate, he scooped a dollop of *poi* onto his finger and lifted it to his lips. He licked it clean and then looked at her. "Your turn."

She sighed. Leilani finished talking to her friend and turned back.

"Go on, Ophelia. It's not that bad. I promise."

Ophelia bravely dipped a finger into the gray sludge, and then, squeezing her eyes closed, inserted it into her mouth. Dane and Leilani exchanged a conspiratorial look and waited until Ophelia's eyes opened.

"It tastes like…" She rolled it around in her mouth. "Like wallpaper paste."

Dane threw back his head and laughed. "How could you possibly know what wallpaper paste tastes like?"

"Well, it's what I imagine wallpaper paste tastes like," she said.

Leilani made a face. "It's an acquired taste, obviously."

Ophelia made another couple of attempts at the *poi* before moving on to some of the other foods on her plate. Dane rose to get them both something to drink and then grabbed a bite to eat for himself. Ophelia brought out her disposable camera and took a few photos. Several times, friends of Dane and Leilani came over to say hello, and eventually, Sam joined them.

Dane found himself floating on the awareness of Ophelia seated beside him and marveling how, in such a short time, she had turned his world on its head. Having her there felt natural, as if she had been born to be at his side. And yet, Hawaii wasn't her dream. She belonged to New York, to Paris, to her job with Reid Recruiting. And his life was here now.

No matter how he might be enjoying this evening, nothing could change the fact that his life and Ophelia's dreams weren't destined to align.

OPHELIA COULDN'T SEEM to stop herself. She felt a swell of emotions roiling beneath her breastbone—expectation coupled with awkwardness. Her senses were heightened with Dane seated so close to her. She tried to think of questions and comments to continue drawing him out and keep any uneasy silences from forming between them.

"There are a lot of people here," she commented after she had swallowed the last of her *haupia,* which was, as Cole had predicted, delicious.

"When Masters throws a party, most of the community turns up," Dane remarked.

"He must be popular."

"The same could be said for your boyfriend."

Her head automatically swiveled to follow his stare to where several well-dressed women surrounded Cole. Did it bother Dane that Cole had come? "Ex-boyfriend," she corrected.

"He came a long way for an ex-boyfriend."

"It wasn't me he came for," she replied.

She felt Dane shifting to watch her. "Are you sure about that?"

Just then, Cole looked up, his stare moving like a missile with a homing signal, finding its way straight to her. He held up his glass in salute, making a show of pointing at the tiny cocktail umbrella resting on the side. Despite herself, she smiled. After a couple of seconds, she realized Dane still watched her. She turned her head, catching herself in his stare.

"Maybe he came to prove something to you," he said.

"How so?"

"Maybe he wants you to know he changed his mind, that he's willing to find his way wherever you are. To be with you."

She wasn't sure if it was Dane's implications concerning Cole or his own direct gaze that sent the warmth flooding into her cheeks. She forced a brittle laugh and shifted her eyes away.

"It's obvious you don't know him very well."

"No," Dane conceded, "but some things aren't all that hard to figure out."

She looked back at him, studying his carefully neutral countenance. What was he getting at? Was he nudging her back toward Cole? Did he think her ex-boyfriend would become a consolation prize, if he chose not to accept the Towers offer?

"I don't expect you to understand."

Dane frowned. "He loses you if he stays where he's at. He has the chance to win you if he goes. What's so complicated about that?"

She stared at Dane, trying to see behind the cool wall of his blue eyes. Was he testing her, trying to determine just how she felt about her ex-boyfriend? "I don't see how Cole's and my relationship is any business of yours."

His passive expression flickered, and she knew she'd wounded him in some way. Before she could question him further, she sensed movement in her peripheral vision. Turning her head, she saw Cole moving toward them.

DANE TENSED AS he saw Ophelia's attention turn, a frown tugging at her mouth. Following her gaze, he watched as Cole Dorset resolutely made his way through the crowd and in their direction.

The band had segued into a soft pop ballad,

the native Hawaiian lyrics blending with a few English ones. The song was a perfect opportunity to hold someone close.

Dane realized Cole planned to ask Ophelia to dance.

A prickle of irritation ran along his nerves. Ophelia might insist that Cole hadn't come to Hawaii for her, but Dane felt otherwise. The other man had the look of a predator about him, and while Dane knew he had no real claim to Ophelia, the idea of her with Cole still chafed.

He should let it go, he knew. He should let Cole have his chance, without any interference. After all, it would solve the dilemma of these complex feelings he was experiencing toward Ophelia. Let the two of them reconcile, let her return to New York and leave him in peace to sort out his own mess.

But watching her, seeing the tiny indent between her brows as she studied Cole's approach, stirred his protective instincts. Before he could think through the consequences, he shifted, his arm brushing ever so lightly against her skin and drawing her eyes back to his.

"Would you like to dance?"

OPHELIA COULD ONLY blink in response to Dane's question. Cole was only a few steps away, and before she could find the words to respond to Dane, he slipped his hand into hers and stood. She followed his lead, and as they brushed by a frowning Cole, she heard Dane utter an insincere apology.

"Sorry, Cole. I already claimed her for this one."

She experienced only the briefest glimpse of Cole's scowl before she was in Dane's arms, his hands around her waist as he drew her close.

Despite her own better judgment, she leaned in, fitting perfectly against the length of his chest and torso. They swayed to the music in a rhythm of their own making.

"So what will you do?" he asked after they had been dancing for a few minutes. "If you can't have Paris?" His breath fluttered the hair by her ear as he whispered into it, and she shivered in response.

It was a question she had refused to allow herself in the last week. "I'll wait," she decided, "until another opportunity arises."

"Will you be happy?"

She lifted her eyes to his, surprised to see a deep measure of compassion there. Happy? When had anyone ever thought to consider her happiness? Her mother had always been more concerned with success. Cole had only cared for appearances. When she thought of happiness, she had always imagined Paris—her childhood, the few precious memories she retained of her father and their time as a family. Could she be happy putting off that dream again for an indefinite amount of time? Until fate and fortune afforded her another chance?

When she offered no answer to his question, he asked another.

"You're leaving tomorrow."

She blinked at this statement. "Yes." She had tried her best not to think about having to leave, but now the weight of that realization settled heavily on her shoulders. "I'll need to be back in the office on Monday with—" she trailed off, searching for an appropriate response "—with an explanation."

"What will happen if you go back empty-handed, as it were?"

Ophelia cleared her throat and turned away from him. She didn't want to consider the possibility so she didn't reply.

"Ophelia." His murmur of her name drew her eyes back to his. "I can't do it."

She felt all the air leave her lungs as her shoulders dropped in disappointment. She squared them up and began negotiating.

"We could arrange an increase on the first year's salary, plus the additional bonus of use of Bianca Towers's private jet. You could fly back here whenever you wanted."

He frowned at her. It was a losing battle, and she knew it. But she had been unprepared for the disappointment that slammed into her chest.

"Is there anything I can say or do to change your mind?"

He shook his head. "I'm sorry. But I can't go back. I don't have it in me."

She felt the faint prick of tears stinging the backs of her eyelids and was appalled at her lack of self-control. What would Lillian think of her if she began crying right in the middle of this luau?

She cleared her throat and blinked several times. "Don't apologize. I can't say you led me on. You're far too gentlemanly for that." She laughed at the words, and to her embarrassment, it came out strained.

"Ophelia…" He moved his hands from her waist to run his fingers along her arm. She jumped, jerking herself away.

"Really, Dane. You owe me no apologies." She still couldn't meet his eyes.

"If it's any consolation, no one has ever come anywhere near as close to convincing me as you did."

It was a small source of comfort until she considered what her mother would say. As a teenager, when she had performed in several school sports competitions, Lillian had a saying. "*Almost* isn't *accomplished.*"

She could hear those words now, in her mother's familiar cool tone, drumming themselves through her head.

Almost. Almost. Almost.

"I appreciate the time and attention you afforded me this week." Too cold. She sounded like her mother. So cold, so distant.

"Ophelia, believe me. It was my pleasure."

He sounded nearly as disappointed as she felt.

"I wish you the best of luck with the plantation." She was having difficulty looking at him.

"This isn't goodbye yet," he softly reminded. "You're not leaving until tomorrow."

But it felt like goodbye. Already, it felt as if she were going away. Without him. Without her dreams of Paris and the future. She took another step back, nearly colliding with the couple dancing behind her.

"I think…perhaps it should be," she said. And when she finally locked her eyes with his, she saw the same remorse that must be reflected in her own. "I'll have to contact Ms. Reid with the news. She'll need to relay your regrets to Bianca Towers." She cleared her throat once more and extended her hand, trying to keep her voice bright. "Again, I wish you all the best."

He looked at her for a long moment before placing his hand in hers for a cordial shake. He held on to her fingers and willfully drew her closer to him once more.

"I hope you know it was worth it," he said, "your coming here. For the pleasure of meeting you."

She barely managed a polite nod before she tugged her fingers from his and hurried away before the tears started.

CHAPTER TEN

DANE FOUND HIMSELF by the luau pit where the pig had been roasted and then excavated. All that remained was the detritus of scorched soil and charred banana leaves within a gaping maw of dirt.

He stared into the dark cavity and compared it to the emptiness he felt inside. He'd been certain that turning down the Towers proposal was the right choice. So why did he feel bereft and dissatisfied? Was it the likelihood that he would be losing the coffee plantation? Or did it have something to do with Ophelia's impending departure? Perhaps it was simply guilt over how he would face Keahi, Pele and Leilani to tell them their jobs were now forfeit.

He kicked at a blackened stick and watched it break apart in a flutter of ash and soot.

"Ah, there you are."

Dane looked up and cringed at the sight of Kenneth Masters approaching.

"I've been looking for you. I thought perhaps

you wouldn't come, feared you might choose to avoid me. I'm glad to see that wasn't the case."

Dane watched the older man as he circled the pit, the coldness in his eyes belying his warm tone.

"So I assume you've brought the payment with you."

Dane stiffened. "I'll have $10,000 for you on Monday. That should make a substantial dent in the loan."

Masters frowned. "Why, yes, that's something. But not even half of what you owe."

Dane forced himself to remain pleasant. "No," he conceded, "but I thought it might be enough to buy me a little more time. You know things can get tight in the months leading up to a harvest."

Masters's frown only deepened, and Dane felt the faint stirrings of dread.

"Of course, if anyone understands your predicament, son, I do."

Dane chafed at the other man's use of the word *son*—it seemed a calculated gesture of feigned concern. "I, too, was once new at this game. However—" Masters trailed off for a bit, and Dane braced himself "—at some point, you have to accept that others know better than you. Perhaps you're not the genius you've been touted to be."

Determined to keep his cool, Dane crossed his arms. "Is that what bothers you, Masters? My reputation?"

Masters shrugged. "You have to concede the irony—the infamous Dane Montgomery has finally been bested."

Dane clenched his jaw in annoyance. "That's how you see this, then, as a competition between the two of us? Do you think if you win my plantation, that it will be enough to accommodate the size of your ego?"

Masters laughed. "I hardly think you're one to talk about ego, Montgomery. After all, why is it that you've stayed here in Hawaii, hmm? Why haven't you returned to New York, taken one of the offers presented to you and salvaged your farm when you had the chance?"

The other man took a step closer and leaned in, his expression smug. "Because of your pride. You can't admit that you're no good at this farming venture. You refuse to confess that you've *failed*."

Dane dropped his arms and ground his teeth together at these words. Could Masters be right? Was it only his own arrogance that kept him from accepting one of the many offers that had come his way? Returning to New York might feel like a defeat but would it be better than signing over his land and property to Masters? The man may have been a mega-lomaniac but perhaps he had a point.

"Think about it, Dane," Masters continued. "The longer you're out of the game, the fewer recruiters will come. They'll begin to recognize your skills for what they were—a brief, flaming star that too quickly died out. Maybe that's why you really left the corporate world? You knew your supposed brilliance couldn't last much longer."

How many more opportunities would come his way? What if Ophelia was the last of them? What if the Towers proposal was the last opportunity fate saw fit to send him? And he had turned it down, turned his back on the last chance he had to save his farm, his friends, his dream.

The taste of bitterness coated the back of his throat. He refused to let Masters defeat him, refused to give up on his farm without one last fight. Moving around the luau pit, he brushed by Masters and headed back toward the party.

"Where are you going?" his rival demanded. "We haven't finished our discussion yet!"

Dane called his reply over his shoulder. "There's something I have to do first."

AFTER LEAVING DANE, Ophelia managed to seclude herself behind a palm tree until she regained control of her emotions. It was ridiculous, her disappointment. Her mother would have disapproved of her self-pity. And yet, she needed some time to shake off her regret and attempt to put things in perspective. Dane would not be coming back to New York. It wasn't as if she were the first recruiter to be turned down. But perhaps she had been the first with so much at stake—her mother's approval, the stability of the company, her hopes for a future in Paris.... She felt the crumbling of her dreams all around her, and still, in the midst of the wreckage, one thought dominated.

Dane wasn't coming back to New York. She would likely never see him again. It dismayed her, perhaps more than all the others combined.

But that had to be her failure speaking. She hadn't known Dane a week—she could hardly be this devastated about never seeing him again. It was only his importance to everything, his role in her success, which caused her to think in such a way.

She repeated this to herself until she accepted it—she wouldn't be missing Dane but only what he represented: her stepping stone to the future.

Well, it was done. He had turned down the offer. Now she had to shift her thoughts back to the mainland and how she would relay the news to her mother. Consulting the time on her cell phone, she noted that it was long past midnight in New York. She felt a swell of relief—too late to call. She would handle it in the morning, before she had to pack for the airport. With this plan in mind, she determined to rejoin the luau and absorb as much culture as possible before she had to begin thinking in terms of the city once more.

DANE SEARCHED THE luau attendees in a careful sweep of faces and postures, seeking out one in particular. His eyes passed over Leilani, dancing with Sam. He saw Pele protectively dishing out squares of *haupia* at the refreshment table, and he caught Keahi's eye as he spoke with one of the musicians. He quickly kept looking. An acquaintance called his name, but he ignored them. He had a mission, one thing in mind… and one person he had to find.

Finally, his eyes alighted on Cole Dorset, a drink in hand as he leaned down and spoke with someone in front of him. Cole's height and frame blocked Dane's view of whomever the recruiter spoke with, but he started in that direction, anyway. His suspicions were confirmed as he drew closer, and Cole shifted, allowing Dane a glimpse of the woman before him.

Ophelia.

He came upon them in several more long strides.

"We need to talk."

She looked startled by this abrupt declaration. Or had it been something Cole had said before Dane broke between them?

"I—"

She looked to Cole, and when Dane glanced at the other man's face, he saw both curiosity and pique written on his features.

"There's nothing like an 'excuse me' when you interrupt a conversation, Mr. Montgomery."

"Excuse me," Dane automatically offered. He didn't have time to feel sorry, embarrassed or even annoyed. He only needed to talk to Ophelia. "Please. I need to speak to your colleague."

Ophelia's eyes were widening, seeming to absorb his desperate tone.

"Cole, if you'd give us a minute?"

Cole hesitated, his eyes flitting between the two of them. Dane willed him to go away.

"If this concerns the recruitment offer, then perhaps I should stay."

Dane cast a glance over his shoulder and saw Masters, some distance away, scanning the party as Dane had been doing.

"Tell her to double it."

He turned back, focusing his sight on Ophelia, though he was aware of Cole's eyes narrowing in his own peripheral vision.

"Double—" she began.

"The signing bonus. Tell Bianca Towers to double my signing bonus, enough to clear my debt to Masters with some left over for Keahi to keep things running until the harvest this fall. Get her to double it, and I'll do it. I'll sign."

He felt an overwhelming sense of urgency, the need to hear Ophelia tell him this was acceptable.

"Will she agree to that?" he asked.

Ophelia slid a glance toward Cole and back to Dane. "I think so. Yes."

Cole gave a snort and then chuckled. "Montgomery, she's interested in the coup of having you on her team. Believe me, she'll agree."

Dane relaxed, feeling a weight lift from his shoulders. He turned to see Masters only a few feet away. By the time the other man was upon them, Dane was grinning.

"Ken, I have good news. There's no need to dole out any more fees to your lawyer. I can repay the loan in full."

And in that moment, his sacrifice was worth it just to see the scowl of defeat on Masters's face.

Ophelia waited until the following morning to place the call to her mother. She rose early, mostly because she couldn't sleep, anyway, her thoughts filled with the realization of a goal accomplished along with the slightly giddying prospect of Dane's return to New York.

She moved to the window, where dawn's light had yet to creep over the horizon, and dialed her mother's line. Even on a Saturday morning, she knew her mother would likely be in the office, and odds were, her assistant was there with her—performing menial tasks. As a workaholic, Lillian believed Saturdays were often the best days to catch up on items overlooked throughout the week.

"Reid Recruiting, Lillian Reid's office."

"Hi, Tamara, it's me."

"Ophelia!" Tamara's voice fell, hushed and slightly anxious. "I was hoping you'd call."

Ophelia suspected her mother had hounded Tamara relentlessly, asking if Ophelia had checked in yet.

"It was too late to call last night. But I have good news. Could you put me through to my mother?"

Tamara's voice was saturated with relief as she told Ophelia to hold. She could only imagine how tense things had been this week for anyone who worked directly with her mother.

"Ophelia."

Her mother's voice cut across the line, her impatience punctuating every syllable.

"Hello, Ms. Reid." She wanted to savor this, to bask in the glory of her success. But in the end, she said it as simply as she could. "He agreed to sign."

There was a sound on the other end, a whoosh of air that Ophelia could only assume to be a sigh of relief.

"He wants Bianca to double the signing bonus, but I didn't think that would be an issue."

"No, no. She'll be so pleased we've accomplished the impossible that she'd probably triple the bonus if he asked."

"Good." Ophelia waited for some word of congratulations from her mother. "Cole and I will be flying back today, but Dane needs another couple of days to arrange his affairs. He'll be coming in on Monday."

"That's acceptable."

"He'll need the bonus sent as soon as possible. He has some debts here to clear."

"I'll begin arranging things immediately."

Ophelia paused.

"And...Paris?" she prompted.

"We can discuss all that when you return."

Ophelia gave a short nod and then realized

her mother couldn't see it. "All right. Is there anything more you need from me?"

"Not right now," her mother answered. "Only...well done, Ophelia. I knew you could do it."

Ophelia closed her eyes and drank in those simple words. "Thank you, Ms. Reid."

"We'll speak more when you're back."

"All right."

"Come to the loft tomorrow afternoon, after your flight gets in and you have a chance to rest up."

Ophelia hesitated. She wasn't sure she had the energy to face her mother so soon after her arrival in New York, but she didn't wish to lose the approval saturating Lillian's tone.

"I'll see you tomorrow, then."

"Have a safe flight."

Lillian hung up before Ophelia could say thank you.

Ophelia made her way downstairs as the morning's light was just beginning to work its way through the windows. The first-floor area was deserted with the lights still off, but she could hear movement from the direction of the kitchen, so she headed that way. She rapped lightly on the door before nudging it open to find Pele, elbow deep in a mixing bowl and already hard at work.

"Good morning, Pele."

The short, round housekeeper gave a short nod of acknowledgment, barely glancing up.

"Do you mind if I get some coffee brewing?"

She offered another nod, which Ophelia took for approval before heading for the coffeemaker. She rummaged for some filters before moving toward the sink to fill the pot with water.

"I suppose Dane told you everything," she said by way of conversation.

Pele didn't respond.

"Pele?"

"I heard you," the other woman snapped.

Ophelia frowned and stood there until she realized the coffeepot in the sink had long since filled and was now overflowing water down the drain. She turned off the stream, decanted the excess from the glass pot and carried it back to the brewer.

"Pele, have I done something to offend you?"

The older woman turned, and Ophelia saw that her eyes were red-rimmed with either sorrow or rage, perhaps both.

"You came here and turned our world upside down. And you have the nerve to ask how you have offended me?"

Ophelia stood there, stunned.

"Dane never would have accepted my offer

if he didn't already owe Masters money. That's not my fault."

Pele didn't reply, and Ophelia finished measuring grounds into the coffee filter before putting it into place and selecting the button to brew. The kitchen remained silent, save for the gentle gurgling of the coffee and the hiss and drip of brewing.

Finally, Ophelia decided she'd had enough.

"Listen, none of this is my fault. You disliked me from the second you opened the inn's door, and you didn't even know me! And yet, you're totally enamored with Cole."

"He's different."

"Yes, more aggressive, more determined, and if he had been the first one to show up here—"

"Dane would have made him leave immediately."

"Exactly, and for that matter…wait a minute." Ophelia stared at Pele. "Is that why you don't like me? Because Dane didn't kick me out right away?"

Pele's gaze skittered away.

"You don't like me because Dane actually listened to my offer."

Pele turned her back, but Ophelia wasn't about to let it go. She reached out, her hand touching the stout woman's shoulder. She whirled at Ophelia's touch, brushing her away.

"Yes, he listened to you! And now he's leaving! If you had stayed away, he wouldn't be going! You were trouble, the moment you showed up here. I knew it. I could see it in the way he looked at you. And now, he's leaving. Because of *you*."

Ophelia took a step back. "Not because of me," she said. "Because of Masters. Because he doesn't want to see you and Leilani and Keahi without a job. Because he wants to make this plantation work, even if it can't be exactly how he imagined."

"He would have found another way. It would have been on his terms, not yours. You should have stayed in New York, where you belong."

These words wounded Ophelia. She could understand Pele's grief at losing Dane, but she hardly felt she deserved such animosity. All of a sudden, she felt rather glum, an emotion that annoyed her. She had accomplished the impossible, convinced Dane Montgomery to return, although she recognized it had more to do with Kenneth Masters than any skills on her own part. Dane hadn't chosen to return based on her recruitment—it had simply been his means of escape from a possible financial disaster. Could her mother have guessed that? Is that why her praise had been so sparse?

"I know you may find this difficult to believe, Pele, but I care about what happens to Dane. And to the rest of you."

Pele snorted in disbelief. "You are sneakier than the others. That's all."

"I'm not being sneaky. I've been nothing but honest with Dane, and with you! You're being entirely unfair!"

"Um, am I interrupting something?"

Ophelia whirled to find Cole in the kitchen doorway.

"No," Pele answered before Ophelia could. "You come in. I'm making you Hawaiian sweet bread like I promised."

Cole grinned at Pele and moved farther into the room, though his eyes remained trained on Ophelia. His expression held a question—what had she been so upset about? But she refused to respond.

"Here, I'll pour you some coffee," Pele told Cole and brushed Ophelia aside to get to the finished brew.

Ophelia stepped back. She had the feeling Pele doted on Cole simply because she knew it would bother Ophelia. She never would have guessed the older woman could be so spiteful.

"How do you take it?" Pele asked.

But Cole wasn't looking at her. His attention remained squarely on Ophelia.

None of it mattered, she told herself. Not

Dane, not Pele's anger, not her mother's lack-luster praise, none of it. Within another month or so, she would be in Paris, settling into a new life and reconnecting with old memories. She would have to try and run down contact infor-mation for her cousins—let them know she was coming. Maybe they could get together for din-ner once she reached the city, share memories of her childhood....

"Fee?"

She straightened to awareness as Cole spoke.

"Are you okay? You look like you don't feel too well."

Ophelia's eyes turned in Pele's direction, but the other woman did not acknowledge her, in-stead focusing on the task of pouring and pre-paring Cole's coffee.

"I'm fine," she told him. "Just fine. I'm going to return to my room and get some packing done before breakfast."

She left the kitchen without giving Cole a chance to reply.

Ophelia moved toward the stairs to the second floor but paused as she saw Dane entering the lanai. She hesitated at first and then headed for the patio, calling a soft "good morning" as she stepped onto the terrace.

Dane stood with his back to her, glancing

over his shoulder as she moved toward him. She stood beside him at the rail, watching as the morning sun covered the trees and shrubs in a hazy golden light, tingeing the world's edges with strokes of burnished copper.

She chose not to burden Dane with the details of her and Pele's conversation, instead focusing on the dawn's brilliance.

"I wish sunrises in the city were as pure and lovely as these," she murmured. Only after she had spoken the words did she realize it was not the most optimistic observation for the journey Dane was about to embark upon.

"Yes," he agreed, his voice quiet. "But I suppose they have their own magic." He shifted slightly, and she did, too, so that they were looking at each other. "Just as I'm sure the sunrises in Paris will."

She looked away at this and made an attempt to memorize the exact shading of the dawn's tones. She should go to her room, get the camera Dane had bought her and try to capture the hues so that she could remember them once she was gone. But she suddenly found this point in time, just the two of them huddled together on this patio awaiting their futures, too precious to leave.

Ophelia didn't know how long they stood together in silence, watching the sun stretch its fingertips farther across the plantation, breathing in the scents of flowers and dew. She wondered how it was she could feel so at ease in this place, so comfortable around Dane. She knew she couldn't afford to explore the feeling any more deeply. They would return to New York, perhaps see each other a few times as he settled into his new position, and then she would be leaving—putting another ocean between them.

She thought of all the things she should say to him—express her gratitude for his hospitality, extend the obligatory welcome from Towers International, offer her mother's congratulations, wish him the best in his new career... but she said none of those things.

She simply stood there, with him, on the lanai and didn't speak another word as the sun brightened the day and eclipsed all other possibilities for the future.

CHAPTER ELEVEN

SAYING GOODBYE WASN'T quite as difficult as Ophelia feared it would be. In fact, her entire farewell to the Okina Inn occurred in such a rush that she was hard-pressed to recall it as Cole navigated her rental car back toward the Kona airport.

Leilani hugged her with admonitions to keep in touch. Cole made a grand show of kissing Pele's hand, but when Ophelia took the other woman's stubby fingers in her own, they remained limp.

"Thank you for the delicious meals and such a wonderful introduction to Polynesian culture," Ophelia said. Pele nodded but said nothing.

Before anyone could notice the cool farewell, Keahi bundled her into his arms and told her to come visit again soon. She had no chance to respond as Cole grabbed her by the arm and tugged her toward the door.

"We need to have time to return the rental car, Fee," he reminded.

And so, she only had a span of seconds to face Dane.

"Call when you get to New York," she instructed, and he nodded.

His face was haggard, uncertain, and she suspected, as she had earlier that morning on the lanai, that he hadn't slept at all the evening before.

"Bianca is going to be thrilled. We couldn't be happier."

She didn't know what else to say, and her words only seemed to weigh Dane down even more.

"O-pheeeel-ia," Cole reminded in an impatiently singsong voice. She didn't turn at the sound but felt the pressure to wrap up her goodbyes all the same.

She stole a few seconds more to meet Dane's eyes and hold them with her own. "You got this, Montgomery. Do you hear me?"

To her relief, a corner of his mouth twitched. Almost imperceptibly but still, she saw it.

"Have a safe flight."

"You, too. I'll talk to you when you get in."

And then, almost without realizing it, she was in the car, with the coastal highway sliding by and the distance between her and the plantation widening with every mile.

She and Cole spoke little on the drive to the

rental return and then on the shuttle to the airport. After checking in for their flight and finding their way to the gate, they sat side by side, with Cole absorbed in his smartphone and Ophelia observing the other passengers. She felt a tug of emotion as she watched a little girl and her mother, heads drawn together in conversation. The child fingered the shells on one of the cheap necklaces such as Ophelia had seen all over the islands, and her mother seemed to be coaching her on counting them, one by one.

Ophelia stretched her mind backward, trying to find a similar memory within the catalogs of her experiences, but she could recall nothing. The closest she had was the memory of the flight from Paris to New York, after her father's death, and the feel of her mother's hand holding tightly to hers as the plane took off. She glanced down at her fingers now and was startled to realize they looked quite similar to how her mother's had appeared, that long-ago day.

"Fee?"

She jerked, suddenly remembering Cole beside her. He had put the smartphone away and was eyeing her with concern.

"They called the boarding for business class."

"Oh." She rummaged through her bag for her boarding pass and stood with Cole to get in line.

When they were both settled in the plush seats with the coach passengers filing by, Cole sighed.

"Well, I'm glad that's over," he announced.

She didn't bother to query him on what he was referring to—whether it was the assignment with Dane, the boarding of the plane or something else entirely. When she didn't respond, he didn't engage her further in conversation, and she closed her eyes, mentally reliving all her experiences in her brief week on the islands.

Six hours later, they changed planes in Los Angeles, and as soon as they were in the air once more, Ophelia succumbed to exhaustion and fell asleep. Some time later, she opened her eyes again and found Cole flipping through a magazine. The overhead lights were dimmed, and the plane purred quietly with the background hum of the engines.

"What time is it?" she questioned as she straightened up and stretched her neck, working out the stiffness.

Cole consulted his watch. "A little after midnight. But that's Hawaiian time. I haven't changed the time zone on my watch yet."

She moaned slightly as she rolled her head around her shoulders.

"Here."

Cole shifted and placed his hands on her shoulders. She tensed, but he didn't seem to notice as he began working his thumbs over the stiff muscles in her neck. As odd as it felt to have Cole touching her after all that had transpired, she soon found herself relaxing under his fingers. She allowed him to work out several of the knots before she pulled away.

"Thank you."

He didn't respond even though she sensed he had something to say. She began to lean her head back against the seat when Cole suddenly spoke up.

"I had a lot of time to kill on the flight over."

She opened her eyes and looked at him curiously. "It's a long flight," she agreed.

His eyes darkened as he leaned in. Their faces were mere inches apart, and she frowned uncomfortably.

"I spent most of it thinking about you."

She felt her own eyes widen in surprise. "You mean, my assignment with Dane?"

"No." He shook his head. "Just you."

"Cole, I…I don't understand."

"I guess it wasn't just you," he continued, "but us. The last four years. And what a great team we make."

She was at a loss as to how she should respond to this declaration, so she said nothing.

"I thought, you know…it would be such a shame to lose that if you move to Paris—"

"Paris is not negotiable, Cole. You know that."

"You didn't let me finish." His voice held a touch of irritability, though it was hushed in deference to the other passengers. "If you move to Paris…*without me.*"

She stared at him. "What are you saying?"

He reached out and touched his fingers to her face, and she resisted the urge to pull away.

"I want you back, Fee. And if it means moving to Paris then so be it. It would be a shame to break up our team now. Look at what we just accomplished, after all! Dane Montgomery! What other recruiting team can say that they convinced the most obstinate man in the corporate world to come back?"

"He's not obstinate. He just knows what makes him happy." She prickled, wanting to point out that Cole had contributed little to convincing Dane to sign the contract. In fact, he had nearly derailed her progress. But she didn't say so, knowing that she hadn't really convinced Dane on her own, either. It was his situation that had compelled him to agree to the Towers deal.

But her defense of Dane had brought Cole up short. He frowned severely at her.

"Exactly what happened between you and Montgomery in the last week?"

She turned away. "Nothing happened. I did exactly what my mother told me to do—I spent some time with him, got to know him, made the offer. Simple as that."

In her peripheral vision, she saw Cole eyeing her suspiciously. "You've spent a lot of time with him the last few days, though."

She rolled her eyes. "Of course I have."

"Fee, you couldn't possibly have gotten… a little too wrapped up in your assignment?"

"Cole!" She sensed the passengers behind them stirring in their seats, and she dropped her voice. "How dare you ask me such a thing! We're not together anymore," she said. "Remember?"

"But that's what I'm trying to say," Cole whispered back. "I *want* to be. I want us to be together again. And…" He paused, seemingly for dramatic effect. "I'm willing to go to Paris if it means we can be a couple."

"Cole…" She had adjusted to the idea of life without him—more easily than she had anticipated. When she imagined herself in Paris, he no longer fit by her side. But she also knew what it had cost Cole to come to this decision—to make the sacrifice of his own wants in order to see hers fulfilled. It was probably the most unselfish thing he had ever done, especially for her.

"I've already spoken to Lillian," he continued, "and she's agreed to let me join you again."

"But…why?"

He reached for her hand, tucking it into his. In one small corner of her mind, she recognized that his touch didn't thrill her. Not like Dane's had. But then again, Dane had been a new, almost-forbidden possibility. Cole was familiar. The newness had worn off. That had to be the difference.

"Because we're perfect together. We could turn the Paris operation into the most prestigious recruiting firm in Europe."

"But what about New York? I thought you didn't want to leave."

"I realized that it won't be the same without you."

"What won't?"

He released her hand, his face flickering with irritation. "Ophelia, I'm doing my best here to tell you that I want us to be together. Four years is a lot to just throw away. I don't want to lose that. I don't want to lose *you*."

She closed her eyes, drew a breath and tried to steady herself. The plane hit a small bump in turbulence, and she opened her eyes.

"So you're willing to move with me to Paris?"

"I am." He reached for her hand once more. "You can show me all the places you're always talking about—the Louvre, Notre Dame, the Eiffel Tower. What better place for us to be together than the city of love, right?"

And without meaning to, another place popped into her mind's eye—the Place of Refuge with its safe haven for those who were pursued or persecuted. For the span of several heartbeats, she could hear the ocean's soft rumble against the shore, the echo of the tribal chants thudding in her chest. She shook her head to clear it, and Cole pulled back once again.

"Is that a no?"

"What? No. I mean, yes. I mean…" She drew a breath. "Can I have some time to think about it? I'm just feeling pretty overwhelmed right now. With everything."

She felt him relax beside her. "Of course, sweetheart. You take all the time you need."

She tried to appear grateful and hoped it came off without looking strained. She must have succeeded because Cole beamed at her.

"I'm going to try to rest a little more," she said.

"Sure. Here, lay your head on my shoulder." She shifted and leaned into Cole, though her body felt somewhat stiff in the action. It took

a long time, but eventually the reverberation of
the plane's engine beneath her and the steady
rhythm of Cole's breath lulled her into a dream
where she was being pursued across shark-
infested waters as she attempted to reach the
Place of Refuge. Her breath came in short gasps
as she struggled through the choppy waves, her
nose and mouth filling with the bitter tang of
salt water. She couldn't see her pursuers, but
she sensed them behind her. She had an overwhelming sense of urgency to stay beyond their
reach.

Her limbs grew tired, and she felt them
weighing her down as she struggled for the
lava-rock-lined shore of the refuge. As she drew
nearer to it, she saw her father, standing on the
platform of the temple and smiling down at her.
She struggled all the harder to reach it, calling
out to him for help, but he continued to stand
there, simply smiling and not moving.

Her pursuers in the water drew closer, and
her sense of urgency rose. She had to reach the
wall. She had to get to the temple platform.

"Help me!" she cried, and still, her father
did not move.

The predators in the water grew close—she
could not see them, but she could sense them,
and her panic grew. The waves washed over

her head, once then twice, and she felt herself slipping under.

They had almost reached her, her fate nearly sealed. She was just succumbing to her fatigue, ready to let the dark water and the monsters within it take her when she felt a hand encircle her wrist.

Looking up, she saw Dane, his arm reaching out and grasping on to her as he tugged her from the waves and onto the shore.

When she awoke, they had landed in New York.

OPHELIA ENTERED HER apartment, dropping her bags at the front door, and headed straight for the kitchen to pour herself a glass of water. After the long hours on the plane and her conversation with Cole—along with a stilted goodbye where he attempted to kiss her lips and she offered him her cheek instead—she needed some time to gather her wits.

She gulped the water and then refilled the glass before carrying it with her to the living room where she sank onto her plush sofa. Cole hated this sofa. She'd had it since her first apartment, and though she'd had it reupholstered in a burgundy corduroy, he still found it "tacky" in her otherwise stylish surroundings.

But it was like an old friend, and she settled

down into its embrace, clutching the glass of water in her hands, as she considered everything that had occurred in the past week.

She replayed her memories of Hawaii, trying to recapture the scents and sights, her lips tingling as she recalled her time with Dane. Then she thought about Cole and their conversation on the plane. He said he would go with her to Paris. What more could she ask from him? He had a point, after all—four years was a lot to just throw away, especially now that he'd agreed to see things through and support her in her dream.

It was more than she had expected from him, and despite some niggling reservations deep in her stomach, she could find no good reason to turn him down.

Except for the memory of Dane's kisses. And she knew that was hardly fair to Cole. Her time with Dane had been fleeting—a dream she must now lay to rest as a pleasant memory and nothing more. When Dane arrived in New York, his time and attention would no longer be hers—as if they had ever really been hers in the first place. It had just felt that way, given the circumstances of her assignment.

She took another long swallow of water and then placed the glass on her dark wood coffee table. She grabbed the snow globe displayed on its surface instead and then stretched out on the sofa, propping her head on one end and her feet on the other. She sank deep within the sofa's folds as she cradled the heavy globe, studying the scene within the glass. There was a miniature Eiffel Tower suspended in the liquid, with a tiny Parisian café at its base. She tipped the entire object on its side and watched as a flurry of white flakes swirled stormily inside.

She could relate to the internal maelstrom. Inwardly, her thoughts churned in a mad rush of decisions and possibilities: Cole, Paris, her mother, her career. And silly as it seemed, she suddenly wished that instead of a Parisian snowstorm within the glass, she could witness a swirl of sand settling along a beach with sea turtles and waves.

A FEW HOURS LATER, Ophelia stood before her mother's door, a gift bag in hand. After ringing the doorbell, she nervously tucked her hair behind her ear. While she normally sported a mature French twist, she had chosen to let her hair down for a change. She had become accustomed to the feel of it, sweeping against her shoulders, and she found she liked the sensation. At least she still wore the business-casual navy slacks her mother preferred to see along with a navy-and-white-striped long-sleeved shirt.

As she heard movement behind the door, she quickly dropped her hand from her hair and straightened to the appropriate posture. The knob turned, and her mother stood in the doorway, bestowing a rare smile.

"There you are." She leaned forward to kiss the air by Ophelia's left cheek and then the right before she stepped back and gestured for her daughter to enter.

"How was your return flight?"

Ophelia stepped over the threshold gingerly, always feeling that she had to move cautiously in her mother's home for all the glass sculptures and crystal bowls on display. She felt her throat tightening in a familiar reaction to the heavy scents of perfume and cleaning products.

Her mother's house was much like a visit to the Guggenheim with its pristine white walls and lighted displays.

"It was fine."

Lillian began moving through the front foyer and hall while Ophelia followed her toward the loft's spacious living room.

"Can I get you something to drink? I have Perrier or some chilled champagne, if you prefer. We should drink to your success, after all."

"The Perrier will be fine, thank you."

She waited as her mother disappeared to the kitchen and shortly returned carrying two flutes of sparkling water. She wasn't entirely sure if this could be considered a familial visit or work appointment and was therefore uncertain how to address her mother. She finally opted for the maternal title.

"I brought you something back, Mother." She extended the handled bag with its sea-green tissue paper.

"A gift? How sweet of you, darling."

She breathed a sigh of relief that she had chosen the correct form of address. Her mother set the bag aside without opening it. Ophelia frowned in disappointment. She only hoped Lillian would be pleased with the item she had purchased at the artist's village in Holualoa—a small sculpture of a dolphin crafted from polished koa wood.

Turning her back toward the gift, Lillian moved to the couch and gestured for Ophelia to join her on it. They sank down together but unlike her own plush corduroy couch, her mother's was an uncomfortably firm ivory brocade. She sat upon it gingerly, fearful of spilling even something so harmless as the Perrier on its flawless exterior.

"So tell me about your trip and how you

managed to convince the irrationally stubborn Dane Montgomery to return."

Ophelia kept her posture perfectly straight as she took in her mother's curious expression. Even in her own home, her face had a look of calculation to it.

"I fear it had little to do with my skills," she demurred. "Dane needed an influx of capital. Bianca's signing bonus will provide it."

"Of course, he's aware that by signing he commits to at least two years in her employ? Probably more, since she's agreed to revise the contract and double the bonus."

Ophelia took a sip of her Perrier, the fizz of the sparkling water tickling her nose. "He read the contract thoroughly. I believe he understands all the—" she coughed slightly into her palm "—details."

She had been about to say *consequences*— a poor word choice, especially in her mother's presence.

Lillian took a small sip of her own beverage. "He certainly is a sharp negotiator, doubling his bonus and pocketing the $10,000 incentive. I hope his skills as a tour guide were supreme, considering that tidy sum for a week's time."

Ophelia thought about her experiences on the islands—from the sacred stillness at the Place of Refuge to the conversation and food with the

Inoas, her tour of the plantation and the cultural festivities at the luau. She hardly thought she could put a price tag on all that she had seen and done, but she didn't say so to her mother.

"It was the trip of a lifetime," she summed up, instead.

"I should hope so, considering I footed the bill for it."

Ophelia gulped down another swallow of Perrier and coughed as the carbonation burned the back of her throat.

"I trust you thanked Cole properly for coming to your aid as he did."

This time, Ophelia choked on her water and sputtered as the glass shook in her hands, spilling sparkling water onto her blouse.

"Oh, Ophelia," her mother chided as she stood to retrieve a towel. Lillian returned to dab at Ophelia's shirt until she handed over her glass and grabbed the cloth, instead.

"As I mentioned on the phone, I had the situation well in hand before Cole's arrival." Ophelia continued wiping at the wet blotch on her top and muttered a silent thank-you that not a drop had reached the couch.

"Mmm," was Lillian's only reply to Ophelia's reminder.

She was too distracted by her personal ministrations to notice at first that her mother had fallen silent.

"Ophelia."

She immediately looked up at the familiarly patronizing tone.

"You do realize that your time in Hawaii was simply a performance."

Ophelia frowned. "A performance? Meaning?"

"Meaning, Dane Montgomery was an assignment. Nothing more."

"Of course. What else would he be?" Despite this flippant response, she felt her cheeks flaming in betrayal of her words.

"From what I've heard, the man can be quite…charismatic."

Ophelia couldn't help herself. She made a noise, a sound of both wistfulness and disbelief and then immediately cut it off. In part, she was striving desperately not to recall the details of Dane's kiss, fearing how her blush would deepen. On the other hand, she remembered Dane's initial hostility toward her.

"I doubt he's the same man you remember."

Lillian shrugged, lifting one elegant shoulder in casual dismissal. "Perhaps. I never really met him—I only saw him a time or two at various benefits and social functions. He always had scores of women and starry-eyed sycophants hanging on to his every word. As if every syllable he uttered carried some great insight." She scoffed. "I think the man is a magician, creating an illusion, a persona. He had great success performing that trick for various companies, and I'm certain he did the exact same thing for himself."

Ophelia felt a prickling of disappointment at this summation. She didn't believe the man she had met, the man who had kissed her, was an illusion. But the thought of Dane surrounded by hangers-on chafed at her. She supposed she should get used to the idea, however. Once Dane returned, he would be in great demand socially. Eventually, he was bound to begin dating—

She stopped herself at that point. Her mother was right, in a way. Her time with Dane had been part of her assignment. He must have realized that. Now that her duties were completed, there would be no reason for him to see her as anything other than his recruiter. The thought pained her, but it couldn't be helped.

"Well, it matters little now." Lillian leaned back against the cushions of the sofa, propping her elbow on the back and leaning her head into her hand. "How are things between you and Cole, hmm? I suspect he felt rather mopey without you around."

Though Ophelia had been longing for a topic change, she wasn't sure Cole was her first choice. Dropping her eyes, she twisted the damp towel she still held in her fingers.

"He's agreed to move to Paris with me. He wants to get back together."

She glanced up to find her mother beaming. "He spoke to me about the possibility, and I've given him my blessing on the matter. I suppose you told him yes?"

Ophelia looked away. "Well, I told him I'd think about it."

"What?" Her mother gasped in surprise, the sound holding a tone of disapproval in it. "That was the very reason you broke up with him. If he's agreed to your terms, of course you and he will get back together."

"They weren't terms," Ophelia said, trying to keep her voice calm. "It was my dream, and he didn't want to be a part of it."

"He only needed time to consider his future here, without you. You have to remember, Ophelia, that just because this is what you've always wanted, Cole has his own career to consider."

Ophelia looked back at her mother. "But he's known I wanted this for years! I talked about it from the day I met him! He knew that if we were going to stay together, eventually we'd be moving to Paris!" She knew her voice climbed toward a petulant whine, and her mother's steely eyed stare confirmed it. She lowered her gaze to her lap once more. "It just…it gave me a lot to think about."

Her mother sat in silence for several minutes. "I'm sure it did. But now that you've both had a week apart, I think his desire to go with you is simply confirmation that you're meant to be together."

Perhaps her mother was right. But then why did this thought pain her so? Before she could consider how to respond, the tinkling chime of the doorbell rang through the loft.

"Ah, that must be him now."

Ophelia blinked. "What?"

Lillian was already rising to her feet. "Oh, yes, dear, didn't I tell you? I asked Cole to join us."

Ophelia felt a stab of disappointment. She had hoped for an afternoon alone with her mother, just the two of them, and certainly she longed for a few hours without Cole. Apparently, it was not meant to be.

DANE LISTENED TO the admonitions from Leilani, taking them all in stride.

"Call us at least once a week so we know how you're doing and email as much as you can."

Dane hefted his suitcase into the back of his Jeep. "Got it."

"I'll text you photos as often as possible so you can keep up to speed on the progress of things around here."

Dane slammed the door closed. "I would love that."

"*Tutu* is going to send care packages of your favorite foods so you don't get too homesick, but you'll have to forward us an address as soon as you have one so we know where to mail them."

"Okay, will do."

"And I need you to do me a favor."

"Sure, just name it."

"You have to tell Ophelia how you feel about her."

Dane froze. "Run that by me again?"

Leilani placed her hands on her hips. "You heard me the first time. You can't let her leave a second time without letting her know how you feel."

"Leilani, I don't know what you're talking about."

But he did. He was just surprised that Leilani had noticed when he had worked so hard to keep his emotions hidden.

"Dane, stop. You're falling in love with her, and you have to tell her that."

"You're just a kid, and you're giving me relationship advice?"

Leilani's nostrils flared widely. "I am *not* a kid, and if I don't advise you then who will?"

Dane sighed. As if he didn't have enough to worry about right now. "Listen, I think Ophelia's great, but...love?"

Just then, Keahi ambled over with Pele at his side. She carried a brown paper bag that Dane knew must hold containers of snacks and other food for his plane ride. Leilani shifted.

"Keahi, how does Dane feel about Ophelia?"

"He's falling in love with her," Keahi promptly replied.

Dane groaned. "You, too?"

Keahi's eyes widened. "What, is it supposed to be a secret?"

Dane looked to Pele. "Help me out here, Pele."

The older woman pursed her lips and said nothing. Leilani looked at him triumphantly.

"Fine. Let's say I did have feelings for Ophelia. Even so, she'll be leaving for Paris. It's hardly fair of me to spring something like that on her before she goes."

Leilani shook her head. "That's the point, Dane. You didn't say anything when she was here, and she left without knowing how you feel. You can't make the same mistake when it comes to her leaving for Paris."

Dane remained skeptical.

"She has feelings for you, too. It's obvious."

A ripple of hope went through him. He looked to Keahi for confirmation.

"Leilani's right, brah. You've fallen for Ophelia, and I'd bet this plantation that she's falling for you, too."

"You'll never know if you don't try," Leilani added. "And you'll regret it forever if she gets away."

Dane considered these words. "Okay, but I'm not making any promises."

Leilani clapped her hands together and began jumping up and down. "You guys are gonna make the cutest couple!"

And even though he tried, Dane couldn't keep from smiling at the thought.

BRUNCH WITH COLE and her mother was a tedious affair, just as Ophelia had predicted it would be.

Ophelia continually checked her watch, wondering what was happening at the Okina Inn right now and wishing she could have spent just one more week there with her new friends.

"…once we get to Paris, that is."

Ophelia snapped to renewed attention as Cole mentioned the word *Paris*.

"I'm sorry, what was that?"

Her mother sighed. "Honestly, Ophelia, you've just sat there like a statue for the last hour."

"I'm sure Ophelia's just overcome by the jet lag." Cole reached out for her hand as he came to her defense. The urge to pull away overcame her, but she resisted, not wanting to draw any more critical attention to herself.

Just then, her cell phone began vibrating. Feeling relieved, she apologized and reached for her phone to check the caller ID on the screen. The name Dane Montgomery flashed across it, and her stomach flip-flopped wildly of its own accord.

"Excuse me," she said. "I should take this."

Pushing back from the table, she headed away from the dining room and deeper into her mother's loft. As she answered the call, she couldn't help smiling.

"Hello, Ophelia speaking."

"Hi, Ophelia."

The sound of his voice sent tingles over her skin.

"Hi, Dane," she replied, hoping her voice remained steady. "Are you at the airport?"

"Keahi and I are driving there now. I just

thought I'd call and…" He trailed off, and her stomach somersaulted with nervousness. Call to…what?

"Check in?" she supplied.

"Yeah." His voice suffused with relief. "I just thought I should check in."

She wondered if he felt nervous about coming back, if perhaps he needed her reassurance.

"I'm glad you did. Everyone here is really eager to meet you."

"Oh. Right."

Silence filled the other end of the line.

"Dane?"

"Yeah. I'm here."

She frowned at the flatness of his tone. Had she said something wrong? Was he having second thoughts? He had already signed the contract, though—she had brought it back with her from Hawaii.

"Did you say goodbye to Pele, and Leilani?" Her voice softened as she said their names, knowing it would be hard for him to leave them.

"I did. Leilani said to tell you she misses you already."

"I miss her, too. She's sort of like the little sister I never had." She laughed lightly and was pleased to hear Dane join in.

"Yeah, she's kind of like that," he agreed.

Ophelia heard a muffled voice in the background, and Dane chuckled again. "Keahi said he misses you, too. His father was asking after you, and Mrs. Inoa said to tell you she wants you to return as soon as possible."

Ophelia felt a swell of warmth at this, the feeling of having belonged somewhere if only for a short time.

"Make sure they know I miss them all, too."

She heard Dane repeating her words to Keahi.

"Ophelia?"

She could hear her mother calling from the other room.

"I have to get going," she said. "Have a safe flight. Call when you get in." Her stomach twisted at the thought of hanging up.

"Thanks. I will. I'm…looking forward to seeing you again."

Ophelia felt a dart of surprise. He was? The thought warmed her. "Um…me, too. Goodbye, Dane."

"Bye, Ophelia."

She ended the call and lingered for several seconds longer, ignoring her mother and Cole for just a little bit more and wondering how she had ever allowed Dane Montgomery to get under her skin like he had.

CHAPTER TWELVE

OPHELIA EXPERIENCED A tide of congratulations as she moved through the halls of the Reid Recruiting offices on Monday morning. The compliments varied in degrees, some expressing awe, others declaring they had known all along that she was the recruiter for the job and several clearly attempting to veil jealousy at her success.

The most gratifying well wishes of them all came from Holly, who jumped from her chair to hug Ophelia tightly when she saw her, and gush about her success, reminding her that she had finally done it—she was going to Paris.

While Holly's sincerity warmed her, she found the reminder of Paris left a bittersweet taste in her mouth. She thanked her assistant, spent a few minutes catching up and then escaped into her office where she devoted the morning to answering a slew of emails, responding to a stack of calls and reading over a dozen memos, all the while smiling falsely at the occasional colleague who would drop in to congratulate her.

After several hours of this, her head throbbed in protest. She drew a breath and looked out her window, drinking in the city's sunshine and noting the metallic difference between the silver light in the city versus the golden warmth of the islands. She checked her watch and noted that in Hawaiian time, the day was just beginning.

She stood and walked to the window, rolling her head to work out the stiffness and stretching onto her tiptoes to relax the tightness in her calves. If she closed her eyes and concentrated hard enough, she could still smell the loamy scents of lava soil and salt water....

"It's a beautiful day, isn't it?"

She whirled to see Cole standing in her office doorway. How long had he been there?

"It's a delightful spring day," Cole went on, "a perfect day to start fresh."

She knew he subtly referred to the fact that she still hadn't given him an answer after their conversation on the plane. She forced a smile.

"I was just thinking how different the light is here in the city compared to the islands. It has more of a silvery cast while everything in Hawaii is bathed in gold."

He moved toward the window, but she noticed his eyes never left her face.

"We should visit there again someday. Maybe…on our honeymoon…"

She started at this reference. Had Cole really begun thinking in terms of matrimony again? There was the reference to the cocktail umbrellas at the luau and now talk of a honeymoon? At one time, this sort of talk might have made her giddy but now she felt only a faint queasiness at the prospect.

She turned her attention back to the New York skyline and didn't respond. He sighed.

"I need to have an answer, Fee. If you want me to go to Paris with you, I need to make arrangements."

"I know." But she couldn't bring herself to say any more than that. After another minute, he turned away from the window.

"I thought we could have lunch together today."

"Oh. Well, I'm not sure I should leave my desk. I have a lot to wrap up here before I can start thinking Paris—"

"Fee." He moved forward and placed his palms on her shoulders. She knew he meant to be reassuring but the weight of his hands felt like a burden, not a blessing. "You have to take a break at some point. Why not now, with me?"

He smiled in that golden-boy way of his—the same grin that had once made her feel singular and special. Now it nearly caused a panic attack in her chest.

"I've already made reservations at Le Petite Renard."

Ophelia felt a ripple of both pleasure and annoyance—the latter for Cole's presumption that she would join him for lunch and the former because he had chosen one of her favorite French-inspired bistros.

"Okay. I suppose I should eat something, anyway."

Cole beamed victoriously and removed his hands from her shoulders in order to extend one, palm side up, toward her.

Quelling any doubts, she placed her hand in his.

Le Petite Renard was an upscale bistro just off Times Square in Manhattan. Ophelia treasured its similarities to the cafés in Paris, from its wrought-iron tables and chairs fronting the glass windows outside to its French and English menu boards hanging behind the glossy cherrywood counter.

Cole had reserved a more private table in the back of the establishment, and when they arrived, she found her favorite appetizer (a salad of mixed spring greens and berries in a tart lemon vinaigrette) already waiting. She was impressed that Cole had gone to such lengths but found her appetite lacking, even in the face of the deliciously flavorful starter. She managed to force down a few bites and hoped her appetite would improve with the main course.

But it didn't. Cole spoke easily throughout the appetizer and into the entrée (a vegetarian wild mushroom and goat cheese tart for Cole and the *Crepe du Jour,* stuffed with brie, ham and seasoned spinach for her) while Ophelia picked at her food. She remembered the lunch she'd had with the Inoas less than a week ago. She wondered how the couple was doing and if they were worried about Keahi now that Dane had departed. She stole a glance at a clock hanging nearby, as Cole rambled on about a particular client who wanted him to continue to handle their account from Paris, and estimated Dane should be landing at JFK airport shortly.

She surreptitiously slid her phone from her purse. "It sounds like they really value your negotiation skills," she said, and checked the display for any missed calls. The screen contained no notices. She hoped Dane remembered to call once he landed....

"Ophelia?"

Her head snapped up, and at Cole's expression, she felt a flush burn across her cheek-bones.

"Sorry. What was that?"

"I asked if you're ready for dessert." He hadn't appeared to notice she'd tuned out his dialogue—he only wondered if she had finished eating.

"Um…I'm not really that hungry."

"But I have something special planned."

"Oh. Well. In that case…" She conceded out of a sense of obligation.

Cole gestured to a waiter, and the two of them sat there, in strained silence—at least it felt strained to Ophelia—until a waiter came over bearing a covered platter. He withdrew the white serviette with a flourish and easily lifted the single dish from the tray, placing it in front of her before whirling away.

Ophelia felt Cole's eyes on her as she stared at the dish of *Crème Caramel,* a creamy custard normally topped with homemade whipped cream. Today, however, in place of the white foam cap sat a biscotti over the top of the dish, and on its surface rested a small, royal-blue velvet jeweler's box.

Ophelia stared, another swell of panic rising up in her chest.

"Go on," Cole prompted. "Open it."

She was going to hyperventilate. Right here.

Right now. She'd never had a panic attack before, but the tightness in her chest surely precluded one. His talk of honeymooning in Hawaii…the cocktail umbrellas at the luau… had he been trying to ready her for this? Priming her for this proposal?

"Fee, it's not going to bite. Just open it."

She swallowed. It was too much right now, with everything else she faced. A promotion and move to Paris was daunting enough, and those were things she'd always wanted. But marrying Cole…did she still want that? Had she ever wanted it?

"Cole, I—"

"Come on. It's not as if I'm proposing or anything."

She froze.

"Oh."

The panic subsided, replaced in degrees by embarrassment. Reaching out, she lifted the box from its resting place and popped it open. A pair of pearl earrings rested inside.

"They're real pearls. I got them in Hawaii. It's to congratulate you. On the Montgomery contract and your promotion."

Someone laughed nearby, a shrill, uneasy sound. It took her a moment to realize it had come from her own throat.

He wasn't asking her to marry him, then.

And she felt nothing but relief and a slight awkwardness that she had misunderstood.

He eyed her skeptically. "You don't seem very pleased."

"Oh, they're lovely! Really!" And they were nice—elegant, simple. In truth, though, they looked like something her mother would have preferred. But she had no desire to hurt Cole's feelings after he'd made such an effort. "It was very thoughtful of you, but…I'm not sure I should accept them."

He continued to stare at her, seemingly in wait for something more.

"I'd hoped perhaps they would help you decide."

"Decide?"

"On me. On whether we could be a couple again. Especially since I'll be moving to Paris with you.…"

Ophelia felt a flash of guilt at his slightly wounded expression. She couldn't string him on, she knew that. And if he had only agreed to move to Paris before she had left for Hawaii, then perhaps things would be different. But something there had changed her, and she wasn't sure she could return to the way things had been with Cole. And yet…she wondered if she owed it to him to try.

"Do you think we could take it slow for a bit? See how things go?"

At first, he frowned, a small indent forming between his brows. And then he shrugged. "Sure. Why don't we go on a few dates and test the waters again?"

She felt relieved. "Yes, that would be a good start."

No pressure, she tried to assure herself. Just a couple of dates.

"You can wear the earrings when I take you out."

"Oh." She looked back down at the smooth, iridescent surface of the pearls. "I don't know."

"I insist."

"Um…okay."

"Excellent." He reached across the table and grabbed the biscotti from her plate. "Do you mind if I eat this?"

She shrugged. She had even less of an appetite now than she'd had before.

OPHELIA FOUND SHE couldn't return to work following her lunch with Cole. She got the entire way to her floor and exited the elevator before she found herself stuck, unable to move. The office air felt claustrophobic, the scents of stale coffee and carpet clogging her throat. She turned on her heel and stepped back into the elevator before the doors could close. She rode it the entire way back to the lobby floor and then rushed toward the sunshine outside like a prisoner seeking release.

Once outside, she began to pace, trying to calm her restlessness. But she couldn't shake the desire to flee, to get as far from this building and her mother and Cole as she possibly could, if only for a few hours.

She was just debating whether to text Holly that she wouldn't be returning to the office when the phone in her hand lit up with a call. The name that flashed across the screen sent a wave of euphoria through her.

Dane Montgomery.

Her heart lurched, even as she bid it not to. His plane must have landed, and he was calling her, as he'd said he would. Suddenly eager to hear the sound of his voice, she accepted the call and held the phone to her ear.

She hesitated for a second over all the witty things she might say to him. In the end, she didn't utter a single one of them.

"Hey," she murmured.

"Hey," he replied.

She could imagine the smile she heard in his tone, one corner of his mouth quirked upward. "Did you have a good flight?"

"Not too bad. I forgot how restless a person can feel, sitting on a plane for that many hours."

Having experienced two of those flights in the past week, Ophelia agreed with this observation.

"I checked in to the hotel," Dane went on. He was staying at the Towers Resorts in downtown Manhattan, near the Towers International office suites, until he found a place of his own in the city. "I have to say, Bianca has a good thing going for her. If all her properties are this nice, it shouldn't be hard to shine up the company's image."

Ophelia found herself smiling with pleasure at his optimism. "It sounds like you're ready to get to work."

"Not just yet. Give a guy some time to recover from the jet lag."

She laughed. "Well, when you do, perhaps you'd like to have dinner with me—as a welcome back to the city."

She felt herself stiffen as soon as these words were out of her mouth. Had she just…?

But Dane sounded nothing but pleased on the other end of the line. "Are you busy right now?" he asked. "After twelve-plus hours on a plane, I'm ravenous. Crackers and pretzels only carry a man so far."

Ophelia knew she had to be grinning a little too broadly and hoped the people going in and out of the Reid Recruiting building didn't report her to security for lurking. She wasn't about to tell him she had just had lunch with Cole. In fact, her appetite suddenly seemed to be returning.

"I'll be there soon."

OPHELIA GIGGLED UNCONTROLLABLY as Dane stuffed a huge slice of pizza into his mouth. He tore it off with his teeth and chewed vigorously, working to swallow as she continued to laugh helplessly at his enjoyment of the meal.

When he finally got the massive bite down, he sighed with contentment. "Okay, I have to admit…this, I missed. There's nothing like a New York slice."

Ophelia's giggles slowly subsided until she could take a sip of her Diet Coke without fear of spraying it all over the table. "Was it worth a twelve-hour flight, then?"

He made a point of looking between his plate and her. "I guess between the pizza and the company, it was worth it."

She felt a tingle of pleasure shoot through her. "I don't suppose there are too many girls you'd spend twelve hours on a plane for, just so you could have lunch."

"Well, some girls are worth it." He winked

at her in such a boldly flirtatious move that she felt herself begin to blush. Perhaps he felt the same way she did—giddy at seeing him again after a day apart. Maybe that was why they were both in such boisterous spirits.

She took a bite of her own slice as he continued to enjoy the pizza.

"So you're okay then, with being back?" She ventured the question tentatively, not wanting to destroy the carefree mood that seemed to have come over Dane. It was probably the lightest she had seen him in all the time she'd known him.

He wiped his fingers on a napkin before replying. "I don't know yet. I'm glad the plantation will be saved. That part feels really good. As for the rest of it..." He shrugged. "I guess I'll have to wait and see."

He picked up his pizza again and gestured it toward her. "How about you? It must feel good to know you're fulfilling your dream of moving to Paris."

She thought about it. "Yeah. Yeah, I guess." Tearing at the corner of her pizza crust, she avoided his eyes.

But she felt him grow still across from her.

"You're not having doubts, are you?"

"Of course not!" she declared.

"Ophelia...can I ask you something?"

Every fiber of her body vibrated at his tone. "Sure."

"Do you really think Paris is the solution to your problems? Do you think you'll be happy there?"

She swallowed. "It's been my dream for as long as I can remember."

He nodded with seeming understanding. "But do you ever think you could be just as happy…somewhere else?"

She cocked her head, studying him. What was he really asking?

"I don't know. I've wanted Paris for so long, I can't imagine giving it up for anything."

"Or anyone?"

She stared at him. "Are you saying—"

"Can I get you a refill?" Their waitress had chosen that inopportune time to interrupt.

Ophelia could only stare at her stupidly.

"Your Diet Coke?" the girl prompted, her eyes conveying her annoyance at Ophelia's slowness.

"Um…no. No, thank you."

The girl turned to Dane, her irritation turning to flirtation. "And how about for you, love?"

"I'm fine, thanks."

By the time the waitress sashayed away, the moment had passed, and Ophelia didn't know how to resurrect it.

"Tell me what you love about Paris."

Ophelia frowned at this question, wishing he would ask her again—whatever it was he'd been asking in the first place.

"What do you mean?"

"It's important to you, and you have a family history there. But what else do you love about it? I want to know."

She considered for a moment.

"The smells," she replied. "Of wet pavement in the morning. Baking bread when you pass a *boulangerie*. Perfumes in a thousand scents with hundreds of notes layered in them. Cigar smoke and flowers. It smells old and new at the same time."

Something in his eyes sparked at her description. "What else?"

"The colors are the same way—everything is muted and ancient or fresh and vibrant. Chic coupled with vintage. There are fashions in every hue imaginable, and they stand out in sharp contrast to charcoal-gray sidewalks, faded red brick and weathered brown walls."

Now that she had started, she couldn't stop. "It's magical. It's not that people go to Paris to fall in love, it's that Paris *is* the city of love. You fall in love with the place, more than the person you're with. Every conversation is a story, and each painting is a new experience. You cannot be there without falling in love—in love with the idea of love."

She suddenly stopped, surprised that these feelings had been buried within her. For a brief time, she hadn't been in a New York pizza shop at all but rather experiencing the streets of her favorite city.

"But is it real?"

Dane's question caused her to physically start. "Real?" she repeated.

"Do you love the city, or simply the idea of it? As you said—are you in love with the idea of love? Are you only in love with the *idea* of Paris, of the happiness it once represented?"

She drew in a sharp breath, disconcerted by such an enigmatic question. "It's the only thing I've ever wanted, Dane."

"But maybe...just maybe," he clarified, "what you want isn't really there. Maybe you want to go back to a time that's gone—back to when your father was alive and your mother was—" he drew a breath "—someone different than she is now."

She felt a prickling of anger. "You don't even know my mother."

"No," he agreed. "But I know you. And I know her opinion matters to you, maybe more than anything else."

She chafed. "You barely know me. We only met a week ago."

She could tell this observation wounded him by the way he winced in response. Guilt wove itself in with her anger, complicating her emotions further.

"I think I know you better than you know yourself, Ophelia."

"And what do you know?" she shot back, wondering how he could possibly think he had her figured out when she couldn't figure herself out.

"I know that you care, more than most in your profession—that you want the people you place in careers to be happy." His voice grew quieter so she had to strain to hear him. "I know you didn't want to coerce me here against my own will. I know you feel bad about how things have turned out."

He reached for her, grabbing her hand in his and holding on even when she tensed. His thumb ran in circles over her wrist until she felt herself relaxing.

"I know you try to hold it all in but once in a while, like with Masters, something more comes out—you don't like bullies. Maybe because you grew up with one."

She jerked her hand out of his grasp then. "My mother isn't a bully," she whispered. She wasn't sure what hurt more—Dane's observation or the ring of truth in it.

Dane only looked at her sadly, and his expression angered her all the more.

"You're just miserable because you had to come back, and you don't want to be here."

"Maybe I don't," he returned. "But at least I'm honest about it. I'm here because I have to be. Why are you really going to Paris? Is it because you truly want to be there? Or because you're trying to recapture something you lost a long time ago?"

She could only stare at him, hurt by his words. She held his gaze for some time before he sighed.

"I'm sorry, Ophelia. I'm not trying to be cruel. I'm only trying…to understand, I guess."

She saw their waitress approaching again and issued her a glare that sent the younger woman scuttling back toward the kitchen. "Understand what?" she asked, turning her attention back to Dane.

"You," he finally responded. "I'm just trying to understand you."

Her lips parted to speak and then she closed them. "Why?" she asked, her voice barely more than a whisper.

He leaned forward. "Because I think I'm falling in love with you."

CHAPTER THIRTEEN

DANE HAD THOUGHT a lot on the flight over from the islands. And mostly what he'd thought about was Leilani's advice— *You'll never know if you don't ask*. He had thought of a thousand things he might say to Ophelia to express his feelings, but he hadn't planned to speak as he had until the words were already out of his mouth. Her reaction, however, was not what he had been hoping for.

"Don't."

"Don't?" he questioned.

"Don't do that. Don't play games."

He leaned back. "Why would you think I'm playing a game?"

She fidgeted in distress, her eyes meeting his and then darting away. "Because you can't be in love with me. You haven't known me long enough."

"You don't believe in love at first sight, then?"

Her eyes found their way back to his. "You're

saying you fell in love with me as soon as you laid eyes on me?"

He shook his head, choosing his words carefully. "No, I don't think so. But in the days since then…yes. I think I have. And I also think…you have feelings for me, too."

She stared at him before dropping her eyes to the table. "Cole's asked me to get back together with him. He's agreed to move to Paris."

"Uh-huh." In truth, this didn't surprise Dane. He'd expected Cole Dorset to realize his mistake at some point and attempt to reconcile with Ophelia. "And?"

"And?" she repeated.

"What did you tell him?"

She frowned. "Nothing. Yet."

Dane found himself breaking into a grin. "Good. Then I've still got a chance."

Her eyes widened. "Wh-what?"

"Let me take you out on a date."

She stared.

"Come on. One date. After all, didn't you once say that you'd read I could be charming? Give me the chance to live up to my reputation."

She eyed him warily. "Is this the jet lag talking?"

He laughed. "What are you doing tomorrow night?"

"I—" She stopped, clearly dumbfounded.

"Then it's a date."

He waved over their waitress, who'd been hovering nearby, and asked for the check.

"Dane, I'm not sure we should…"

"Should what?"

Her eyes remained fixed on the tablecloth. "I'm not sure we should pursue something when I'm going to be leaving for Paris. Long-distance relationships are difficult, especially when the distance is continental."

"Were you happy when we spent so much time together in Hawaii?"

Her stare immediately rose to his, and he saw the truth in her eyes. He grinned. "Then it's a date," he repeated.

He could see she was struggling with herself, but a small smile crept onto her face, anyway.

"Okay," she agreed, her voice soft. "It's a date."

OPHELIA HADN'T EXPECTED to be so nervous.

Or so excited.

She had skipped out of work for the rest of the day to go home and decide what to wear for her date the next night, discarding numerous outfits until she found one she thought Dane might like. She kept her cell phone on silent, and when she finally stopped to check the screen, she felt a swell of uneasiness. There were two missed texts from Holly, asking why she hadn't returned from lunch, a missed call from Cole and then a voice mail from her mother. Fortifying herself with a glass of red wine, she listened to the message.

"Ophelia, I find it highly inappropriate that you're not in your office this afternoon. There is so much to be arranged concerning your promotion, and Cole is simply beside himself at your disappearance. Holly never saw you return from lunch, although Cole assures me you reentered the building with him. He told me about giving you the earrings, which I thought was a perfectly lovely gesture on his part. What were you expecting? A proposal? I hope you're not out sulking. I expect to see you back here shortly."

The call ended on that note, and Ophelia defiantly deleted the message. She thought about what Dane had said earlier, about her mother being a bully. As much as this observation chafed at her, she knew it was true.

Her mother was a bully. She had been for nearly as long as Ophelia could remember. Certainly from the day her father had died, and her mother had been left to carve her own way in the world. She could have asked for help from her family, but she'd refused, knowing how they had disapproved of her marriage to a much older man. Ophelia well knew, from the few strained visits she recalled with her maternal grandparents, how they had chastised her mother.

"What did you expect?" she remembered her grandmother saying. "For the man to live forever?"

And then she recalled her mother's words, from the message she had just played.

"What did you expect?"

What *did* she expect?

Her mother had experienced love and marriage to a man Ophelia suspected she still secretly mourned. The loss of him had turned her hard and ruthless. And ever since he had passed, she had spent her life trying to intimidate Ophelia into doing as she saw fit.

That included a relationship with Cole. She could only imagine what her mother would say if she knew about her date tomorrow night with Dane. In an uncharacteristic gesture of further defiance, Ophelia turned her phone off completely and laid it aside for the rest of the evening.

THE NEXT NIGHT, Ophelia found herself feeling more relaxed than she had since her time on the island. That morning, she had managed to make excuses and apologies to her mother, Cole and Holly concerning her absence the day before, and she had sailed through her day in anticipation of her date with Dane that evening.

Now she happily strolled hand in hand with Dane through Central Park, enjoying the warm spring evening air, her stomach full with the Italian dinner Dane had ordered for them and her spirits light as Dane expounded on his first day at Towers International.

"She's just nothing like what I expected."

"You mean Bianca?" Ophelia clarified.

Dane nodded. "I feel really sorry for her, actually."

"Sorry for her? Why?" Bianca Towers was the heiress to a fortune, plus she had managed to secure Dane Montgomery as part of her team—Ophelia couldn't imagine why the young socialite should be pitied.

But Dane stopped walking at this question and turned to face her, his expression thoughtful. "You should have seen how they treated her in that board meeting today. The directors have no respect for her, or her ideas. They see her as this vapid, clueless girl, and the truth is…she's actually really smart. She has a lot of solid ideas, and she's working very hard to change her image from the one the media projects. But the board has no faith in her."

"Do you think you can help with that, change how they see her?"

"I'm already trying. I pointed out the merits of some of her strategies, emphasizing to the board that she has the right idea, and they should give her suggestions a chance. I think it helped. In fact, I think that's why she wanted me here so badly."

"What do you mean?"

Dane released her hand to pull her arm through his own, and she leaned into him as they began walking once more. It was a lovely feeling, being drawn protectively into Dane's side. She savored his nearness.

"She's sharp, Bianca Towers. She knew that if she could get me back here, she'd have done what no other corporate professional had managed to do. I think she also recognized that if she won my support, the board would have to take notice and start seeing her in a different light—as a peer instead of just some silly girl they needed to indulge."

He shook his head in amazement, and Ophelia could tell he was impressed. "Bianca Towers is going to go further than anyone could have imagined."

"Well, she's lucky to have you on her team," Ophelia stated.

"You're my recruiter—you have to say that." He nudged her, and she laughed.

"Even so...it's true."

He turned the intensity of his stare on her, and she felt her skin warming as he scanned every one of her features. "Thanks for coming out with me tonight. I'm having a really great time."

She felt pleasure course through her. "Me, too," she agreed.

On a whim, just before walking out the door earlier in the night, she had tucked the disposable camera from Dane into her purse. She still had a few photos left on it, and she'd used most of them up throughout the evening. There was only one more in the roll.

"Do me a favor?" she asked.

He was leaning close. "Sure," he breathed.

"Take a picture with me?"

His eyebrows rose in surprise at this request. "A picture?"

"Yeah. I've taken pictures of just about everyone and everything since I met you, but I don't think I got a single one of you and me together, just the two of us."

The fact that she had pointed this out seemed to please him immensely. "Well, we're just going to have to fix that," he declared.

Approaching another couple strolling through

the park, Dane asked if they'd be willing to take a photo for them. Ophelia brought out the disposable camera and handed it over, then she returned to Dane's side to pose with him. He drew her against him, his arms wrapping around her.

And she realized, for that brief moment before the camera flashed, what it was to feel like she had come home.

Now they approached her apartment building, and Dane insisted on walking her to the door, as any proper gentleman should, he said.

When they reached her floor, she asked if he wanted to come in for coffee.

"I brought some Kona that Leilani gave me."

"Oh, thank God. I've been going through withdrawal."

She laughed as she unlocked the door, and they entered her apartment. Dane followed her, and she moved toward the kitchen as he looked around. She suddenly felt self-conscious of all the Parisian decor on the walls and shelves. Her apartment was a veritable Paris shrine—a constant reminder of her goal to return. She had begun to wrap up some of the smaller items, sorting them for storage and packing, but most of her possessions still remained unwrapped. She was finding it hard to begin the actual process of boxing up her life.

As she began to move around the kitchen,

Dane appeared in the doorway. Her stomach churned madly as she felt his eyes following her movements—opening the bag of Kona, measuring the beans into her coffee grinder, pulsing them into grounds, measuring water for the coffeemaker.

"It smells like home," he commented, and her eyes found his in understanding. He looked slightly forlorn as she finished preparing the coffee and hit the button to brew.

"Feeling homesick already?"

She moved closer to where he was standing.

"I was homesick before I even boarded the plane," he confessed. "The only thing that made it bearable was knowing you'd be here."

She felt a tug of sympathy. "Dane, it'll get better."

"Not once you're gone."

Her stomach did a somersault as he reached out a hand and rested it against her jaw, his thumb stroking her cheek and sending tingles along her skin. She was relaxing into him, her eyelids sliding closed when his next question brought her to attention.

"If I asked you to stay…would you?"

Her eyes widened as she looked at him, the earnest desperation on his face, the flicker of longing in his eyes. "Dane, I—I can't."

"Why not?"

She licked her lips, searching for an answer, until she realized…she didn't have one.

"I just can't."

He released her, and when the warmth of his touch was gone, she shivered.

"I'm sorry. It was unfair of me to ask. Just because I had to give up my dream doesn't mean I have the right to ask you to do the same."

"Don't be sorry." She stepped toward him, bridging the distance he'd created and ending up in his arms. "I wish…"

He brushed his fingers along her hairline and moved them down to tuck a sweep of hair behind her ear. "What do you wish?" he murmured.

She looked into his eyes. He loved her. This man really loved her. The way he looked at her now left no doubt. It startled, frightened her, even. Because for a minute, she had the overwhelming sensation that she might just love him back.

She stiffened and stepped away. This was a dangerous game to play. It risked everything.

"Nothing," she whispered and went to pour the coffee. "Never mind."

Her chest ached as he fell silent. She sensed him moving away from the kitchen and into the living area. When she carried in a tray with the coffee, he was settled deep in her couch. She placed the tray on the coffee table.

"If you're planning to get rid of this couch when you move, I'd take it off your hands."

She stared at him after this announcement.

"Really? You mean that?"

He eyed her. "Yeah...why?"

She moved to sit beside him. "Cole hates this couch."

Dane straightened up and reached for a mug of coffee. "It's comfortable."

"Exactly!"

She felt a bit embarrassed as he smiled with bemusement. His next words, however, caused an even greater embarrassment for her.

"Do you love him?"

She hesitated. "We've been together a long time."

"But do you love him?" Dane repeated.

She shrugged and looked away, wishing she could change the subject.

"Ophelia."

Her gaze jumped back as she felt the warmth of his leg brush against hers as he shifted.

"It's okay if you love him. You just need to be true to that."

Despite these words, his voice sounded sad.

"Have you ever been in love?" she ventured.

He took a sip of his coffee and sighed—

with pleasure or regret, she wasn't sure which. "Once, I guess. But I was so young, I'm not sure it even counts."

"Who was she?"

"A girl I grew up with. We dated in high school, but once we graduated, I wanted to move on to bigger and better things. She was content where she was—in the town where we grew up. I never faulted her for that." He shrugged. "We should all be so lucky. Last I heard, she was happily married with two kids. It's the life she'd always wanted."

Ophelia considered this. "Do you ever…envy her?"

He thought about this. "No. She got what she wanted out of life, and so did I."

Ophelia reached for her own mug of coffee. "And you've never loved anyone since?"

"Not in the same way. I've dated women, some of them wonderful, some of them not. But ultimately, I never felt that…that thrill around them that goes beyond pure attraction—the feeling that this is the person you could spend the rest of your life with."

The way he looked at her then caused her hands to tremble so that she had to place her mug back on the table to keep from spilling her coffee.

"I don't know if I feel that with Cole, either,"

she confessed. "I've always thought we were more...more compatible than romantic. Does that make sense?"

"I think that makes perfect sense."

"But he's willing to move to Paris with me, and that's saying a lot for Cole. I don't think it was ever something he wanted."

She settled against the back of the couch and, after placing his mug beside hers on the coffee table, Dane leaned back with her. She found herself nestling into his side and relaxing as his arm came around her.

"I wish...things were different," she said.

Dane stroked his fingers along the length of her arm, making her feel, at least for now, secure.

For the next few weeks, Ophelia didn't see Dane at all. Her days were filled with tasks relating to her upcoming promotion—transferring clients, reassigning her current workload and meetings with her mother about the Paris branch. She assumed Dane's time was filled with settling into his new role, getting to know his creative marketing team and consulting for Bianca.

On several different occasions, she composed texts and emails to him.

Hey stranger, wondering how you're settling in?

Or

Dear Dane,
How are you adjusting to your new role? If you have any questions or concerns, please feel free to contact me at my office.
Sincerely,
Ophelia

But she sent none of these because not one of them said what she really wanted to express. Those were words she dare not voice aloud, nor put into print. So she carried on, trying desperately to put Dane out of her mind and focus on Paris, instead. She kept waiting for the anticipation to kick in, the realization that she was actually doing this—moving to Paris…but it never came. She reassured herself that the reality of the situation hadn't sunk in yet, and once she was in Paris, her happiness would know no bounds.

She went on a couple of dates with Cole, but each one only seemed to solidify for her how little affection she felt for him. She couldn't help comparing every word, every gesture, to

Dane, and each time, Cole came up lacking. She tried to express how she felt without wounding his ego, but it was an impossible task. Cole had decided they were destined to be together, and he had her mother's approval in that thought—disagreeing with the both of them proved to be more than Ophelia was capable of doing.

She had determined that she had to break things off for good with Cole, that she couldn't continue stringing him along, and that was when she received her mother's invitation. It came to her apartment, in a creamy white envelope embossed with silver accents. The script within was printed on pristine ivory cardstock, requesting her attendance at a dinner party that Friday evening. It was to celebrate Reid Recruiting's recent success—which left Ophelia uneasy but unable to decline the event. Of course, Cole would be in attendance, and she could hardly break up with him right before the party occurred.

So, steeling herself for the occasion, she pulled her vintage black dress from the back of her closet and prepared to attend her mother's dinner that Friday night.

DANE STARED AT the invitation in his hands as Bianca looked over his shoulder, her gaze fixed on the same creamy white stationery with flourished silver accents.

"A date with the dragon lady," Bianca said, and he couldn't help laughing.

When he didn't speak, however, Bianca moved from behind to stand in front of the desk where he sat.

"Do we attend, then?"

Dane sighed and tossed the invitation onto a pile of correspondence. "Of course. It would be in bad form to turn down Lillian Reid."

Bianca made a show of shuddering violently. "It'll be like a scene from *The Godfather*."

Dane uttered another small laugh, but a part of him sank even deeper into sadness. He felt certain Ophelia would be in attendance at her mother's party, and as much as he missed her, he dreaded seeing her on Cole's arm.

Bianca must have noticed his glumness because she settled into the seat in front of his desk and eyed him curiously.

"Come on. It won't be *that* bad. If you handled my board of directors so effortlessly, then Lillian Reid will be a breeze. She seems tough, but she's kind of sad."

Dane perked up at this. "What do you mean?"

Bianca leaned back in the chair with a shrug. "She lost her husband when she was young, you know? And she had that daughter to raise all by herself. She never remarried, and she rarely dates. It's like she's…insulated herself. Against feeling. Against love. Don't you find that sad?"

"I hadn't thought about it," Dane confessed. "How do you know so much about her?"

Bianca frowned. "I keep telling everybody to stop thinking I'm clueless. I went to college. I have degrees in both business and economics, remember? I'm capable of doing a little research, you know."

Dane found himself smiling with genuine affection. "I know." He had been pleasantly surprised to discover Bianca Towers was not the vacuous girl he had assumed she would be. On the contrary, she was bright and hardworking with a solid business sense. She only needed some direction and the ability to change the world's perception of her. Her first battle had been with the company's board of directors, who'd assumed, as Dane had, that her party-girl reputation was an inherent part of her personality. But over the past few weeks, the two of them had worked to change her persona and the future of her company through networking events, charity benefits and interviews. He had the utmost faith that Bianca Towers was going to be just fine in her new role.

"Well?"

Stirring himself from these thoughts, he blinked in confusion. "Well what?"

"Don't you feel sorry for Lillian Reid?"

Dane thought about Ophelia and how she craved her mother's approval and affection. He found it difficult to feel truly sorry for someone who could so callously withhold love from her own daughter.

"Not even a little bit," he answered Bianca's question.

Her eyes widened in surprise. "What? Not at all?"

"No," Dane declared.

"Well…why not?"

"Because," he said, "being hurt by love is no reason to reserve it from others."

Bianca cocked her head. "What are you talking about?"

Dane purposely shifted his attention to his desk and began sorting through paperwork there in order to avoid his young employer's eyes. "I think what makes Lillian Reid such a tragic figure is not that she lost her husband so young or had to work so hard to build her business…but that she had a treasure right in front of her all along that she neglected, not recognizing the worth and love of her own daughter." He looked back up, surprised by the depth of his own feelings on the matter. "I don't feel sorry for her. I can't."

Bianca stared at him until he forced himself to look back to his desk once more.

"I'm meeting with the advertising team in an hour, so I better prepare."

"Sure, I'll let you get to it."

He looked up when she stood, and he felt her hesitating. When he met her eyes, she gestured toward the invitation left lying on his desk.

"Are we still attending?"

His gaze shifted to the creamy stationery once more. This might be his last chance to see Ophelia before she left the country—and his life—forever.

"Yes," he reaffirmed. "We're attending."

LILLIAN REID'S CELEBRATORY dinner party took place in the Azure Room of the prestigious Indigo restaurant on the Upper East Side. Ophelia entered the room that evening on Cole's arm, her eyes scanning the dusky-blue walls with their black sconces and silver accents. The atmosphere was relaxed but also a little dark, and it took Ophelia's eyes a few seconds to adjust to the dimness. Her mother stood out in sharp contrast to the deep blue shades as she sat in a pale gray scoop-necked blouse.

"Cole, Ophelia," her mother greeted and rose

to her feet so she could brush a kiss against each of their cheeks. "I'm glad you made it."

"Sorry we're late," Cole apologized with only the faintest trace of irritation. "Ophelia couldn't find her pearl earrings."

Ophelia was glad for the dim lighting after this remark. Cole had insisted she wear his pearls to the evening's dinner, but when she went to put them on, she couldn't remember where she'd last seen them. Of course, this hadn't done much for Cole's mood in starting the evening.

"It was worth the wait. She looks lovely."

Ophelia felt every nerve ending come alive at these words, spoken by a delightfully familiar voice. She shifted her attention to the other guests, scanning their faces more carefully now that her eyes had adjusted to the dim atmosphere.

There he was. Seated four chairs down from her mother's right. Bianca Towers sat beside him, on his left.

Dane.

"Thank you," Ophelia murmured and offered a look that she hoped he knew was just for him.

"Well, at least you made it. Honestly, I don't know what Ophelia would do without Cole to keep her on time for things." Lillian laughed, and a few of the other guests—all senior members of Reid Recruiting, she noted—joined her in polite chuckling.

Ophelia frowned, feeling this statement to be a trifle unfair. She was occasionally late for social functions, mostly out of her reluctance to attend. But Cole had little to do with her promptness in any situation.

"Take a seat, you two, so we can begin the first course. I'm sure you're all starving."

Cole placed a hand under Ophelia's elbow to guide her, and she couldn't help easing out of his grip to find her way to her own place at the table. She ended up across and two seats away from Dane, making any sort of conversation with him difficult. But she caught his eye as Cole insistently pushed her chair in for her, and he managed a commiserating smile. Suddenly, at least, she didn't feel so alone.

THE DINNER WAS every bit as tedious as Ophelia feared it would be. The food tasted superb but did nothing to make up for the conversation. At a table filled mostly with recruiters, the discussion was filled with the biggest placements of each person's career. Given Dane's presence, Ophelia had the best story of them all, but she had no desire to brag. On the contrary, she caught Dane's eye several times, silently apologizing that he had found himself in the midst of such a scene, but each time, he gave a slight shake of his head as if to reassure her that he didn't mind. More than once, she turned her head to find him watching her. When that happened, she had to redirect her attention elsewhere, lest the warmth she felt seeping through her cheeks be visible even in the dim light of the room.

Dane was seated just beyond the reach of comfortable conversation, but at least she managed to exchange a few words with Bianca Towers. For her part, Bianca seemed as bored as Ophelia felt, but she handled the situation charmingly, laughing at all the right places and commenting just when she should. Clearly, Bianca had a good sense of the social scene.

And Ophelia found that she liked her all the more for it. Perhaps Dane was right—maybe they had all misunderstood Bianca. She had needed Dane to prove her point—that she could bring things to the company others had never suspected. Well, if having Dane at her side had made her board of directors see past the media hype and take her seriously, bravo for her.

Ophelia was musing on this very point when she suddenly realized the table around her had fallen silent. The waiters had brought dessert, but as Ophelia looked down, she realized hers was different than the others.

Instead of the chocolate soufflé on every other plate, Ophelia's contained a small, black jeweler's box. At first, she could only stare at it, and then she looked at Cole beside her. She could tell by the look on his face that this was no pair of earrings before her.

Involuntarily, her eyes went to Dane's, only to find his face blank, his eyes dark. She looked back down at the box.

"Ophelia, dear, aren't you going to open it?" Though voiced as a question, her mother meant it as a command. She reached for the box and found her fingers were trembling with so many eyes on her.

To her mortification, Cole pushed back his seat and got down on one knee.

No. Not here. Not now. Not with all the senior recruiters and Dane Montgomery watching.

"Ophelia," he began, "even though we've experienced a few differences in the past month, I need you to know that my feelings haven't changed. After all we've been through, as we face this new chapter ahead, I want us to do it together…as man and wife."

Fingers still trembling, she eased back the lid of the box and found a large, square-cut diamond resting inside, its edges lined with smaller emeralds. It was something worthy of a princess and had probably cost more than she could imagine.

And it wasn't the kind of ring she would ever wish to wear.

She didn't look up right away—she needed a minute to breathe. Everyone around her held their breath, as well; she could feel them frozen in anticipation. If she looked her mother's way, she knew what she would see—a silent demand to answer appropriately, to grasp this chance, to claim Cole as her own, once and for all.

And then, because she knew she had to do it quickly, before she could allow any fear to make her hesitate, she looked Cole straight in the eye.

"I'm so sorry, Cole. But I can't marry you."

CHAPTER FOURTEEN

DANE FELT EVERY bit of tension drain from his body as Ophelia rejected Cole's proposal. Before anyone could react, Ophelia snapped the lid of the ring's box closed, stood and fled the room. He waited only a split second before he rose to follow her.

He caught up to her as she was heading for the restaurant's foyer, her face flushed and her eyes wide.

"Ophelia." He called her name softly at first and then, when she didn't respond, a little louder. "Ophelia!"

He sensed others turning to look—Indigo's patrons as well as staff, but he ignored them as she turned to face him.

"I can't breathe," she announced. "Dane, I c-can't breathe."

"Here." He placed his hand on her back and steered her into the foyer and then outside the restaurant. Ophelia began gasping, drawing in great gulps of the cool night air.

"It's okay," he said, his hand making small

circles of reassurance on her back. "You're okay."

She shuddered slightly and then stilled. "I didn't expect that." She drew another deep breath and then ran a hand over her hair. Her fingers brushed her ears, and she gasped. "The earrings. I need to give him back the earrings." She moved like she was going to go back inside and then stopped in her tracks. "I can't face him. I can't face *her.*"

"You mean your mother?"

She met his eyes. "Dane, she's going to kill me."

He frowned. "Because you turned down a proposal from a man you don't love?"

"You don't understand."

He didn't respond to this. "You can return the earrings later. Ophelia. Ophelia, look at me."

She did as he commanded. "I think you did the right thing."

Whatever she saw on his face must have arrested her attention because she stopped her nervous fidgeting and held on to his gaze. "I did," she affirmed. "I don't love him."

Dane couldn't help it. He grinned. "No. I didn't really think you did."

She relaxed, whether in relief or in response to his words, he couldn't be sure.

"Dane—"

"Ophelia—"

They both exhaled and laughed softly. A couple emerged from the restaurant and eyed them curiously before moving on down the sidewalk. Dane took her hand and pulled her away from the Indigo entrance.

"You first," he said.

"I…um, no, you go ahead."

"Oh. All right." He cleared his throat, debating where to begin. "I've missed you."

She took a step closer to him. "I've missed you, too."

He still held her hand and now he reached for the other one, as well. "I wanted to apologize."

"Apologize?"

"For everything I said about Paris. That's your dream, and I had no right to grill you so hard about it. You don't need to be able to explain it or justify it. If you believe in it, that's enough."

She stared at him.

"Thank you," she murmured.

"And I wondered…" He shifted his weight from one foot to the other. "If you'd be willing to share it with me."

Her eyes widened once more, and he found himself automatically squeezing her fingers in his.

"Ophelia, I mean it. I've missed you these

last few weeks, more than I ever could have imagined possible." He drew a breath. "When I first met you, I didn't really see you. I only saw your purpose in coming to Hawaii and the fact that you were from New York. But during that week in Kona, I had the opportunity to get to know *you,* and after that point, there was no going back. I fell in love with you. I'm in love with you, Ophelia." This was it. "I love you."

She didn't respond so he forged ahead.

"I've never met anyone like you before— you challenge me at the same time you let me know you care about me. You have faith that I can find my way to any solution. You…make me better, as cliché as that might sound. And the thought of you leaving, of being separated from you…it's more than I can stand. So…" He licked his lips. "I'd like to come to Paris with you. If you'll let me."

She pulled her hands from his and took a step back, her lips parting in surprise. "You want to come with me? To Paris? But…you can't. You have to stay here, with Bianca."

He shook his head. "It doesn't matter. I'll give it all up. I'll sell the coffee plantation. I'll go back to square one. I'll do anything I have to if it means I can be with you."

"Oh, Dane."

"Ophelia." He took a step forward and

reached for her hands once more. "You changed everything. I could never imagine the woman I'd want to wake up to every day for the rest of my life. But you're that woman. And if I have to go to Paris to prove it to you, that's what I'll do."

"No. I can't let you do that."

His grip on her fingers tightened as he tugged her close. She didn't resist.

"You said it yourself. Paris is my dream, not yours. I can't let you give everything up like this. What about Keahi, Leilani and Pele?"

"I'll make sure they're provided for somehow."

"And your contract with Towers Resorts?"

"I'll break it. I'll return the signing bonus."

"How? Hasn't it already gone to pay back Masters?"

"Then I'll sell the plantation to pay back the bonus."

"What if I gave you the money?"

"What?"

"I have some money set aside. It might not be quite enough to pay back the bonus, but we could find a way."

"No, Ophelia. No, I'm not taking your money."

"Dane, listen to yourself. Think about what you're doing—you'd be giving everything up. *Everything.*"

"Not you. I'd still have you." He reached up to wrap his palm against the back of her neck and leaned his forehead into hers. "Please, Ophelia. Let me come with you."

He could feel her tears falling onto his own cheeks.

"You would hate me," she whispered. "Maybe not at first, but eventually…it would change everything."

"No. It wouldn't."

"It would." She pulled back to meet his eyes. "You love me."

She didn't deny it.

"Tell me you don't love me."

"I can't," she said, the tears continuing to well in her eyes. "But, Dane, I can't ask you to do this, either."

"You asked Cole," he pointed out.

"It wasn't the same. It's *because* I love you that I can't ask you to do this. You can't give up on the plantation, not for me."

"Ophelia."

She shook her head, and he held her all the tighter.

"Then what happens next?"

"I'll go to Paris, and you…" She sniffed. "You'll do what you came here to do and then, in another few years, you'll retire again to run your coffee plantation, which will be known all over the islands as one of the best farms in Hawaii."

"And where will you be when that happens?"

She frowned and finally pulled out of his arms.

"Ophelia." He said her name again.

"I have to go, Dane."

He watched her for a long moment before she turned to leave.

"Ophelia."

She turned back.

"It was a pleasure."

It might have been his imagination, but it looked as if fresh tears rose into her eyes just before she turned away and hurried down the sidewalk.

WHEN DANE TURNED to reenter the restaurant, he found Bianca Towers standing several yards away.

"That was painful to watch."

He felt a prickling of irritation, knowing he and Ophelia had had an audience.

"No one asked you to," he stated.

"I know. I'm sorry. But I couldn't leave."

He gestured toward Indigo's entrance. "Did the party break up?"

"Oh, it's a whole roomful of awkward in there. I already asked for the car to be sent around. I don't think you want to go back inside."

"Cole's licking his wounds?"

"Lillian is doing damage control. Maybe you were right, about not feeling sorry for her. I don't envy Ophelia Reid. My mother may be a raging alcoholic, but at least she's not trying to control every aspect of my life. I have a board of directors for that."

Her dry tone caused him to smile despite the lingering ache in his chest. "But you're handling them like a pro."

She gave a little bow and just then, their town car pulled up to the curb. Dane took care of tipping the valet before he slid behind the wheel. He drove in silence, even as he felt Bianca's eyes occasionally studying him.

"Is it true?" she asked after a while. "About your plantation? Is that really your dream?"

He glanced her way. "You didn't know that?"

She looked out the window of the passenger's side. "I didn't think you'd be that serious about it." She turned to study him again. "It's a big change from what you used to do."

"That's exactly why I love it." Perhaps he shouldn't have been speaking so freely in front of his young boss, but after the conversation he'd just had—the loss of yet another dream—he no longer had the energy to be tactful.

"So why give it up?"

He focused his attention on the road. "I needed the money."

"Oh."

In a family like hers, he couldn't imagine that money was ever an issue.

"So…it wasn't because you wanted to work for me?"

He hesitated, uncertain how to respond to this. Suddenly, Bianca laughed.

"I'm just teasing you, Dane. It's okay. Only… I'm sorry."

"You're sorry?" He knew his tone was incredulous.

"I am. Is that so hard to believe?"

"Why should you be sorry?"

Bianca shrugged. "I didn't think about it—about you having to leave behind your own life to come here. I guess it was selfish of me, but you've actually really helped me." She drew a breath. "For a long time, all I've wanted was to contribute to the family business. I guess that was *my* dream, but the board of directors seemed pretty determined to push me out." She looked at him. "Your coming here made all the difference."

"Someone once told me that no one should be bullied into giving up on their dreams." He felt a pang in his stomach, missing Ophelia all over again.

"Wise words," Bianca agreed.

They rode in silence for several minutes more.

"Bianca," he began and then stopped.

He felt her eyes on him, and he tore his attention briefly from the road to look at her face. She was young, ambitious and eager to take on the world around her. She reminded him of himself, so many years ago. But he wasn't that person anymore. And New York was not his home.

"I want to go back to Hawaii."

He looked back at the road before he could witness her reaction.

"What, for like, a visit? To check up on things?"

"No." He felt his stomach twist itself into a knot at the same time he felt the burden lifting from his shoulders. "No, I want to go back... for good. It's my home now. The people there, they've become my family."

She fell silent, and he didn't at first have the nerve to look her way. When he did, she was staring out her window again.

"I'm sorry, but I can't do this."

"You signed a contract," she reminded him, her words accusatory. "You asked me to double the bonus, and I did. You took the money."

"I know."

Silence descended between them until Dane finally flicked on the car's four-way flashers and pulled to the side of the street. He turned to face her, but she presented him her shoulder and kept staring out the window.

"Bianca…you don't need me."

She shifted to look at him. "Yes, I do. Nobody thinks I'm anybody without you. You're the one thing I did that they can't argue with— I convinced you to come out of retirement."

"You did," he agreed. "And nothing's going to change that. I came back." He drew a breath and then released it. "And now it's time for me to leave again."

"No," she repeated. "No, I won't allow it."

He felt both irritation and pity for her. "I'll have to break the contract," he admitted, "and find a way to pay back the signing bonus." He swallowed hard at the thought of where the money would have to come from—no more plantation, no more inn. But at least he could be with the people he loved.

Except for Ophelia. He felt a stab of pain at the thought but ignored it.

"You can't keep me here," he reminded her gently, "if I don't want to stay."

He watched her struggling with these words and felt sympathy for her. He had grown to genuinely like Bianca. But it wasn't enough to make him want to stay.

"Take me home," she said.

He hesitated. "Do you want—"

"Take me home," she repeated, turning cold, clear eyes on him. "I'll have the lawyer begin drawing up the termination papers in the morning."

He looked at her for only a heartbeat longer before putting the car back in gear. And while a part of him felt relieved to be free, a cloud of uncertainty cast a shadow over his relief.

What had he just done?

LILLIAN RECEIVED THE news the following morning on her personal cell phone before she'd had any coffee. She'd tossed and turned most of the night, annoyed by Ophelia's rejection of Cole's proposal and wondering how she had raised a daughter so absolutely different from herself. Cole may not have been the man of Ophelia's dreams, but that was exactly why she preferred him for Ophelia. Her daughter would have less risk with a man like Cole—he had proven himself to be solid and stable, not to mention capable. He would never leave her, never break her heart, as Lillian's own had been broken.

The same could not be said of a man like

Dane Montgomery, who had thrown away a promising career in favor of some wild scheme to cultivate coffee in paradise.

Lillian's own experience with love had taught her that it was not something to give oneself over to completely. She had worked hard to keep her daughter from the tragedies she had encountered in life. And to see Ophelia so carelessly disregard Cole's offer left a bitter taste in her mouth.

The feeling still lingered when she awoke the morning after her dinner party with a splitting headache, a dry mouth and not an ounce of coffee in her loft apartment.

The chirp of her cell phone set her temples throbbing even harder, and when she saw Bianca Towers's number on the display, she wanted to toss her phone into the garbage disposal and grind it into oblivion.

She ground her teeth together instead and began searching for a bottle of aspirin as she answered the call.

"Why, hello, Bianca. I was so disappointed when you rushed off last evening without saying goodbye. I recognize the dinner didn't end as intended, but I hope my daughter's antics didn't scare you away."

Lillian located a half-full container of painkillers and began fiddling with the childproof cap. She had never understood why pharmaceutical companies couldn't offer their products with two different cap options—one for those with children and another for those who didn't need to worry with such inconveniences.

"He quit."

The cap popped off, shot across the kitchen and rolled beneath the fridge. Lillian suppressed a sigh as she shook a couple of tablets from the container and into her palm.

"I'm afraid I don't understand," she mumbled as she reached for a tumbler and filled it with water from the tap.

"Dane Montgomery." Bianca's tone fell flat over the line. "He. Quit."

The aspirin stuck in Lillian's throat, and she coughed violently, drawing more water and chugging it to wash down the offending tablets in her throat.

"Excuse me?"

Bianca sighed with what sounded like exasperation. "He's going back to Hawaii, breaking the contract. My lawyers are drawing up the paperwork as we speak." She paused before delivering the final blow. "Towers International will no longer require the services of Reid Recruiting. To make myself clear... you're fired."

LILLIAN REID HAD once lived by the old adage, "If you want something done right, do it yourself."

So when all phone calls to her daughter went unanswered, she took it upon herself to make a visit to Dane Montgomery. She knew the man had yet to find an apartment in the city and currently resided in one of the suites at Towers Resorts in Manhattan. She sent for her chauffeur service and then took the time to shower and dress in a formidable business suit before pocketing a few more aspirin and heading out the door.

Using her most authoritative tone with the concierge, she learned Dane's suite number and then took the elevator to his floor. Once she reached the door to his rooms, she steeled herself for battle before lifting a hand and knocking resolutely. Long minutes passed before the man who had caused all these problems for her of late answered the door.

She had to confess that she could understand why her daughter found him attractive. His height and frame, the morning scruff dusting his jaw and those clear blue eyes all served to present a picture of attraction that had surely been the basis for more than a few women's fantasies throughout his time as an executive.

"Ms. Reid," he said, more as a statement of fact than a greeting.

"Mr. Montgomery." She inclined her head, adopting his tone. "Might I have a word?"

"I'm not changing my mind," he declared with apparent sincerity.

She stared him down. "What makes you think I'm asking you to?"

This statement obviously caused him sufficient confusion so that he finally stepped aside and gestured for her to enter.

She crossed the threshold and took the opportunity to appreciate the ambience of the suite. Its sitting area featured plush armchairs in chocolate-brown suede, a glass-topped table and a dark wood desk. Ecru-and-ivory-striped wallpaper contributed to the impression of sophisticated luxury.

"Can I get you anything?" Dane asked.

"A glass of water. Preferably sparkling, if possible."

Dane nodded and moved toward the suite's kitchen while Lillian slid a finger along an end table's surface before taking a seat. Dane returned shortly with her drink.

He hesitated before taking the seat across the coffee table from her own. She sipped her water and then placed it on the table between them.

"May I ask what changed your mind?" She finally opened the conversation.

Dane eyed her, rather warily, she thought. His blue eyes were distrustful. "I don't belong here. I never claimed that I did."

"No," she conceded, "but you agreed to return, which indicated you had made your peace with it. I only wonder what changed."

He said nothing, and she found herself growing impatient.

"Did it have something to do with my daughter?"

He went very still, his entire frame taut, but he said nothing.

"Are you in love with her?" Lillian demanded.

This question seemed to deflate him. "It wouldn't matter if I was."

"Why? Because of her—" Lillian stopped short of the word *fiancé,* remembering it didn't apply. "Because of Cole?" she corrected.

Dane shook his head. "She has her own plans, her dreams for Paris. They don't involve me."

Lillian straightened with interest. "Then you'd give her up? So she could pursue her own interests?"

Dane leveled his stare with hers. "Yes," he answered. "I'd let her go, if that's what would make her happy." He paused for a long moment. "Could you do the same?"

The question stunned her, rocked something deep within. "That's an absurd question," she retorted. "I'm her mother. I'd do anything for her."

"Anything but release your hold on her."

She clenched her jaw and stared at him. "I'm allowing her to move halfway across the globe. I hardly think I'm clinging to her."

He shook his head. "It isn't the physical distance. It's the emotional strings you hold."

She scoffed at this, but his words reverberated somewhere deep inside. No one had stated it so candidly before; no one had ever dared give it voice, but Lillian knew, in the most secretive corner of her heart, that she did indeed hold Ophelia tighter than necessary. She feared letting go of her—feared losing the only person left in this world who loved her.

Perhaps it was why she had always approved of Cole for her daughter—she knew that any love Ophelia had for Cole would never displace the love she bore for her mother. She would never be replaced or made less important in Ophelia's eyes, when it came to Cole. But Dane.

Dane Montgomery was far more dangerous. Someone like him would steal her daughter away from her, make her second best. Then she would have no one. Perhaps it would be best if Dane returned to Hawaii, after all. Then Ophelia could forget about him.

Lillian got to her feet, and Dane followed suit.

"Well, I can see this has been a waste of time for us both," she announced.

"I disagree."

She blinked in surprise.

"I see the problem now, I think," he went on. His gaze was far too penetrating, and she reached for her purse.

"I wish you the best of luck in your future endeavors, Mr. Montgomery. I'm sorry we were unable to work things out."

She turned to go.

"It's never safe, you know."

She froze at these words. Despite her reluctance, her curiosity overwhelmed her. She turned back around.

"What isn't?"

"Love," he replied. "Love isn't safe. There's always a risk to it, the fear that the one you love will leave—either of their own accord or be taken away. To give your love to another is to risk your heart." He drew a breath. "But it's not just a risk. It's a refuge. Loving someone changes you, makes you better if you let it. It holds you when you're afraid you'll fall. It carries great risk, but it's a place of safety, as well." Those piercing blue eyes met hers. "Loving Ophelia doesn't necessarily mean losing her. If you let her go, you might be surprised what you'd gain."

She tried to make a face in response, tried to roll her eyes or give some indication she found his logic too idealistic and naive. But she couldn't move, couldn't utter a word in reply. It was as if his words had sharpened tips that had found their way straight into the center of her soul. He had seen more of her than she had intended.

"Goodbye, Mr. Montgomery." She headed for the door, half in desperation, wanting to leave before Dane said anything more.

She nearly made it, but he caught up to her on the threshold of his suite, gripping the door before she could escape through its frame.

"I haven't had a chance to thank you."

"Thank me?" She knew her tone must have been incredulous because a corner of his lips twitched in what appeared to be amusement.

"Yes, thank you."

"Whatever for?"

"For sending Ophelia to Hawaii. For giving me the opportunity to get to know her. I wouldn't change that for anything."

His tone, as much as his words, melted something within her she had long thought unable of softening. Suddenly, she had to know.

"Do you love my daughter?"

"More than anything or anyone else in the world," he replied without hesitation.

"And does she love you?

At this, he looked away, and Lillian escaped through the doorway without waiting for an answer.

OPHELIA DIDN'T LEARN about Dane's resignation until Monday morning. She had kept her cell phone off the entire weekend. She hadn't checked her email, she hadn't listened to her messages and hadn't read her texts. She'd needed time to herself, to process everything that had occurred. She'd spent the time packing up her apartment for storage and had made every effort to keep her mind focused on Paris and her upcoming move.

But with each item that went into a box, she'd found herself growing more and more despondent. Instead of excitement, she felt only a flat indifference. After all this time, working toward her goal, she now was unable to experience any joy in it. She contrasted each mental image of Paris against her recent experiences in Hawaii and was disappointed to find Europe lacking in comparison to the islands.

When she turned her phone back on Monday morning, she experienced a long sequence of alerts and chimes, all telling her of Dane's decision and departure while she had isolated herself from everyone. She felt a moment's panic when she realized his plane had already taken off according to a text from Holly, and that he was, right then, across the Pacific on his way back home.

She didn't bother heading into work that morning. Instead, she took a cab to the Towers International offices, using a confidence she didn't feel to get past security and then reception until she found her way into Bianca Towers's office on one of the top floors.

The younger woman looked up and then stood as Ophelia entered the room unannounced. A receptionist trailed behind her, protesting the intrusion but Bianca gave a curt nod of dismissal and a command to close the door so that soon, it was just the two of them.

"If your mother sent you," Bianca began, but Ophelia shook her head.

"She didn't. I'm not here for Reid Recruiting. I'm here for Dane."

This statement must have caused sufficient interest for Bianca because she moved out from behind her desk and offered for Ophelia to sit beside her on a leather sofa with damask pillows against the far wall.

"Please don't blame him," Ophelia began as soon as they were seated.

"He chose to resign before the terms of his contract expired. Just who else am I supposed to blame?"

"Blame me, if you have to," Ophelia replied.

"I don't see how it's your fault."

Ophelia sighed. "I should have known he wasn't ready, that it wasn't going to work."

"It was his decision, Ophelia. Not yours."

"But he was pushed into it, and I knew that." She paused. "I shouldn't have let him go."

The younger woman cocked her head. "What does that mean?"

Ophelia hesitated, realizing how the words sounded. "Just, please…give him another chance."

Bianca emitted a scoff of incredulity. "And how am I supposed to do that?"

She hadn't even known she had the answer until Bianca asked the question. "Let him work from Hawaii. Retain him as a consultant with biannual meetings here in New York. Arrange for him to meet you at the new resort in Waikiki when you're there. You can reduce his salary, but he can keep the signing bonus. And you both *win*."

When Ophelia first began speaking, Bianca shook her head. But by the time she was finished, the other woman appeared to be considering the suggestion.

"It could still be said that I got Dane Montgomery out of retirement, that he works for Towers International."

"Exactly." Ophelia felt a swell of triumph and excitement. "It's not so much the work that's the problem," she explained. "He wants to be near his coffee plantation, and he feels like Hawaii is his home. So compromise. And then you both get what you want."

Bianca stood and began pacing. "He'd have to be available on my hours, though. The time difference can't become an issue."

"It wouldn't," Ophelia reassured. "It's only six hours, so it could be arranged."

"And he'd come to New York twice a year?"

"That sounds perfectly reasonable to me."

Bianca paused in her pacing, turning to Ophelia with narrowed eyes. "How do you know he'll agree to it?"

Ophelia stood, topping Bianca in height by a couple of inches. "Because I know him."

"Didn't you just meet him for the first time when you flew to Hawaii to recruit him?"

Ophelia nodded but remained confident. "Yes. But I know him," she repeated. "He'll think this is a perfect solution." She decided to take things one step further. "Plus, I have another proposition."

Bianca resumed her seat, and Ophelia followed suit. By the time she finished outlining her second proposal, she could see Bianca growing more and more excited.

"If you ever choose to give up recruiting, Ophelia Reid, perhaps you should consider becoming a defense attorney. You're pretty good at negotiation."

Ophelia felt herself relax with the knowledge that Bianca approved. "Negotiation is all part of a recruiter's job."

"I just have one question."

Ophelia felt a ripple of uneasiness.

"I watched you turn Dane down, outside the restaurant on Friday night. Why are you negotiating on his behalf now? As far as I see it, both your professional and personal relationships were terminated that night."

"Personal, maybe. But I'm still his recruiter."

"But I'm no longer a client of Reid Recruiting."

"Well, perhaps that can be renegotiated, as well."

Bianca grinned. "Okay, fair enough."

And Ophelia knew she had won.

THE WORD SPREAD quickly, and within a matter of days, the corporate world was buzzing with the news of Dane Montgomery's return, departure and then the revision of his contract, which allowed him to work from Hawaii. Bianca reinstated the Towers account with Reid Recruiting, and once the hotel heiress contacted Dane—Bianca had requested to speak to him herself concerning the new contract terms—it seemed everyone had found the perfect solution.

Everyone, that is, except Ophelia. She still felt little excitement about Paris, and she recognized, perhaps too late, that while the European city would always hold a special place for her, it wasn't where she belonged. She wished she could somehow renege on her position there, but she couldn't find the courage to tell her mother she no longer wished to move and oversee the European branch.

So she continued with the charade, packing her items for storage and transferring the last of her clients to others within the firm. She received a handwritten note from Dane, postmarked from Hawaii, containing a pressed hibiscus flower and only two words.

Thank you.

Her heart squeezed at the sight of his handwriting, her fingers delicately tracing the fragile flower she knew his own fingers had touched. She was still holding it when Holly paged her through the phone's speaker.

"Ophelia, you have a caller. She wouldn't give a name but insisted I put her through. She's on line one."

Ophelia frowned, puzzled, but moved her hand toward the blinking line to take the call. As she reached for the phone, her eyes fell on a thick blue envelope lying in her inbox tray. She recognized the logo from the photo printers two blocks away. When she lifted the packet, two dozen photos spilled across her desk. They were the images from her disposable camera. She had forgotten she'd given it to Holly last week and asked her to get prints made. She'd begun to sort through them when a beep sounded from the phone, reminding her of the waiting caller.

She continued to rifle through the images, feeling a pang of both pain and nostalgia as she lifted the phone's receiver and pressed the button for line one.

"Hello, this is Ophelia Reid."

"You should come back."

Ophelia was so absorbed in the photos that the words didn't immediately register. There was the Painted Church and then the Inoas, some of the local craftsmen at Holualoa, coffee cherries waiting to ripen, sunsets, Leilani in a hula pose, Keahi holding his arms out as if preparing to embrace her and Dane smiling at her with a sideways glance... And then the words of her caller penetrated.

"Excuse me?"

"He misses you. You should come back."

"Pele?" A wave of surprise washed over her. "How did you find my number?"

Pele clicked her tongue. "You're not the only one who can use the inn's internet to look up things."

Ophelia couldn't help the small laugh that escaped. Her hand brushed through the photos and found one of the feisty housekeeper. She remembered that Pele had tried to wave her away while she took the picture so that her hand was extended in a dismissive gesture. The photo captured every bit of her spirit.

"He is not the only one who misses you. We all miss you."

"All of you?" Ophelia asked with skepticism.

There was a short pause on the other end. "All of us. I should not have said the things that I said. It was not your fault he chose to leave. I'm sorry."

Ophelia felt tears rising. "It's okay. Thank you." The tears continued to come until the images on the desk before her were a blur of vibrant colors.

"You made him happy. He is not the same without you."

And she wasn't the same without him. Dane had restored something for her—a sense of family, of belonging. But by the time she'd realized exactly what she was giving up, Dane had left and her chance had passed.

"I miss him, too," she whispered. "I miss all of you."

"I know."

She didn't even bother to ask just how Pele knew this, but she believed it.

"Can you be happy without him?" Pele asked.

Ophelia held her breath and looked around her office. Her gaze fell on the window, catching the morning light streaming inside. Soon, she had planned to trade one office for another—in Paris. But suddenly, the lights of Paris no longer seemed so bright. Instead, she longed for the golden cast of the islands.

Blinking away her tears, she looked back down at the photos. The first one her eyes found was the last from the roll—the image of her and Dane in Central Park. His arm was wrapped tightly around her, and they were both smiling with such happiness that Ophelia barely recognized herself.

It was then that she knew. She loved him. Nothing, not even Paris, compared to that.

"Ophelia?" Pele spoke again. "Can you be happy without him?"

"No," she answered. "I can't."

OPHELIA INVITED HER mother out to dinner to break the news. She would have preferred to have an intimate conversation in her own apartment, but given the state of it with boxes and packing tape and half her kitchen already packed, she decided a restaurant would be better. They agreed to dine at Le Petite Renard after work, but Lillian had been waylaid by a last-minute phone call, so Ophelia found herself sitting at the bistro alone for thirty minutes, twisting her napkin into a wrinkled mess as she anxiously awaited her mother's arrival.

It didn't help that her last memory of Le Petite Renard involved Cole giving her the pearl earrings.

She had returned the present earlier that week. He had taken a few days off work, which left her feeling guilty. She couldn't remember the last time Cole had called off. Her rejecting his proposal must have impacted him more than she'd imagined. So she had stopped by his apartment with the earrings and an apology. All things considered, it had gone well. She suspected his pride had been more wounded than his heart, and they had parted amicably. She knew Cole would eventually rebound and hopefully find someone he could love in a way he hadn't quite been able to fully love her.

All thoughts of Cole dissipated as she saw her mother enter Le Petite Renard, speak with the maître d' and then find her way to Ophelia's table. She seated herself in a cloud of perfume and a sigh.

"My apologies for running late."

"That's all right," Ophelia automatically replied.

"Have you ordered?"

"I was waiting for you."

Lillian nodded in approval and waved down a waiter without looking at the menu. She placed her order, and Ophelia followed suit, asking for the same grilled lamb chops, steamed vegetable medley and side salad with house dressing.

The waiter wrote down their beverage requests as well, but this time, Ophelia decided to forego her mother's glass of chilled white wine in favor of simple sparkling water. She wanted to be as clearheaded as possible for this conversation.

After their orders had been placed, and the waiter moved away from their table, Ophelia faced her mother. Her stomach tightened with apprehension, and she dropped her gaze again so she could find the words to begin.

"It's fortuitous you asked to meet," her mother said, instead. "I think it's time you and I have a chat."

Ophelia twisted her napkin into a knot once more and then tried to smooth it on her lap so she had somewhere to look other than into her mother's eyes.

"I'm proud of you."

The words were so sudden and unexpected that Ophelia's head jerked up of its own accord.

"Wh-what?"

Lillian drew a small breath and held it for several seconds. "I always assumed it went without saying, but perhaps I was wrong. I am proud of you, Ophelia. Not just for what you did this week, in renegotiating the Dane Montgomery contract to find an acceptable compromise for both parties, but for how committed you've been to the company and to this job."

Ophelia nearly winced openly. What she wouldn't have given to hear those sentiments one month ago. But now…now they only made what she had to do even harder. She licked her lips and chose her words carefully.

"Thank you, Ms. Reid. I really appreciate—" She stopped herself. "That means a lot to me. More than you can possibly know. Thank you."

Lillian nodded without smiling.

"But there's something I have to tell you."

She had to do it quickly, as she'd done in rejecting Cole. She had to say it before her head tried to dissuade her heart.

"I don't want to move to Paris."

Lillian blinked, and Ophelia rushed to fill the silence.

"It was a childhood dream, to live there. But I think it's one of those ideas that makes a better dream than a reality. I don't want the promotion. I'm sorry."

The waiter reappeared just then with their beverages, and Ophelia sat in misery until he moved away once more. Lillian took her time in responding, reaching for her wineglass and taking a sip before returning it to its spot on the table.

"Does Dane Montgomery have anything to do with this decision?"

At the mention of his name, Ophelia's breath caught. She decided to be as honest as she could be. "Yes and no. I don't want to move to Paris anymore, no matter what happens with Dane. At the same time, I have to admit that it was meeting him and traveling to Hawaii that helped change things for me."

"I see." Lillian didn't look at her. Instead, she fiddled with the stem of her wineglass. "And is that why you rejected Cole's proposal? Did Dane Montgomery have anything to do with that?"

Ophelia felt herself flushing. "I turned Cole down because...I don't love him."

"And Montgomery? Do you love him?"

She hesitated and then decided it was best to come clean. "I do," she murmured. "I love him very much."

Lillian relaxed and leaned back in her seat. Ophelia wasn't sure how, but she sensed that her mother had been waiting for something—and that Ophelia had just delivered it.

"Then you're fired."

Her jaw dropped.

"Excuse me?"

"You're fired," Lillian repeated, and despite the words, Ophelia saw a rare glint of humor in her mother's eyes.

"Although I'm sure the arrangement satisfies Bianca, I won't have a recruiter working for me from Hawaii. You'll have to find some other way to occupy your time." She reached for her wineglass once more as Ophelia stared. "I'm sure you'll have no trouble putting your talents to good use, however. I heard you negotiated a fabulous deal with Towers International for exclusive rights as the Kona coffee supplier to their Waikiki resort. Dane's money problems should be over with that sort of coup." She clicked her tongue and met Ophelia's eyes. "I hope he knows your true worth. Because it's never anything he could measure in dollars."

Ophelia felt a warmth blossom in her stomach and spread outward. Tears touched her eyes.

"He does, Ms. Reid. He does."

Her mother shook her head. "You don't work for me anymore. So enough of that Ms. Reid nonsense."

Ophelia grinned, reaching out to grip her mother's hand in her own. The touch seemed to startle Lillian, who looked at her daughter with something akin to both awe and regret.

"I know this can't be easy for you. So thank you…Mom."

EPILOGUE

OPHELIA FELT A different sort of anticipation than she had experienced the first time she'd stood on this doorstep. The Kona breeze was just as deliciously balmy, but this time, she felt in no way weary from her long flight. On the contrary, she was energized and eager for the days ahead.

She rang the doorbell of the Okina Inn and waited, the waves in her stomach rising with each second that passed.

Moments later, the door opened, and Pele stood before her.

The older woman looked her up and down.

"You're still too skinny."

Ophelia broke into a laugh, and she knew the sound must be a mixture of relief and giddiness.

"You're still too bossy," she shot back.

Pele pursed her lips at this sassy comeback, but then, to Ophelia's surprise, the other woman grinned. Before either of them could speak further, Leilani ducked around her grandmother and threw herself into Ophelia's arms.

"You made it!"

Ophelia tightened her grip on Leilani and looked at Pele over the younger girl's shoulders.

"I did," she confirmed.

Just then, Keahi appeared behind Pele, his round face all smiles. "Aloha, Ophelia Reid."

"Aloha," she greeted.

Keahi swept her into one of his bear hugs, and she felt a swell of homecoming—of belonging.

"*Tutu* has been cooking like crazy for you! Banana-nut pancakes with coconut syrup and pineapple wedges, *huli huli* chicken, taro rolls, *haupia*..."

"All at the same meal?" Ophelia asked in astonishment.

Leilani giggled. "Of course not! We'll have plenty of meals together, now that you're here to stay."

"It all sounds delicious."

Ophelia surveyed her new family: Pele's sturdiness, Leilani's bubbly nature and Keahi's warmth. There was only one person missing.

"I can fix you a plate right now," Leilani rushed on, but Ophelia shook her head.

"Not now. I wondered...if he's here."

All three of them grinned at her, like children waking on Christmas morning, knowing the best was to come.

"He's here," Pele assured.

"We didn't tell him you were coming, just like we talked about," Leilani said. "It's our surprise."

"He's in the orchard," Keahi said. "I'll bring in your bags. Go find him."

Ophelia felt a swell of anticipation wash over her. "Thank you. I'll see you all later."

When she looked back over her shoulder, all three of them were standing on the porch, watching her walk away.

DANE FELT SLIGHTLY guilty for all the time he was spending in the orchard. He had informed Keahi that he wanted to run yet another test on the pH level of the soil, just to be on the safe side, but in truth, the dirt's acidity was perfectly balanced. Dane simply needed more time to himself these days.

Since he'd returned to Hawaii, things were both better and worse. His mornings were devoted to brainstorming and consulting calls and emails with Bianca and her team, while his afternoons on the plantation were productive and energetic. It was a perfect balance, and he felt confident that after this autumn's harvest, the plantation would remain permanently in the black. His debt to Masters had been paid within the first few days of his arrival in New York, and while it obviously chafed at the other man, he appeared to have decided to let bygones be bygones.

Everything had turned out better than Dane could have expected with one exception.

Ophelia.

He missed her more than he wished to admit to anyone. In such a short time, she had completely changed the balance of his world. And even though he still loved Hawaii, and more than ever, it felt like home, he couldn't help feeling that there was a small piece of paradise she had taken with her.

And he feared he would never get it back.

His thoughts were so intent on Ophelia, wondering where she was right now, whether in Paris or New York, that it didn't surprise him at all to see her walking toward him through the coffee orchard's lanes. He found himself staring, welcoming this mirage, until he realized…

It was really her.

He closed the distance between them in several measured strides.

"You're here," he whispered in disbelief.

Her smile was the most beautiful thing he could ever remember seeing.

"I'm here," she confirmed.

"But…Paris?"

If possible, her smile grew even wider. "But you're not in Paris."

"Me?"

She lifted a hand and rested it against his chest. "You." She drew a breath. "I love you."

His heart thundered against her palm.

"Pele's going to insist we get married, you know."

She leaned into him, lifting her face to his. "Well, we wouldn't want Pele to be unhappy."

He knew then that it was true. She was staying here in paradise, with him.

"I don't suppose your mother took the news very well."

She lifted her arms to wrap them around his neck. "Better than you'd think. But she's already insisting we fly to New York for the holidays. She refuses to spend Christmas in 'the tropics,' as she put it."

He laughed at this. "It's okay. We'll bring her back a muumuu."

"Those long dresses like Pele wears?"

"One with big orange flowers."

Ophelia shook her head. "Have you learned nothing?"

He wrapped his arms around her waist. "I guess you have your work cut out for you."

"More than you know. I spoke to Bianca

Towers, and I already negotiated a deal for the Towers Resorts in Waikiki to exclusively serve Kona coffee from your plantation."

He felt a swell of tenderness toward her. "You're really all in with this, aren't you?"

"Completely."

"And you have no regrets…about Paris? You're sure?"

She met his eyes and held them. "I'm sure. I don't need to go to Paris to find out where I belong."

He took another moment to savor the feel of her in his arms.

"You belong right here. With me."

"I wouldn't have it any other way. Now kiss me and remind me why it's called paradise."

He did exactly as she commanded.

* * * * *

LARGER-PRINT BOOKS!

GET 2 FREE LARGER-PRINT NOVELS PLUS 2 FREE MYSTERY GIFTS

Love Inspired®

Larger-print novels are now available...

LILPDIR13R

ReaderService.com

Manage your account online!

- Review your order history
- Manage your payments
- Update your address

---

*We've designed
the Harlequin® Reader Service
website just for you.*

Enjoy all the features!

- Reader excerpts from any series
- Respond to mailings and
  special monthly offers
- Discover new series available to you
- Browse the Bonus Bucks catalog
- Share your feedback

Visit us at:
ReaderService.com